From Grandeville – A Tale - Tale 11.

E'Nilt

Being The First Tale of Mythology.

Of A Sort.

George R. Mead

E-Cat Worlds Press

Comments and questions? –> gmead01@gmail.com

E'Nilt

Everything is fiction, nothing more, nothing less. No real people are in these tales nor do any real life clones of the characters exist.

LCCN 2011932365

Mead, George R. , 1934 -
E'Nilt. Being The First Tale of Mythology. Of A Sort. / George R. Mead.
p. cm. – (From Grandeville, a tale; Tale 11)
ISBN-13 978-0-9817446-7-4
            1. Fantasy. I. Title. II. Series.

E-Cat Worlds established its publishing program as a reaction to the large commercial publishing houses currently dominating the book industry and the smaller intellectual clones. It is interested in publishing works of fiction and non-fiction that are often deemed insufficiently profitable or commercial or that are not necessarily reflective of literary trends and fads.

E-Cat Worlds, 57744 Foothill Road, La Grande OR 97850
www.ecatworldspress.com
SAN 255-6383

In the middle of nowhere - Creativity.

First Edition:
Printed in the United States of America

From Grandeville.

Portal
Lair
Search
Not Again
And Again.
Magiwitch
Rebirth
Offspring
Holiday
Treasure
E'Nilt

A Tale of the Feyra

Jonathon and Dee
Dee of the Fontala

Nonfiction

A History of Union County
The Ethnobotany of the California Indians
A History of the Chinese in the West: 1848-1880

He had told them.
　　　More than once he had told them.
He had told them.
　　　He was done with the hero business.

And they listened.
　　　And smiled.
　　　　　And tickled his ribs.

And they knew that he was just being a grump.
　　　And he knew that they knew.
And they knew that he knew that they knew.
Etc.
　　　Etc.
　　　　　Etc.
　　　　　　　Etc.

That was the problem being what he was, being what they were. At times, it was hard to know where he ended and where they began.

So, long ago, or maybe not all that long ago, he had decided to help a friend, one of his very best friends. It was something that had needed doing. But one small action leads to another, as it is said, and then another, and then another.

And then, there you are.
　　　In it again.
Willing or not!

That is the real problem with the hero business. It seems as if you can never retire. No matter what.

Well, he told himself, never again! That was the last time!

It was something that he said every once in a while.

He had told them.
More than once he had told them.
He had told them.
He was done with the hero business.

And they listened.
And smiled.
And tickled his ribs.

And would kill anything that attempted to harm him.

After all, he was their hero as well.

Chapter One

Beginnings

Grandeville. Tinker's Place.
It was New Year's Eve.
Once again.
It was a party, a relatively quiet party.
Once again.
It was a relatively quiet party on New Year's Eve.
Once again.

A family gathering.
For them.
Just for them.

All in all, it was a fairly typical activity in this corner of rural, northeastern Oregon. For New Year's Eve.

This particular party was happening not far outside the small, isolated community of Grandeville. The large, sprawling house was just a short drive from the edge of town. Up on a high bench, off by itself.

However, as family gatherings go, as family parties go, one might say, given the cultural values of the nation, and the cultural values of this corner of the state, that this was a somewhat unusual family to be gathering together this New Year's Eve, for a relatively quiet party.

So, as we just said, it was New Year's Eve. And it was a gathering of his family. And they were gathered in the large living room. They were mostly occupying the three large couches that had been shoved around until all could face the large Christmas Tree. And some chairs as well.

He sat on one of the couches, one arm thrown around Smoke's shoulders and looked around the room and at the gathering. Besides the rest of himself, there were his children, Je'leel, Eulin, Rorx with his wife Szaifeh, and Sedeem and her husband Farth. And standing here and there were the mothers of Je'leel, Eulin, and Rorx: Dat, Sa'ar, and Imdar.

Sliding his arm from around Smoke's shoulders, lightly brushing his fingers over her thick, jet black hair, he stood and hoisted his glass high into the air. "A toast, I propose a toast." And stood close to Sedeem.

Everyone quickly refilled their glasses with whatever they wished.

"It is a custom," he stated, "somewhere in this world to toast on New Year's Eve those close to us who are no longer here. Therefore," he looked at Sedeem, "to your mother, R-Bar," and scanned the rest of the faces watching him, "and to Ran, and to Flar, and to Ferrelden." He tossed his drink into his throat, dropped the glass on the couch, and hugged his first child. Sedeem hugged him back.

"I miss them all," he murmured, blinking back the tears he didn't want starting.

"It has been a year, Dad," she whispered gently, "since Mother died."

Chantal joined them and hugged them both. "Fourteen months." And kissed each of them on the cheek.

"One more toast," rasped Tinker.

Chantal leaned close and growled in his ear, "It better be upbeat this time, Cowboy." She gave him a friendly pat on the rear pocket.

He winked at her, retrieved his glass from the couch, smudged away a small spot on one cushion, and held the glass out while Chantal refined it.

"Sip it, this time," she ordered.

"Sure, Boss." He nodded and smiled at her.

Then he held his glass high. Everyone did the same thing.

"To wives and to children." He took a sip. "Love everyone of ya." And quickly set his glass in a safe place as Chantal wrapped herself around him. "Give us a big sloppy kiss, husband. It's New Year's Eve."

He did.

Smoke tapped Chantal on the shoulder. "Next." Then he worked his way through the line that had quickly formed. And finally kissed three daughters on their foreheads and hugged one son.

Then he hugged Farth in a very formal sort of a way, thumping him on the back. There was a lot of back to thump. And after that, he was draped with and by Szaifeh, who grinned wickedly, black eyes twinkling, as she held him. "Me too, Unc, you old hunk."

So he kissed her too. And laughed. "May I sit down now?"

Sha'gar and Chicken dragged him to one of the couches.

"OOOOOF."

"Thou art a jewel, Husband King." Chicken handed him his glass. Refilled. Sha'gar nodded.

Chantal tossed an arm around Smoke as they sat in one of the other couches. "He is positively glowing with happiness."

Smoke nodded. "Fourteen months of peace and quiet and just us." She tickled Chantal. "You were right to insist on that. He is calm and healthy and totally at ease with everyone here."

"Yep. And it certainly didn't hurt that all his kids could get here for Christmas and New Years."

"And his other . . . wives."

Chantal laughed. "And them too. How did you arrange it?"

"Three-S," stated Smoke, meaning Sha'gar, Sgenn, and Szart.

Szart walked across the room and joined Chantal and Smoke on the couch.

"Don't look so serious," said Chantal, looking

into her deep black eyes.

Szart nodded, and said ever so softly, ever so carefully, "There is one more who wishes to be here."

"What!" Chantal looked around the room. "Who?"

"I think that he can handle it." Smoke grinned broadly, orange-gold eyes glittering.

Szart looked over at Sgenn. Who looked back.

Sha'gar, now sitting very close to Tinker, slid her arm around his waist. Just in case. And nodded.

Szart nodded back.

She faded in, soft as a summer breeze. A tall woman with her arm around a young boy who looked to be around fourteen or fifteen years old. They both wore shirts of a soft fine material colored a pale rose. Over each left breast there was embroidered, in fine detail, a black dragon in full flight. Their black trousers were draped neatly over soft boots of a light tan color.

She stared at Tinker. And stated, firmly, Royally, "Greetings! To Our Great King Husband from your Most Dutiful Queen Wife, The White Warrior, Daughter of The White Warrior, who does now present to thee, Our Noble Son, Prince Frahn, Realm of the Dragon."

She bowed her head and nudged her son toward the man sitting on the couch, staring at them, mouth slightly open.

"Holy Cow," whispered Chantal. "Her!"

"By George," gasped Chicken.

"He is handsome," cooed Messenger, grabbing

two glasses from a tray. "Really really." She jumped up and handed one to Lurin who was waiting, watching Tinker, and her son.

Slowly he stood, eyes jumping from the boy to the woman. "My. . . son?"

Rorx grabbed Szaifeh and hissed in her ear, "Say nothing."

The boy stopped and bowed formally. "Father, I am Frahn, Prince of the Realm." He looked up, bright blue eyes looking into bright blue eyes.

Lurin looked pointedly at Szart. "Sook, her sister, Mine Own Brother's Queen, did say that We must come." She looked back to Tinker. "We are here. If thee does so order it, We shall flee."

"NO!" He shook his head. "No." And smiled, a wobbly weak sort of a smile, still somewhat unsettled by their sudden appearance.

Sha'gar and Chicken jumped to their feet. "Sit thee here," said Chicken, waving at the couch, "for now all his family do be gathered herein."

Lurin glanced over at the younger folk, and nodded, recognizing his features in the daughters and the son. She walked over and sat next to him and sipped at the liquid Messenger had poured in her glass.

"It does appear that We do have much to learn, Our King." She grabbed one of his arms as Frahn, now standing in front of them, frowning slightly, asked, "I have three sisters and a brother?"

"Wow!" gulped Tinker. He nodded. "Yes. You

do."

Messenger hurried over and handed a glass to Frahn. "It is called root beer."

Chantal looked at Smoke.

Smoke nodded. "It is what she wanted. Some time has passed in her elseplace."

"She knows?"

"Sook told her what little that she knew."

"Sneaky of you." Chantal jabbed Smoke in the ribs with an elbow.

Smoke winked. "Szart did it. Your idea, fourteen months ago, to get him to accept his . . . harem." She looked around the room. "And they are all here. And he does." She leaned close, her lips tickling Chantal's ear. "And there will be no more, I think." She laughed. "Could be more kittens, though. You, Szart, Sha'gar, and Sgenn are fertile. Also that Queen."

"Don't get any ideas," snarled Chantal. "Let's go get the cake and ice cream." She stood and headed for the kitchen.

Chicken went along to help.

In the kitchen, Chicken winked at Chantal. "Fair dragon pon Fair Queen's shirt do fair fly." She grinned. "Most pointedly."

Smoke cut the cake. "She has grown. Some."

Chantal leaned back against the counter top and stared at Chicken. "Do you realize, given the age of her son, that your brother, her father, must be nearly fifty years old now? And his Queen. And Hanred and

Ripple."

Chicken frowned. "Me'thinks We do need most closely question Fair Queen pon Fair Prince training and upbringing. Tis most bothersome a'fact, that."

Smoke shook her head. "Ask Szart. Let's not bother Lurin. Or him."

"Right!" Chantal grabbed the large cake tray and headed for the large living room.

As she walked into the room, she saw Rorx, Sedeem, Je'leel, Eulin, and Frahn sitting in a tight group, deep in earnest conversation. The older four were very anxious to visit with each other, and a new, never before met, brother.

Messenger was bubbling around, refilling glasses and smiling happily.

Tinker was talking softly with Lurin while Fair Morn, now sitting by his other side, ran her fingers through his hair. She winked at the dessert servers.

Dat, who was large for the holiday, was talking with Sha'gar, Szart and Szaifeh.

Sa'ar, Imdar, and Sgenn formed another small cluster.

As Chantal approached their children, a golden dragon poked its head from somewhere, licked Frahn on the side of the face, and yanked away. Frahn laughed and grinned at Eulin.

"Have some cake." Chantal shoved the tray at them and waited while they took which ever piece looked best. "Where's Farth?"

"Went to bed," replied Sedeem. "He is not much for parties. And he is tired. We have been very busy building Silver Ranger facilities and housing on Frander's Dan. He needs a long vacation."

Chantal nodded and headed for the next bunch.

Sedeem looked at Frahn. "How would you like a wing of Silver Rangers for your personal troop? We are ready to begin stationing some of them elseplace."

Frahn straightened up, frowning as royally as he could muster. "None would dare attack Hahn Dohr Kahn, the Realm of The Dragon."

"Probably not," agreed Rorx.

"They would only be stationed there," explained Sedeem. "But could be sent to aid other elseplaces if needed."

"A Prince requires training in arms from the best," suggested Rorx.

"They would obey me?"

"Unless you do evil."

"Never," snapped Frahn. "Only me?"

"Or me. Or Farth as he is their, ahh, General. Or your Mother."

"Then," stated Frahn, standing up, all Royal Prince. "Let it be so."

"They will require lands for their town and farm fields." Sedeem suppressed her smile at her brother's stern visage.

"There are vast empty lands near M'Ban's Mount."

Sedeem rose to her feet and hugged him. "Then, Brother Prince, we will send The Dragon Fang Wing."

Frahn blushed and stepped back. "I better tell Mother." He hurried in that direction.

Sa'ar took a bite of her cake and said softly to Sgenn. "It grieves us all deeply. Ran and R-Bar were good friends of the Vander, of us all."

"We were a long time healing," said Sgenn. "It is good that all gather here."

Imdar nodded.

Sa'ar looked over at him and smiled. "When did he, umm, find that Queen?"

Sgenn told them all about that.

"I think that it was an after effect," explained Imdar. "The additional shock of the loss of R-Bar right after Ran died lowered his resistance and the Vander Heal still had some, ahhhh, residue. The Princess was unguarded."

She smiled. "So now we have a very handsome Prince."

Sgenn smiled, a soft half-smile, and looked from face to face. "Smoke says that in a pack with this many females that the Consort will probably no longer attract outside his cluster. She says that is The Velvetmist Way."

Sa'ar laughed, a deep in the throat laugh, her eyes twinkling. "Many Vander will be sad to hear that." She touched the sparkling purple gem hanging from a fine chain around her neck.

Imdar wore one just like it.

Sgenn shrugged.

"Well," said Tinker, "your kingdom ought to be pretty well established by now."

Lurin shook her head. "We have much work to do and even greater amounts of exploration yet before us before we know all that there is to know of our vast lands."

"Really? Must be a huge place you've got there."

"We know but a small portion. You should come and visit and explore with us." She smiled warmly.

Frahn joined them, but stood, at just the proper distance away, being carefully contained, projecting being The Prince of the Realm.

"Our Prince?" asked Lurin, recognizing the look in her son's eyes. In this aspect he reminded her of her brother.

"My sister, Sedeem, has offered, for my own, the Dragon Fang Wing of the Silver Rangers. Her husband, Farth, is their General." His eyes sparkled.

"I suppose," said Tinker, "that a Prince needs his own men."

Frahn tried vainly to suppress his grin. "The only Prince in all the kingdoms of Bahn Duhr Tohr, Old Kingdoms or New Kingdoms, who would command such."

"True." Lurin smiled, the hand resting on Tinker's thigh tightened, slightly. "What say thee, Our Lord King?"

"Silver Rangers?"

Frahn nodded. "They may have lands for town and fields near M'Ban's Mount, an unsettled, mostly yet to be mapped region." He looked at his mother. "Thus we settle and map a new portion of Our Kingdom."

Lurin looked at Tinker, merriment crinkling the corners of her eyes.

"Sounds good to me." Tinker winked at her.

Frahn snapped rigid. "Great King, We salute thee." He did and bowed. And then relaxed and grinned broadly, eyes dancing. "Will you come and see them? Umm, once everything is settled?"

Tinker laughed. "Sure. Other than Je'leel, I have never had an offspring that I could watch grow up, more or less."

Frahn spun on his heels and hurried back to tell Sedeem.

Lurin clenched Tinker's hand in one of her's as she watched her son stride away. "'Tis sadness shared then, for Our Prince did just shortly return to Us, a young Prince, a new not new son, to a mother that did but bare hold and suckle him."

"What?" Tinker twisted around and grabbed her by the shoulders. "What?"

"Our Brother's Queen Sook did tell Us of great witch training did We but agree." Lurin blinked wet. "So We did agree to this, as it was much as we did, Our Brother and I. For the good of Our Kingdom and for the good of Our Son, Future King, We sent him away."

He released her and gently caught the tears with his handkerchief.

"But we did weep weak woman's tears in Our Private Chambers, We did."

"How long?" he rasped, "has he been gone?"

"From thy mighty conception has passed but two hard cycles of seasons with no word as to good or ill. Handsome Prince Our Son left as mere babe in Sook's arms and then appeared most grown, not long after came thy request for Our attendance here. He is a Prince, grown and witch raised."

He kissed her. And sat back. Then he stood, grabbed a hand of Lurin's and Fair Morn's and tugged them to their feet. "Come on, let's eat some cake and ice cream."

Chicken grinned at Chantal. "Woooooosh, a mere years two."

"No wonder she looked so young." Chantal headed for the kitchen. "Let's get the rest of the goodies."

Smoke went with them.

Chicken headed down into the cellar. And not much later, headed for the living room, arms holding several large cardboard boxes. She ripped them open and began to extract bottles of champaign and set them on the tables. Then grabbing two by the necks, after shooting the corks across the room, she headed for Tinker who was standing next to the table with the cake and ice cream. She banged one bottle against his chest and let go. He caught it.

Spinning around, Chicken held her bottle high. "To arms, to arms, for We do propose a toast." She waited until everyone was prepared.

"Tis the end of one year in this Our world and the beginning of a'new. We, His Queen," she glanced over at Lurin. "His Verra First Queen, do Ourself Most Royally toast all the Lords and Ladies herein gathered."

She looked around the room. "Who he, and we all, do love most endlessly." Tilting up her bottle she took a very long pull from it. And leaned back, knowing that he was right there, thudding back against his chest.

He threw one arm around her. "Let's go outside and look at the stars, Slim. It is a strangely balmy night for this time of year."

"Jolly good idea, Our Own Bonny Prince."

They headed for the front deck.

"A queen?" asked Frahn.

"Let's sit in a corner," suggested Sedeem. "Each of us will tell you about your father and our parents. And you can tell us about your mother."

She laughed. "We can watch them get all rowdy."

They sat on the edge of the front deck, looking up at the midnight sky and the silver specks decorating it.

"Beyond counting, LordLove." Her bottle gurgled as she took another drink.

"I told Frahn that we would visit." His bottle

gurgled counterpoint to her's.

"Indeed?"

"He wanted to show off his unit of Silver Rangers."

Twisting around so he could lean against one of the deck pillars, he wrapped his arms around her as she leaned into his embrace.

"Fair Prince, thee does Us nantle most outrageously."

He kissed the side of her neck. "Cause you are there."

She squirmed. "Indeed, Me'Lord, indeed."

Chantal squinted at Smoke. And mumbled, "Going to bed, sneaky got to him first."

Smoke winked. "Yep."

Chantal headed for the hall, veered, grabbed Lurin and hugged her. "Really glad that you came. Someone will show you to your room." Spinning away, she headed for her own bedroom.

And soon the living room emptied as all did the same thing.

Fair Morn led Lurin and Frahn to their rooms. Fair Morn's high metabolic rate burned off everything so fast that she was unaffected by large quantities of drink.

Rorx and Sziafeh said goodbye. They were staying with her parents in town

Sa'ar took Imdar to her parent's home, first telling Smoke that any not having rooms could come along as her parent's house could hold all that wished to come.

"Me'Lord, tis most chilly out here."

He stood, gathered her into his arms. "Hot tub'll warm you up." And laughed. "Comes from running around with your shirt mostly off."

"Thee did Us disrobe, sirrah."

He scooped her up.

"We can walk."

"Sure, Slim. Get the door." He carried her inside, through the empty living room and hall and into the tub room. And stepped over the edge. "Happy New Year!"

Water surged in all directions.

"We do be clothed," sputtered Chicken. "Mostly."

And soon, they sat on one of the corner benches, steaming water up to their necks. Soggy piles of clothes lay on the wooden decking near the edge of the great hot tub. She was nestled inside his arms.

"Be thee sleeping, SweetLove?"

"Dozing."

"Our Verra Own skin do be a'puckering most prunishly." She stood. "We would lounge in thy warm, dry bed we would."

"Right. Let's go. Grab some towels."

Chapter Two

Just The Family and All That

Grandeville. Tinker's Place.

He had shoved the couch around. It was the over-stuffed green one. And now sat slumped in it, watching the TV, the sound off, waiting. One of the many quilts was draped over his lap and legs. Both hands held the steaming cup of coffee perched on his stomach. He was oozing into the day. Slowly.

It was morning.

Far across the valley, visible through one of the large living room windows, the sun could be seen, up above the mountain ridge lines, coasting into the sky, casting long lines of gold into the valley.

"Bright Dawn, Husband King." She stood and stared at the TV set. "Truly, it is as We were told by Hanred, Our Parents Advisor, and by Our Royal Father. This is an elseplace most magical strange."

"Morning." He smiled up at her. "Join me? Watch the parade?"

She lifted the quilt and sat next to him, dragging over another.

"Coffee and cup are right there."

She took a cup, filled it and refilled his. And kissed his cheek. "Chantal gave Us this bed garb to wear. Most pleasant."

"Silk."

"She did say these be men's but that here all do wear such."

He nodded. "They decided long ago that men's pajamas were comfortable." And laughed. "So that is what they wear. What you are wearing we had made in Bahn Duhr Tohr at a specialty clothing shop. Got that tricky seam."

"My King?"

He sat up, set his cup on the floor and turned toward her. Pulling the quilt aside, he reached out and with one finger touching the seam at her neck and slid his finger down to the bottom edge of her top. The seam parted, the garment fell open. "Like that."

She looked down and smiled. "Just so. But it is no surprise."

Sliding the garment aside, he reached out and touched her. "I don't remember that scar."

A jagged line ran from just below her right armpit diagonally across her chest.

"Frown not, tis mere memento of the building of the great span. We did help, as did all, in mighty construction. Some support timber did rupture and smite us as we did work." She grinned. "It did ruin mine garment."

"Queens should be more careful," he grumbled.

"We do be most careful." She lifted his hand and kissed it. "It did ruin nothing else. In Our Kingdoms, it is expected that all will share in the building."

"Fair Morn, Me'Lord, Me'Lady." Chicken sauntered in and around the couch and sat by his other side, yanking another quill around. "Fine parade do itself start do thee but wish to watch? It!"

He reached out, held the lower edges together and ran his finger upward, reclosing the seam. "Guess we had better watch the parade."

"As thee wish, Our Own." Lurin looked over at Chicken. "Bright Dawn, Highness." She rearranged the quilt.

"Coffee, please," said Chicken, batting her bright blue eyes dramatically at him.

He handed her his cup. "Here."

"Most kind, Our Heart."

Waggling the controller at the TV set, he brought the sound up, dropped the device into his lap, and slumped, and watched the Rose Parade start.

Chicken wiggled into a more comfortable position.

"You done squirming?"

"Most comfortable enow." She dragged the comforter up to her neck and settled under his arm.

Lurin looked over, and slumped until she could do the same thing.

He sighed.

The parade wandered on until interrupted by one of the many commercials. Messenger bubbled into the room. "Morning morning morning morning." She carried a tray with cups and a large pot of cocoa. Setting the pot on the wood stove, she filled a cup and joined the trio, sitting next to Chicken.

Then Je'leel came in, stood near the group and smiled at them over her cup of cocoa. "Morning Father, Mothers."

Lurin smiled at her. "Sit thee here, Fair Daughter, by Our side." Je'leel did.

Suddenly his hair was violently mussed. "Morning, Dad. WOW, couch is filling up." Sedeem laughed as he grumbled at her, freed his arm from Chicken and swiped at his hair.

Filling a cup with coffee, Sedeem dropped next to Messenger. "Morning, Mom." She glanced over at the clock. "Must be about half over."

Smoke slipped silently by and checked the several pots and looked toward the hall as Fair Morn entered, dragging on her top. "We will make breakfast."

Messenger bolted from the couch, quilt tumbling to the floor. "I'll help." And looked back from the dining room door. "Oooooopsie."

Sedeem laughed and slid next to Chicken, rearranging the quilts. "Been a long time since I watched the parade."

"Indeed," agreed Chicken.

"Shhhhhhhh," hissed Tinker.

By the time the parade was nearly over, almost everyone had risen and wandered into the living room.

By the time the parade was over, breakfast was ready and all but one had settled themselves around the dining room table.

As the last platter was set on the table. Chantal walked in, dropped into her chair, dragged her cup over and sipped, eyes mere slits.

"Walking dead," mumbled Tinker.

Lurin gasped.

Imdar leaned over and whispered in her ear, explaining what he had meant.

Dat slipped into the room and sat next to Chantal, taking a cup of cocoa. She eyed Lurin and nudged Chantal. "A real yum."

"Shhhhhh," growled Chantal.

There was a soft poof of black and they were there.

"Morning, Unc." Szaifeh bent over and kissed his cheek. "Morning all."

"Morning, Father, Mothers." Rorx walked around and kissed Sa'ar and Imdar. "First Greetings."

"First Greetings," they replied.

Rorx fetched two more chairs and sat, Szaifeh by his side. "Temperature dropped last night. It is starting to snow pretty good."

"Oh boy." Messenger giggled. She enjoyed winter and playing in the snow.

"Bout time," said Chantal, now mostly awake,

glowering at Chicken. "Last night was rather balmy for this time of year."

"Most chilly," stated Chicken.

"Happens when you get your shirt snuck off," said Fair Morn. "Pass the toast, please."

"I am going to vegetate on the couch," announced Tinker into the several conversations rattling around the table. "And watch football games."

Imdar leaned close to Lurin and explained what all that meant as well.

Lurin nodded.

And so the day wound on.

Tinker melted into the couch properly armed for a day of football games. Things to munch, things to drink. People scattered everywhere to talk. And to do this or that.

Part way into the first game, Chantal came in. "Gimme room, Cowboy." She yanked blankets, quilts, and pillows around. "I like football too."

"There are acres of couches," he grumbled as she thumped and flopped everything into place.

"Only one hot-water bottle named John," she grumbled back, snuggling close.

He twitched. "How'd you get so cold?"

"Outside, moving fire wood around."

His head snapped up. "In your pajamas?"

She kissed him. "Of course not. Changed back." And slid one hand up under his top. "Umm, nice and warm. Tug that quilt up a little, will ya?"

He did. "There, boss."

"Damn right."

By the start of the second quarter, Chantal had fallen asleep.

The light was fading in the room by the time the second game was tied in the last of the third quarter.

"Husband King, may We join thee?"

"Huh?" He jerked and looked around. Lurin stood behind the couch near one end. "Oh sure." He yanked everything away from his free side.

She sat and pulled things back into place and slipped her arm under his. "Explain this game to Us."

"Sure."

The game paused and amidst the noise of the commercials, Chantal woke and thrashed upright. "I'm cooking dinner." She lurched up and toward the kitchen.

"We like this game." Lurin slid her arm around him. "Football. It reminds Us of our knights assaulting in test combat. Somewhat." She hugged him. "Be thee with Us disgruntled?"

"Huh? What?"

"We did be most forward and We did make thee both a Father and The King."

"Oh." He slipped an arm around her. "It was a shock, ummmm, both times."

"We are more warrior bold than princess subtle." She twisted around and slipped her hand up under his pajama top. "And most ill-trained in coy and sly tricks."

"I suppose."

"There were none in all the kingdoms would We wed." She frowned. "And with Our great new lands many Royals would have come, smiling and speaking sweet words, wanting Us the Kingdom, not Us the Princess."

He reached up and brushed her hair with one hand.

"So. We made Our choice. We did see you and them on occasion and decided after escaping from that great cavern to solve Our problem. T'was most sudden a feeling and most powerful a one. Our Son will be King in time, Our Kingdom has succession and none dare come a'slithering about Our Court visiting Us, for all have heard of thee, The Chosen One, Legend, and Terrible Warrior."

He smiled. "Seems pretty sly to me."

She nodded. "Perhaps. Howsoever, with thee We would be mere plain maid, straight and true." Her eyes held his. "Wouldst lovingly forgive Us with a kiss?"

"Sure."

She slowly tugged him over.

"Oh my gush," gasped Messenger as she ripped a head of lettuce into shreds for the salad she was making. "How are we going to keep everyone out of the living room?"

"Everyone is in the private spaces," said Smoke, reaching out with her mind. "They are visiting in various of the bedrooms. Fair Morn can keep them from leaving."

Fair Morn stood in the great open space, the three story high open space that they called The Chamber, her great butterfly wings open, and flapped vigorously. Every now and then she lifted off the floor and glided a little, forward and back. She needed the exercise to keep her great wings from itching after being folded for long periods of time. It was much too cold outside and this was the only space in the house large enough. But she thought that it was a very dull thing to do to just stand in one spot flapping wildly. However, it sure beat the pain of stiff cold wings. One experience like that had been enough.

"Ummmm?" he said. "Princess?"

"Husband?"

"We had better watch the remains of the game. This house has an awfully large number of people in it and this room gets lots of traffic."

She frowned. "Yes?"

He nodded and sat up, swinging his legs around and dragging quilts and covers up and over them. She did the same and kissed his cheek tugging one of the quilts up to her chin. Then she leaned against his side and watched the game.

He slid his arm around her. "Where's your top?"

She shrugged.

He sighed. "Oh well, just keep that quilt in place."

Chicken walked in and turned on some of the

lights. "Dinner do be ready in but one hour."

The wrong team had won and he clicked off the TV.

"Husband, show Us thy great hot tub." Lurin smiled. "Fair Morn did describe this thing and thy room of shower and We would try these things."

He smiled. "O.K., let's go. Hang onto that quilt."

They stood on the edge of the hot tub. "O.K., out of those pajama bottoms and slip in." He tossed his aside and slipped in.

She followed. "Most warm."

"Yep." He walked into the deep end and settled, water up to his neck.

She followed. "We did find some springs like this." And stood close.

"You could turn one into a spa."

"Explain this thing."

So he did.

She nodded slowly. "We shall have this done when the seasons allow. We shall name it Spa."

He smiled and pulled her close.

Chantal opened the oven and checked the sweet potatoes. "Wonder if it will be a boy or a girl?"

Smoke patted her as she peered over Chantal's shoulder. "Neither. She is in her safe time."

Chantal shut the oven and turned around as Smoke stepped back. "You can tell that?"

"Yes."

"We need to reschedule things around here. Us

fertile babes need to know things like that."

Smoke winked.

"How come you never said anything before?"

Smoke shrugged.

"Foods ready." Fair Morn turned off the last burner on the range.

Everyone gathered around the dining room table.

Lurin halted Tinker by the doorway and whispered, her face held close to his face. "What manner of folk be Dat?"

"She is an indjinn."

"From what elseplace did thee her capture? Never have We seen a wench with eyes all purple, and with fangs, and with hands and feet be'clawed small."

Taking her hand, he tugged her back into the living room and over to one of the book shelves. Picking up an ornate ring he held it out for Lurin's inspection. "This ring is called The Eye of Dat. She lives, lived, in there. The ring was a gift, bought at a witch Foregather. Indjinns are some sort of magical being that apparently live forever as far as we have been able to find out."

Lurin slowly turned the ring over and over, then looked into his eyes. "Je'leel is Our Daughter? The Dat indjinn is her mother?"

He sighed. "Yes."

She stepped even closer. "Husband King, what manner of share wives are these? All of them? Those that We did first believe were naught but warrior women, thy own personal guard, now do appear to be more than that!"

"Stay here." He walked into the dining room. "I want each of you to come into the living room, one by one, starting with you, Princess."

Chicken stood and went with him.

Facing Lurin, he threw his arm around Chicken's shoulders, and explained. "The Princess Chicken, recreated Easter egg toy, changed by Big Red into this lovely person." He kissed Chicken on the side of the face, and sent her back to the dining room.

And they came.

One by one.

"Smoke, of The Velvetmist, a race of telepathic and very large carnivores, changed by Big Red into this luscious form."

"Messenger, who's life we saved. She never knows darkness. To her there is no such thing. She also sees magic emanating from those sorts of people."

"Fair Morn, a magical jest, created by Big Red. She has gigantic butterfly wings and flies. Messenger broke the bonds holding her to B.G., and she became a real person."

"Chantal, a native of this elseplace. Veterinarian. She has her own business in town doctoring all kinds of animals. And, on occasion, us."

"Sha'gar, Faan magician."

"Sgenn, Faan theurgist, Sha'gar's sister."

"Szart, Faan witch, a cousin of Sha'gar and

Sgenn."

"Dat, an indjinn."

She kissed Lurin and asked, "Does he like to play with your body?"

"Indjinns have sorta one-track minds," he grumbled as she walked away.

"Sa'ar, Heart of the Vander, also known as The Purple Mage."

"Imdar, Vander Healer."

"Eulin, Daughter of Sa'ar, also called Dragon Force, trained as Dragon Master, one day Heart of the Vander."

"Je'leel, as you know, Dat's daughter."

"Sedeem, my first child. Her mother, R-Bar, a Faan witch, is dead." He blinked back a tear. "Farth, her husband, is The General of the Silver Rangers."

"Rorx, Warlock of the Vander, Imdar's son. His wife is Szaifeh, Faan witch. Sha'gar and Sgenn are her sisters."

Then they were alone again.

"So," he sighed. "Now you know." He looked at her. "And, Lurin, Princess and Queen. And my son, Frahn, future King."

He took her hand and said, "There is one more." He pulled her over to a dark corner. A great, two-handed black sword leaned there, point down. "Slayer, my weaponkin."

She reached out. One fingertip touched the hilt. The golden jewel set in the base of the hilt began to pulse.

"DON'T TOUCH IT!"

She jerked her finger away.

"You're not going anywhere," he growled at the weapon. The glow faded away.

"It," gasped Lurin, "is alive!"

"Yes," he whispered. "It is, in a manner of speaking. It likes to kill."

She yanked him into a different corner. "When My Brother and I did wander, we heard many tales." She stared at him. "Had we believed those tales never would We have dared act as We did with thee."

He grabbed her, hugged her, and kissed her. And said gently, softly, "I am just a very ordinary guy who happens to have had his life go in some very strange directions." He laughed. "So, here I am. With a harem and five lovely children." He kissed her again. "And you know what?" He smiled broadly. "I like it. In spite of everything, all the strangeness that we seem to get involved in, I like it." He held her tightly and murmured, "And I love you, all. Regardless of how it. happened." He rubbed his hand up and down her back gently. "It is really true. Let's go eat. They are waiting for us."

They strolled into the dining room and sat down. Lurin shoved her chair between Dat and Sha'gar. Everyone beamed happily and began to send dishes and platters around the table.

Lurin turned toward Dat. "Very nice. Does he

like to play with your body?"

Dat smiled, long canines protruding over her lower lip. "Of course. Indjinns are very beautiful."

Lurin sat back and began to fill her plate.

"Pass the cranberries," he grumbled.

Eulin leaned sideways and said something io Frahn. He blushed. Sa'ar wiggled one finger, ever so slightly. Eulin quickly sat up and looked ever so Vander proper. She winked at Je'leel when Sa'ar turned her head to say something to Imdar.

They were working on dessert, several types of cheesecake, when Sa'ar stood and bowed to Tinker. "Vander Lord we must return shortly after this meal. I am very happy to be one of the number here visiting." She sat and smiled warmly at him.

"Short visit," he grumbled.

She nodded. "We are building new quarters, more bedrooms. We decided all should have larger private rooms. The original Vander were rather monkish in a sense. We have decided to be less so."

She beamed at him. "Come visit, Vander Lord Husband."

"Ummmmm."

She laughed. Then she looked across the table at her daughter. "Eulin wishes to stay and visit with her siblings."

"Of course." He nodded and looked around the table. "You all staying for awhile?"

"A few more days, Dad," replied Sedeem. "Then

we must return and ready the Dragon Fang Wing for relocation to Hahn Dohr Kahn."

Lurin looked at her and asked, "Daughter, how many folk will this be?"

"A Wing has 345 rangers plus girl friends and the families of the married. The village will have Wing farmers, artisans, craftsmen, etc. Another two hundred or so." She smiled. "I'd say that there is around one thousand or so total, including children."

Lurin nodded. "They will conform to Our laws and customs?"

"Yes. With two exceptions."

"Oh?"

Sedeem leaned forward. "Mom, the Silver Rangers are committed to the good folk. They will never obey any command that they feel is a breach of that oath. And, if necessary, the wing may be called elseplace, temporarily, Other than that, your kingdom will be their home base. Their allegiance is, in this order: the Silver Rangers, and your kingdom."

Lurin nodded and smiled. "Then We are satisfied to have such a mighty host come to Us, Daughter."

Frahn beamed. "Three hundred and forty-five."

Lurin looked at Farth. "Great General, We do wonder whether these artisans and crafts guilds do work their arts only for The Silver Rangers?"

"No," said Farth. "Beyond the needs of the Wing, and their community, they sell or barter, with others. The Rangers choose to be self-supporting. As much as possible."

Lurin nodded. "Then we would have their spokesman meet with Our Guild Heads to correlate their wares with these others." She held up one hand. "And Mine Own Brother's as he does specialize in weapons and armors."

"Of course," replied Farth. "They will be instructed to do so. There should be no tensions in these matters."

Lurin smiled. And thought that once things were settled that this new group would be a welcome addition to the Kingdom. Both in new skills and new economic endeavors. To her folk.

And to her treasury. Her First Lord would be very busy settling all these matters. Her eyes traveled around the table as she listened to this and that snippet of conversation and finally settled on his face, looking at him with new sight.

Chantal leaned close to Fair Morn and whispered, "And I thought that Smoke had a predator's stare."

Smoke leaned forward, peered past Messenger and winked at Chantal.

"Yep," said Fair Morn, eyeing the remaining piece of cheesecake.

"Nothing subtle about that gal," added Chantal.

"Yep," said Fair Morn, replying to Chantal. This yep was a little muffled as she was finishing the last piece of cheesecake.

Then everyone headed for the living room.

Sa'ar and Imdar halted Tinker before he could leave the dining room.

"We must go," said Sa'ar. She hugged him. And stepped back so Imdar could do the same.

"Come visit." Imdar kissed him. "We are building a special suite to accommodate you and them." She hugged him tightly. "We, Sa'ar and I, see you too infrequently."

"I know."

She stepped away.

Sa'ar threw her arm around Imdar's waist. "We would like you to visit when it is not important." She smiled. "It would be ever so much more . . . relaxing."

And they were gone.

"One game to go," he said flopping onto the couch, grabbing the control and turning on the TV.

"Good night, Father," said Rorx. "We are going back to Doc's to visit."

"Night, Unc." Szaifeh bent over and kissed him. "Mom doesn't say much but she does like to be visited." She straightened up and looked pointedly at Sha'gar and Sgenn. "By her daughters."

Sgenn looked at Sha'gar. Sha'gar nodded and grabbed Sgenn's arm. They faded away.

"Ptar tik tik," snapped Szaifeh, grabbing Rorx' arm and yanking them elsewhere.

Tinker laughed. "Bet J.C. and Reep weren't expecting that much company."

Lurin sat on the couch and slumped alongside him. He was already slumped comfortably. It was a new experience for her. Royalty were not supposed to slump.

She leaned against his side. "Parents and children should visit. Often."

"Ummmmm," he replied. The game had already started.

"Hum hum," said Szart from another couch.

"Gosh!" gasped Messenger. "I don't think that she meant that." Then she giggled and blushed. "Well, maybe she did."

Chantal looked around the room. "Where's Dat?"

Je'leel pointed at the shelf. "Mother said that she was tired. She retired to her ring."

Eulin bumped Je'leel with her elbow. "Frahn is going to do wander. He said that we could come along."

"Think that we should?"

"He could use the protection."

"I don't think he would let us come if he thought that was why we came along?"

Eulin grinned. "We won't tell him."

Je'leel looked doubtful.

"I think Father would like the idea of his children spending some time together."

"Vander sly," suggested her sister.

"Of course," laughed Eulin. "I am The Heart To

Be."

"Let's take a walk. After that meal, I feel like a slow stroll outside."

"Sure," said Smoke, going with Chantal down the hall. And after dressing warmly, they headed into the first pasture and beyond.

Eulin leaned close to Je'leel. "Let's go to your room. I'll ask some of the tiny dragons to come. I found a whole group of them, all colors, on Dikto Flow. They sing just like your birds do here."

Je'leel nodded. They left the room, arm in arm.

"If it wasn't so cold, I'd go outside and fly." Fair Morn wrapped a turkey leg in a paper towel.

"We could go to my room and watch a movie," suggested Messenger. "I took the old TV from his former den to my room. It has a player."

"I select the movie?"

"All right." Messenger giggled. "Get two." She headed toward the Chamber, scooping up two of the cats as she walked along. They were two males, the grey and the black.

"We would with thee go," stated Chicken, peering around to see what Fair Morn was selecting from their large collection of videos.

"Sure," replied Fair Morn, grabbing the second of her two choices. "Let's go." Szart joined them.

The game had ended and now they were lounging in the hot tub. Lurin had insisted. She had argued that it was necessary as she required another time in order to know how to build Spa.

They stood in the deep end, water up to their necks. He was leaning back against the wall. She was leaning next to him.

"What do your folks think about you having an off-campus king?"

She moved sideways, up against his side. "We do not know as the folk rarely express those types of views to Us. Nor do We know what off-campus is."

His hand slid around and up her rib cage. "I meant your parents. Ahhhh, about not having your king, errrrr, not living there with you."

"The Queen and The King said little though We feel both would have preferred Most Royal a ceremony such as that done for Own Brother."

"Ah, well."

He tugged her around and pulled her close, both hands on her waist.

She smiled. "Most mighty a King."

"Ummmmmmm."

Eulin burst into a fit of laughter. "See, I told you. They are like birds."

Je'leel kissed her.

Tiny dragons were perched and flying everywhere in the bedroom. All colors. All singing.

"Woweee," laughed J.C., trying to hug three daughters at the same time, "the gang's all here." He grinned. "So, Rorx, keeping her in line?"

He released them and tossed his arm around the slim woman standing so quiet and still by his side.

"Healthy and happy," whispered the shadows as she leaned against his side, looking at her daughters.

Rorx sat in a chair. Szaifeh sat on Rorx who quickly wrapped his arms around her. "No one keeps witches in line," he said.

"Mik tik," mumbled Szaifeh.

J.C. picked up Reep and held her cradled in his arms and sat in another of the chairs.

Reep curled against his chest. "So," asked J.C., "what's the occasion? Don't ever remember seeing all of you in one spot before, like this."

"His Queen Lurin Wife said parents and children should visit," explained Sha'gar, dragging over a kitchen chair.

"So we came," added Sgenn, doing the same thing. "Here."

The great black staring eyes of their mother carefully looked at each of her daughters. "Hum hum," she said, soft as air.

"The Princess of the new lands," explained Sgenn, sitting as still and calm as her mother.

"All of his are visiting, Dad." Szaifeh shifted into a different position. "And his children." She kissed Rorx on the cheek.

Sha'gar nodded. "That Princess of one of the new lands birthed him a son."

"Frahn named," added Sgenn.

J.C. laughed. "That boy does seem to get around."

Reep nodded. And looked at Rorx.

"It was nice to be able to visit with all my sisters. and brother," he said.

"Must be quite a gathering," said J.C.

Rorx smiled. "Sedeem and Farth are sending one of the Silver Rangers Wings so Prince Frahn will have a Prince's Own Guard."

"Eulin is going to visit and teach him some dragon lore," said Sha'gar.

"They found a Great Black living in a dormant volcano," explained Sgenn.

J.C. leaned his head close to his wife's. "I think that Sgenn is as quiet as you are."

The faintest of movements occurred at one corner of Reep's mouth.

"Bet that she has a bigger smile."

Reep tickled his stomach, having slipped her hand inside his shirt.

"Sgenn," he said, "smile."

"Yes, Father." A soft, half-smile formed and faded away.

He laughed happily. "See," he said to Reep.

"How is our niece?" whispered the quiet. "Szart?"

"Very happy, Mother" replied Sha'gar. "A powerful witch."

Szart waved in big bowls of popcorn. And laughed.

"I don't think that it is funny at all," said Messenger. "Really really."

The monster had just finished doing horrible things to a minor character and was now threatening the heroine. Szart smiled.

"Ghastly," agreed Chicken.

"Sorry," said Fair Morn, taking one of the bowls. "Next movie is just good old fashioned action. Airplanes." She enjoyed movies with flying in them.

Then the movie ended. The hero had won. Szart frowned.

"Don't look so grumpy," said Sedeem. Frahn was looking unhappy at her and Farth. They had just explained why they would not accept a gift for stationing the Ranger Wing in his elseplace, in his kingdom.

"It is not proper," he stated, all Prince proper, "to accept such without some, umm . . . response."

"The Wing could not come," mumbled Farth.

Frahn sat straighter. "General?"

Sedeem propped her head on one hand and suggested very carefully, to both of them, that perhaps something small of little or no monetary value would be appropriate.

Farth fizzled. And thought about it.

Frahn looked at Sedeem and suddenly smiled.

He twisted a ring from a finger and held it out to her. "Here, take this."

The ring was black metal with a square cut rose gem whose face was artfully etched with the same dragon design as on his shirt.

"This ring has little value in coinage. Yet all who see it in Our Realm will know the bearer is of The Royal House."

Sedeem took it and smiled at Frahn and then at Farth. "A noble gift." She slipped it on one finger. "Don't you think so?" she asked Farth, holding out her hand so he could admire the ring.

"It will be acceptable," said Farth.

And with that piece of business completed, they relaxed.

Frahn smiled at them. "I will give the head of The Wing a ring just like that one. Thus, all will know and honor them accordingly."

Farth nodded. "That will be acceptable. Also. Prince."

Frahn jumped up and thumped Farth on the shoulders. "It is Our Great Honor, General." And sat down again. He beamed at Sedeem. "I am going to do quest," he stated, "as soon as we leave here."

"Really?"

"Yes. All Royals who wish to rule must do this. Quest." Frahn beamed at her. "Eulin and Je'leel want to come along."

She nodded. "I thought that Eulin and Je'leel had

already done wander."

He nodded. "Eulin was on the Dragon Master search. Je'leel went with her." Then he looked all serious and stern. "I will see that no harm comes to them. They are my sisters."

Farth's eyebrows shot straight up. Sedeem killed the smile that she felt forming and stifled her laughter.

"Oh," she said. "Ahhh, I am sure that they will feel quite safe, mmm, with you."

"I am well trained. Mother's Brother's Queen, Dark Sook saw to that."

Farth looked at Sedeem.

"I am sure that she did," agreed Sedeem, giving Farth a small sign to say nothing.

Farth stood and bowed to Frahn. "Great Prince, we, The Silver Rangers, salute you." He looked at Sedeem. "Perhaps there is some of that coffee stuff still available?"

She rose to her feet. "In the kitchen." She looked at Frahn. "Eulin and Je'leel are in Je'leel's room."

He nodded and hurried away. To discuss the quest with his sisters. And to assure them that they would be quite safe journeying with him.

Je'leel cautioned Eulin. "Our younger brother approaches."

Eulin told the dragons back to their elseplace a moment before a soft knock came on their door.

"'Come in," said Je'leel, rising to her feet. She had

been sitting on the floor surrounded by a cloud of the petite dragons. And waggled a finger at Eulin.

Eulin fastened her upper garment and sat on the edge of the bed, looking her proper best, as Frahn opened the door and came in. "Sisters."

"Hi," said Je'leel.

"Brother," responded Eulin.

His eyes twinkled as he sat on the end of the bed. "Once we leave here, I am going to do quest." He looked from face to face. "You are coming, aren't you?"

"Yes," said Eulin.

"I will have to ask Father," said Je'leel.

"Good." Frahn nodded, and then looked at Je'leel. "Will he refuse?"

Je'leel shrugged. "He is very happy because I live and grow here." She looked from Frahn to Eulin. "Unlike any of his other children." Then she sat and hugged him. "Don't look so worried. I think that he will agree."

"Most sleepy a'looking King," she purred.

His eyes popped open. "Let's go to bed before I fall asleep. And drown." He heaved himself from the hot tub, grabbed one of the large white robes and slipped it on. The material was thick and easily absorbed the water on his body. Shaking open another robe, he held it out and open for her as she stepped from the steaming water.

She smiled and slipped into the robe. "If one of those panting courtiers had looked at Us like that, We might have wed them." She tugged him into motion. "Through this door?"

"Yep." He led her into the Chamber and to his bedroom.

"Most different." She eyed the king sized bed set flush with the floor.

"I suppose." He tossed his robe to one side and crawled under the covers. And flicked off the light as she joined him.

Soon, everyone else wandered to their rooms.

The house became quiet.

And still.

Chapter Three

A Quest Can Be Very Interesting

Grandeville. Tinker's Place.

He stood at one of the large windows in the large living room and watched the soft start of a snow storm as it began dusting white specks past the glass. And sighed. It had been two weeks. The house was back in order, all the furniture back to where it belonged, holiday stuff packed away for another year in the storage space for things like that.

She walked in, leaned against his back, wrapped her arms around him and peered over his shoulder at the white becoming whiter.

"Pretty heavy sigh, Simba Leader."

"Just wondering how the kids are doing. It has been a couple of weeks."

Chantal patted his stomach and leaned her chin on his shoulder. "Should do just fine, should be all right. Eulin and Je'leel are with him. Anyone messing with them would have to be a raving idiot."

Ginde's Giome. Fair. Sunny.

The raving idiot was doing just that.

Raving.

Actually.

He was screaming.

Frahn stared round-eyed at the market spot. It was littered with a number of bodies. He jerked. Not fear, adrenaline rush.

They had attacked without warning. His sword was gory, his clothes stained and splattered.

Eulin kicked the large screaming man not too gently in the side of the head. "Be quiet. You are not hurt. Yet. Mostly."

The screaming descended into subdued blubbering.

Eulin scratched the large green and yellow dragon on the side of the neck. "Keep him there." One great, blue taloned foot was covering the man's stomach. The toes flexed in and out. Just a little. The dragon warbled liquid sound at her.

"Maybe," she replied.

Je'leel looked around the market spot. People were peeking through windows and out barely opened doors. They thought that they knew what that monster was and had decided that it looked hungry.

"Whoever they were," she said to Eulin, "they were not nice." She bent at the waist and spoke to the man held in place by the dragon. "You will answer our questions." And straightened up.

"Our brother," mused Eulin loudly, "appears to be becoming a mighty warrior. But he certainly needs more training in planning."

Je'leel and Eulin had arrived at Frahn's elseplace, and the Queen had said that Her Prince had already set off on his quest. So the two sisters had searched for him.

They had arrived in the midst of a real brawl.

Je'leel looked over at Frahn, He was much taller, slightly over six feet tall, broader in the shoulders. "He has grown."

Eulin nodded. "Very nice."

Frahn sucked in a deep breath, blew it out loudly, and walked over to them, still clenching his dripping sword. "Sisters! It has been some time since last we visited."

Eulin nodded. "It appears to be about three years or so."

"Closer to five." Frahn smiled. "I have learned much, studied much, traveled much." He carefully looked them over. "You look . . . unchanged."

"Our time has been short," said Eulin. "But you have certainly grown."

"We have been searching long and far." Je'leel frowned at him. "Why didn't you wait for us?"

Frahn ducked his head, looked sheepish, and mumbled, "I, ummm, thought that I might, ahhhh, find a, errm, Princess."

Eulin grinned. "And you thought that two sisters coming along might not approve of you taking her?"

Frahn blushed.

Je'leel looked at the mess in the market spot again. "Well, Brother? What made all this? Mess."

Frahn wiped his sword clean on a nearby body and looked at his weapon. It was chipped and beat up.

"There seems to be few of them, Princesses, in the elseplaces." He looked up, frowning. "Royal is uncommon."

Eulin waved his clothes clean and then hugged him. "But there should be lots of young women attracted to handsome warriors." And laughed.

His face flushed even brighter.

"Eulin," cautioned Je'leel.

Eulin released him and stepped back and grinned at him. "Well, if you can't find a Princess, I know lots of willing Vander."

"Brother," interrupted Je'leel before her sister could expand upon that line of thought. "What shall we do with that?" She pointed at the man beneath the dragon's foot. "And this mess?" The dragon had lowered his head and was now sniffing at him.

Frahn nodded. "Yes." He strode over and knelt next to the fellow. "Do I know you?"

The man stared at him.

"Answer or be eaten," stated Eulin, walking over, joining the little group.

"NO!" gasped the man.

"Fast learner," said Eulin to Je'leel.

"Money?" Je'leel looked past her brother's

shoulder.

"Yes."

"There are six dead men here," said Frahn. "Are there more in your, ummm, group?"

"No."

"True?"

"Yes."

"Just money?"

"Yes."

Frahn stood and looked at Eulin. "Let him up."

Eulin nodded. The dragon stepped back.

"Stand up," commanded Frahn.

The man slowly did, watching the great monster carefully.

Frahn unhooked a small sack from his belt and banged the man in the chest with it. "Here!" And thumped him again with the sack. "Take it!"

The man hastily grabbed the sack.

"Now, leave us."

The man spun and ran, stopped, turned around, stared at them, and whirled back around and down a narrow street.

Eulin said something. The dragon was gone.

Frahn nodded. "If they had asked, I would have given it to them."

"Most generous," said Eulin.

Frahn shrugged. "I think that I will go find a way home."

"Empty-handed?" asked Eulin.

"In The Realm, I have all that I can ever spend."

"And Princesses?"

Frahn sighed. "There are many Old Kingdoms in Bahn Duhr Tohr. I suppose." He sighed again, very heavily. "I suppose one of them will do. Mother said that I must wed soon after returning. I am afraid that she will pick someone if I do not.""

Eulin tossed her arm around Je'leel. "We can not allow our Brother to settle for just any Princess."

"It is his decision!"

"Of course," agreed Eulin.

He frowned at her. "Eulin."

She shrugged. "Well, at least we could get you a Hephira blade and armor, special made." Eulin looked at his equipment. "Much better than that stuff you have."

"Well," said Frahn, somewhat bothered by what his sisters may, or may not be up to. It was just a small feeling of unease.

"Let's," said Je'leel. "You require, Brother Prince, much better than that thing you now carry. I have heard that the Hephira make some of the best in all the elseplaces."

"Ummmm," he said, and nodded. That sounded like a good idea. "All right."

Wenl Fzar. Mid-Day.

They appeared on the road not far from a massive dark stone castle constructed from ancient grey bamir. It was obvious that this castle had once been rather heavily battered. There were many lighter grey areas where the repairs had been made.

Four guards stood by the gate eyeing these suddenly appearing large folk with great suspicion. They watched carefully as the trio approached. The golden scale mail armor of the guards gleamed soft tones in the sunlight. Their golden swords glittered sharp edge.

"Well," observed Eulin. "A little shorter than Messenger and Szart moms described."

"Beautiful armor," said Je'leel.

The large, round, dark brown eyes of the male hephira carefully judged these tall strange folk walking up to them. They popped their swords back into their sheaths.

"I am Je'leel, daughter of The Chosen One. This is my sister and this is my brother. We are here to visit Prince Helf."

One of the guards called into the dark space behind the gate, told the courtier something, and sent him running.

"Wait. And wait," said the guard.

"Father helped them free their lands of great evil," explained Je'leel to Frahn. "I am sure that they will help you gain better armor and a much better weapon."

Frahn studied the guard's armor. "In all the kingdoms I would be the only one wearing such as that." He nodded, and smiled.

They waited.

His smiled broadened as he imaged himself standing in front of the ranks of The Silver Rangers. A golden gleam with glistening silver behind.

A courtier hustled through the gate, dressed in billowing ornate court robes. "Welcome, welcome, welcome. Our First Prince and His Princess bid you welcome. They would see you now. Please, follow me. Please?" He waved one arm at the dark space inside.

They started back into the interior of the castle. And sooner than they had expected, they stood in The Audience Hall. The Prince and The Princess, seated in rather plain looking chairs, watched them approach. The courtier scurried away, having been told that this was to be a private audience.

"Welcome, children of our savior," said Helf, rising and bowing deeply. "Ask and it shall be done ." He waved one hand at the room. "In here, it is our custom that none shall be seated but My Princess and I."

The Princess smiled at the trio. "Stay awhile? With us? In more comfortable surroundings?"

Frahn looked at his sisters and nodded. "It would be a great honor, Princess."

"Please," asked the Princess. "Give us your names?"

"Je'leel, daughter of Dat."

"Eulin, daughter of Sa'ar, Heart of the Vander."

"Frahn, son of Lurin, Queen of Hahn Dohr Kahn, Realm of the Dragon, one of the new Kingdoms of Aahn Dohr Tohr."

The Prince stood. "I am Helf. This is Nandau. I am formally called Andarl sa Helf, First Prince. She is Nadarl ca Nandau, First Princess." He waved one hand. "Come, our quarters are this way. Allow us to show you to your rooms." He looked at Frahn. "It appears that you are in need of clean water and sweet smelling lotions."

Frahn nodded and thanked him, for the three of them, and then said, "If possible, I would like armor such as I saw on your guards."

Helf laughed, stopped a passing courtier and told him something and then led his company around a corner. "The golden scale mail is some of the best in the elseplaces. We will have The Armorer make you some. And a new weapon as well? Suitably sized. Perhaps?" He smiled. "Would you like one?"

Frahn grinned. "Yes."

After a few more turns, a few more doors, down a few more halls, they stood in a large room. A young woman stood waiting, dressed in warriors garb, gleaming golden tones.

"My younger sister," said Nandau. "Irinl of the House of Nadarl, whose proper title is Nadarl ca Irinl, Princess."

Irinl bowed. She stared at these three large folk.

"These," explained Helf. "Are children of The

Chosen One. Frahn, Eulin, Je'leel."

Irinl nodded. "Brother and . . . sisters."

"Yes," said Eulin. "Brother and . . . sisters."

Irinl looked at Frahn, at his travel stained clothes, and his weapon, and then slowly walked around him. "A warrior?"

Frahn looked down at her eyes. Then he realized that the male Hephira had deep brown eyes, the females were azure bright.

He stood taller and straighter, dwarfing her. "I am Prince Frahn, Commandant Dragon Fang Wing of The Silver Rangers, one day King of The Realm of The Dragon, Hahn Dohr Kahn." He bowed slightly. "And a warrior, trained and trained."

She stared up at him, folded her arms across her chest, and stated, firmly, "I am Nadarl ca Irinl, Princess, un-mated, Raz of The Royal Arm." She bowed slightly. "And a warrior trained and trained."

She spun on her heels and commanded him to follow. "We will measure you for your armor and a better weapon. Now!" She strode out through a side door calling over her shoulder, "A much better weapon! Come! This way!"

Frahn had to hurry to catch up with her.

Helf laughed. "The Princess is . . . " And shrugged.

"Herself," said The Princess. Then she explained that in the Land of The Hephira that there could only be one First Princess, what other elseplaces called Queen.

Her younger sister Irinl had always been a little brusk. And had spurned all Princely suitors. So far. As unsuitable. She was too much a warrior to accept most that came seeking her hand.

Helf led them to their rooms and told them, as he showed them everything, that the last Prince who had dared to put his arm around Irinl without asking had been heaved down the Grand Staircase. By her. Few Princes had come visiting since that event.

The royal pair left Eulin and Je'leel to relax and to refresh themselves saying that Frahn's rooms were next door. A courtier would come when the meal was ready.

Eulin flopped back on the bed, testing it, and pinched Je'leel when she sat next to her.

"What?"

"My question," replied Eulin.

Je'leel looked down at her sister, stretched out by her side. "That First Princess wants something."

"What?"

Je'leel shrugged. "I could feel it. She will have to say it."

Irinl gestured over The Chief Armorer. "This large Prince requires the finest armor and weapon that you can make."

"At once," said The Chief, calling for assistants, looking over this large person. He had already received word.

Irinl stepped back and stared at Frahn and what he was wearing. "Take that ugly off," she ordered, poking at his stained and well worn garments.

"No."

"DO IT!" she snapped. "Why not?"

"I wear nothing else," said Frahn. "It would not be proper with you here, Princess."

Irinl whirled away, barking commands. And in quick order, other assistants rushed in carrying arm loads of cloth, tools, and measuring devices. They swarmed around and over Frahn, pushing, poking, bending him this way and that way. And then, in a remarkably short period of time, they handed him a new set of garments, bowed to Irinl, and hurried away.

"Now," stated the Princess. "You have a proper set of garments to wear beneath our armor." She turned her back on Frahn. "Now, get dressed," she demanded, folding her arms over her chest, one foot tapping a steady rhythm, a slow steady beat. "NOW!"

Frahn quickly shed his clothes and yanked on his new trousers.

Hearing the rustle of the material, Irinl spun around and stared at him. He quickly tugged on the rest of the garments.

"What are those scars?" She pointed at his chest.

"Training," he said, hastily yanking his shirt closed. "Hard training."

She nodded. "It will be two suns before your armor and weapon will be ready. They will work hard, and steady, night and day, to make it so." She glanced sideways at The Chief.

He bowed. "It will be so, Princess." He knew an order when he heard one.

She nodded. And beckoned Frahn to follow her. It was a very imperious gesture. "I will take you to your rooms, Warrior Prince Proper." She strode rapidly out a door and down a hall. "COME! This way!"

He had to hurry to catch up with her, stuffing in his shirt as he went.

Later, much later, the Hephira ate the final meal of the day, only after it had been dark for the proper amount of time. Helf related to them how he had been rescued by their father as well as his princess and his kingdom. And then he told how he had taken the armed might of his kingdom to fight alongside the combined armies of Bahn Duhr Tohr and the Silver Rangers to help them eliminate an evil kingdom that had kidnaped The Princess of the Queen of Bahn Duhr Tohr.

Frahn gasped.

"Prince?" asked Helf. "There is something wrong with your drink? Or your food?"

"NO! Not at all. That was my mother you helped rescue."

Helf, Nandau, and lrinl stared at him.

"How is that possible?" asked Helf. "It was but some not long ago time."

"Time flows at different rates in the elseplaces," said Eulin.

"Our brother was witch-trained," explained Je'leel. "Taken as an infant, returned as a near grown man. And did quest adding four or five years to his then grown age."

Frahn nodded. "No one truly understands how the witches do this. Or how it works."

"I fought in that battle also," stated Irinl. "Your mother is beautiful." She stared at him. "That explains your handsomeness."

Frahn's face flushed. "Why thank you, errrrr, Princess." His eyes jumped from Hephira to Hephira.

"My sister," explained Nandau, "was warrior determined even then."

"And quite young to command and fight as such." Helf frowned at Irinl.

"But I did that." Irinl frowned back. And took another serving from one of the bowls.

"She would be the same age as you, Prince Frahn," said Nandau, waggling her hand. "If I understand your time reckoning system." She frowned, just a little. "Well, perhaps two years older."

Irinl nodded and glared at Frahn. "How fits our garb?" She chewed on the leg of something.

Frahn plucked at his shirt. "Soft feeling, snug yet not constricting." He grinned. "These are royal garments. Ummmmmm, would it be possible to, eeeee, acquire a few more assemblages? I would wear such as this at home. And perhaps see whether our tailors might copy them?"

Helf laughed. "We will gift you all that you wish, just name it to us."

Nandau smiled. "Prince, no tailor will be able to do that for it all lies in the material not the cut. And only we, in this land, produce such a cloth."

For a moment Frahn's eyes unfocused as his thoughts took him away. Then he looked at Nandau and smiled. "Ummm, perhaps we may discuss, tomorrow, some way to link our kingdoms together in a mutually advantageous trade system?"

Nandau looked at Helf. She nodded. He smiled at Frahn.

"Prince," said Helf. "I hear the voice of a shrewd ruler who asks to improve his lands and the fortunes of his people." He thumped one hand lightly on the table top. "After the morning audiences, we shall gather together and see if your lands have something we would seek not already here available. Think you on this."

Frahn nodded. And wondered what could be in their undeveloped country that the Hephira kingdom might want.

Hours later, he thumped a fist on their door and after being invited in, dropped heavily into a chair. "I am in trouble," he sighed.

Eulin sat up, dragging a blanket up over her shoulder not wishing to further bother her obviously deeply bothered brother and leaned back against the head board of the bed. "That was fast," she said, smiling at him. "Which Hephira have you impregnated?"

"What?" He stared at her.

Je'leel sat up and banged Eulin on the shoulder. "Behave."

Frahn shook his head. "I can't think of anything that we can offer in trade."

"Oh." Eulin forced her smile away.

"If only I knew everything The First Lord did." Frahn sighed heavily.

Eulin ordered on clothes and disappeared.

And reappeared.

Frahn leaped to his feet and gasped. "FIRST LORD!"

The large, angry man stared at him. "Prince Frahn?"

"I am."

"Why has one of these play ladies of your's brought me here?" He glared at Eulin.

She glared back.

"First Lord," stated Frahn coolly, all regal and royal. "Meet two of my sisters, Eulin and Je'leel."

"Sisters?" The First Lord dropped to one knee. "Humble forgiveness, Noble Ladies."

"You are forgiven," replied Je'leel. "An honest mistake." She smiled at Eulin.

The First Lord cleared his throat. "You look, um, different that last I did see you."

Frahn headed for the door. "Come, First Lord, we have much to discuss and discuss and not many dark hours to do it in."

The First Lord stood, bowed to Eulin and Je'leel and hurried after Frahn, closing the door as he left the room.

"Play ladies," snarled Eulin.

Je'leel shrugged. "You could have worn something less clinging."

"This is proper Vander night wear."

"Play Lady," stated Je'leel, crawling back under the bed covers.

And well into the middle of the next day they met.

"This is The First Lord of Our Realm," said Frahn. "He knows every detail of everything our people make and do. Perhaps if he might discuss our trade with your similar office here, then our business might proceed all that much smoother and faster."

Helf smiled at Frahn. "Well done." And ordered a courtier to take The First Lord to the appropriate person.

When they were alone, Helf touched Frahn lightly on the arm. "We are impressed, Young Prince, and see much of your father in you."

"You will be a good King," added Nandau. Taking his arm, she led Frahn to one side of the room. "We wish to ask a favor."

"If I can, I will."

"You agree too fast." Nandau's smile faded away. Then she told Frahn how three rulers back, the Hephira had lost the Cross-Star Wand. There was learned debate still going on about this event as it was not supposed to have been possible. Some blamed it on dark powers. Some whispered that The Evil One was involved.

"Not long ago past, a wandering merchant saw the artifact in the hands of the Gray Orz on Lelty and had offered to buy it. The Gray Orz beat him and threw him to Farac. Now," explained The First Princess, "the Princess Irinl means to travel to Lelty and retrieve the Hephira relic with cash or the might of arms."

Frahn nodded.

"Prince," said Nandau, her grip tightening on Frahn's arm, "we ask you to accompany Our Sister and to aid her in this quest for we fear for her health and safety."

"Ummmm, my sisters will want to come."

Nandau carefully studied his face. "Will they be safe?"

Frahn bent his head and spoke very softly. "Eulin is a Dragon Master. Ummm, Je'leel is just Je'leel, I think."

"If you believe that your sisters must go with you, then it is so." She had no idea what he was referring to, nor had she ever heard such a title before.

He started to turn away. She held him back.

"What?"

"Only if Irinl agrees. However, not I, nor My Prince may ask her. If we ask, she would instantly refuse."

"Oh."

"At some opportune time and place, Prince."

He nodded. Slowly. "I see."

"I believe that you do." Nandau smiled at him.

Sometime later and later when the sun hovered directly overhead, Frahn looked over at Princess Irinl.

"Princess?"

"Prince Frahn?"

"We have long discussed affairs of state and of business and now we are done. My armour and weapon will not finished until next day."

His eyes watched her face and those large azure eyes watching him ever so carefully. "If you would be so kind, I would see more of this castle and grounds as I am tired of sitting."

Helf nodded. "We have Audience all afternoon, Prince Frahn."

Eulin stood. "Je'leel and I are going to visit the shops. You could come with us." She smiled at Frahn.

"Perhaps," suggested Irinl, "your Warrior Prince would rather visit our training halls and walk the high walls?"

Frahn stood. "I would." He smiled at her. "If you would be so kind." And bowed as well as he could.

Irinl jumped to her feet. "This way!" She strode

rapidly for a side door. "COME!"

Frahn had to hurry to catch up with her.

Je'leel slipped her arm under one of Eulin's as they walked down one of the halls. "He is going to ask the Princess if we may accompany her on her journey to recover the Hephira relic called a Cross-Star Wand."

"How do you know that?"

"Indjinn hearing. I heard what Princess Nandau told him. I have more indjinn than Father knows." Je'leel tightened her grip on Eulin's arm. "And he is not to know. He believes that I am mostly human. Mother was very clever to birth a daughter who looks so correct. But I am indjinn more than I am human, ah, his race."

"Certainly don't act like one."

"I know and understand Father's culture. All his children are born of elseplace females and live and grow in the elseplaces. I live at home. He has a strong need for family, and a home. His kind of family and home."

Eulin slipped her arm free and tossed it around Je'leel's shoulders. "His elseplace is the most backward and isolated that I have ever visited. It must be hard."

Je'leel slid her around Eulin's waist. "Indjinns have few needs or wants. Mother loves him, thus I am. So, I choose to live there. To me, this Hephira elseplace, or any other, are as backward."

Eulin jerked to a halt and wrapped her arms around Je'leel. And hugged her.

"What?" asked Je'leel.

"What?" asked Irinl, leaning back against the wall, wiping the sweat from her face with her sleeve. She had convinced Frahn to parry with her once they had reached the training hall. So he had.

Now he stood back, out of range, and did the same thing. "I will require new clothes. Now." His garments were sweat stained and soiled.

"Easily done." She watched him carefully. "What did you say?"

His practice sword flicked here and there. "I said that I would like to accompany you on your quest." He lunged. The sword tip chipped the wall as she danced away, striking for his legs. His legs pulled up as he jumped, spun, and landed, swinging. The flat of his blade caught her on the side of the head, sending her stumbling, staggering, crumbling to the training hall floor.

Dust puffed up around her as she hit.

"PRINCESS!" He ran over, dropped to his knees, and bend over the still form checking for damage.

She stabbed him with her dagger.

"OUCH!" He sat back and glowered down at her.

Irinl looked up and glowered back. "It was just a touch." And slipped her secondary weapon away. "That was foolish."

"I was afraid that I had hurt you. Badly."

She glared. "The blow was to my head. Why were you fumbling with my upper garment?"

"I was loosening your neck cover as a slight touch of fingertips to the side of the neck can tell much as to health."

"Show me this skill."

Bending back over her, he fumbled with the fastenings on her collar and then gently rested his fingertips on the side of her neck. "Like this."

"Am I healthy?"

He nodded. "Very much so."

"Lie down," she commanded. "I would try this thing."

He nodded. And did. Irinl sat up, bend over him and unfastened his collar. Soft fingertips fluttered on the side of his neck.

"This way," he said, taking her hand.

"Ah," she said, "a steady bump thump. Are you healthy?"

"Very much so."

She nodded. "You may accompany me."

"And my sisters as well."

She nodded. "If you wish them to do so, then they may." She leaned back.

He sat up. "Are you hurt?"

"You did not inspect my head."

"Sit closer and hold still!"

She sat as close as she could.

He reached out and gently turned her head to

one side. Then, with trembling fingers he brushed the matted hair aside and leaned close.

"Well?"

"The skin is unbroken. But there will be a sizable lump and strange colors." He released her.

She turned her head back, nose almost bumping into nose. All he could see were those enormous azure eyes filling his sight.

He cleared his throat. "Ummm, perhaps we should stop practicing for now? Do something else?"

"As you wish Warrior Prince. Did I break your skin?"

"I forgot to check."

She sat back. And reached out and touched a splotch on his chest. Then she looked at the stain on her fingertip. "True sorry."

He smiled. "A scratch to remember you by."

"Fancy words."

"I must practice those skills as well. They are necessary for court business."

"You may practice those skills on me as well. If you wish."

He nodded. And stood up, reached down and helped her to her feet. Then he handed her the primary weapon and bent over to retrieve his. "OUCH!"

She had slammed him across the backside with the flat of her weapon. "That was also foolish." She headed for the door. "In the training hall, training does not stop until you leave."

He leaped, fingers sinking into her hair, yanking her backward as his other arm wrapped around her, pinning her arms, lifting her off her feet. "Yield or die!" he snarled as she thrashed in his grasp."

"NEVER!" Using only her wrist she tried to slash at his legs. Unsuccessfully.

He struggled to restrain his squirming captive, wrapping her ever more tightly in his arms as he banged through the door into the outer hall.

"I yield," she snapped.

"That was foolish," he said. "Turning your back on me in the training hall."

"You may release me now, Prince. There is no longer a valid reason for clutching me so tightly."

"OH!" He released her, arms flying wide. She hit the floor with a thud. He offered her his hand and helped her stand.

She tugged her garments back into some semblance of order.

He took a quick step backward. "Princess?"

She took a quick step forward. "Prince?"

"What?" He wasn't sure whether she was going to attack him or not. She had a strange look in her eyes. Maybe he had breached some terrible royal code of the Hephira by his actions. She hadn't explained anything before they had started practice.

"What do I look like to you?" She hung her sword on her belt.

"Ummmmmm," he replied, struggling to find an

appropriate reply. She was a Princess after all. "Dirty. A sweat stained, dirt dusty Hephira princess." He figured pure description ought to be safe.

She frowned darkly.

He gulped and knew that he was in trouble now, somehow. "Very messy. Clothes, eeeee, disorganized, oh, ripped open. Sorry."

She glowered.

Now he was sure that he had broken some Hephira code. "Hair is matted and tangled. Face is dirty. One eye is puffy. The side of your head is more swollen."

She quickly stepped close and kicked him.

"OUCH!" He leaped back, out of range.

"That is what you see?" she demanded, glaring up into his face, taking a quick step forward. "A dirty, messy Princess whose clothes you have ripped open. One with a dirty face, beaten and made swollen by a large beast of a warrior."

"Ummmm," he said, taking a step back. He banged into the wall.

"Yes?"

He cleared his throat. "If it would be permissible to say so, as Prince to Princess, eeeee, as Warrior to Warrior?"

"SPEAK!" She jammed her hands on her hips, brows furrowing in a dark glare.

"Princess Irinl, I think that you are truly beautiful."

She blinked and spun away. "The wash facilities for warriors is this way!" She stomped down the hall and around a corner. "THIS WAY!"

He had to run to catch up with her.

Two turns in the hall later, she stopped and threw open a door. Steam billowed into the hall.

Irinl poked her head inside and bellowed, "OUT!" She stepped back, crossed her arms over her chest as her foot began to tap.

In moments, three burly Hephira warriors hurried through the door, hastily fastening their clothes on still wet bodies.

"It is empty, Princess," said the last one out. She halted him and spoke softly. He nodded and rushed after his companions.

She looked at Frahn. "I will call you when it is, eeeh, proper." She hurried inside.

The three warriors cast furtive glances as they turned at the first intersection. They had heard rumors about the guests of The First Prince.

"You may enter," called Irinl.

Frahn stepped into billowing steam and soft shadows.

"Throw those filthy rags into a corner by the door and step into the water."

He did as he was ordered. The water came up to his chest. "My Father has something similar to this in his house. Only not so steam filled."

"That green cloth resting on the edge will wash.

Bring it here!"

Grabbing the cloth he surged in the direction of her voice. And gasped. "PRINCESS!"

The water lapped just under her chin. "I am clothed up to my neck. Wash my hair. Gently!" She turned around. Water surged over her bare shoulders.

He moved close, dipped the cloth in the water and carefully, ever so carefully, began to wash her hair.

When he was done, she plunged beneath the water and came surging back up, blowing water, facing him. "Now I will wash your hair. It is a custom among our warriors. Warrior to warrior."

"All right." He settled until the water was up to his neck and closed his eyes tightly as she poured water and cleansing suds over his head. When she was done, she tapped him on the forehead. "Rinse!"

He sank to the bottom, ran his fingers back and forth through his hair, and opened his eyes. And burst upright. "Princess!" he gasped, having managed to suck in some water in his surprise. "You lied!"

"How did I lie, Prince Frahn Proper?" She glowered up at him, water still lapping under her chin. She noted that he was as well muscled as she expected a warrior to be. And that it was only a small cut.

"You said that you were clothed up to your neck."

"You peeked," she snapped.

"Not deliberately," he snapped back. "Princess Irinl Improper."

"I did not lie! I was, and am still, clothed up to my neck." She pushed back away from him. "In water." And hit him in the chest with the green cloth. "And if you had kept your eyes closed as you should have, you would not be so upset now."

"I am not upset."

"RILGAR!"

"What?"

The door opened and someone cleared their throat.

"Speak," snarled Irinl into the steam fog.

"New clothes. Here? As requested. And towels." The door closed.

She turned and surged away from him. "The stairs are over here. You just wait there, proper Prince Frahn."

Through the steam fog he could just see, faintly, golden skin gleaming wetly as she stepped up and out and into the fog. Then he heard the door open and close. And then, in quick moments, the door opened again. "Your things are here by the door. I will wait outside." The door slammed shut.

As he stepped from the door, she frowned up at him, arms crossed over her chest, foot tapping slowly.

"What?"

"What do I look like to you? NOW!" She jammed her hands on her hips.

"Clean." He laughed. And hastily added. "Like a princess, Princess."

"That is it?"

He wondered how he was ever going to get out of this trouble, whatever it was, that he was in, and which seemed to be getting ever worse. "Ummmmmm, errrrrr," he said, quickly searching for the correct words. "Even more beautiful when clean?" He frowned. "And dressed." He tried a smile.

She stared at him. "I suspect that I am beautiful undressed." She held out her hand. "Come! Prince. I will lead your clean and very proper royal self to a filling meal and comfortable surroundings."

She took his hand and guided him back to the housing area. She had a very strong grip.

"Before we eat, I will instruct you in how to properly brush and braid my hair. If we are to travel together this will be a skill you will need to know." She towed him into her rooms.

He had just finished the braid when a soft knocking started on the outer door.

"Enter!" she snapped.

A courtier carefully stepped in. "The First Prince," he said even more carefully, "wishes both to eat the meal with him and His First Princess, your sister."

"We will," growled Irinl.

The courtier hastily backed away and out.

She hustled him down the halls and into the correct room. He almost had to run to keep up with her. Prince Helf and Princess Nandau, Je'leel and Eulin looked over as Frahn hastened in.

Irinl stomped past him and dropped into a chair, shoving another sideways at Frahn. "We are here," she announced.

Helf smiled at her as his eyes carefully inspected the swelling on the side of her head and the discoloration on her cheek.

"What?" Irinl filled her cup and Frahn's.

"We have heard," said Helf, making a small signal to a hovering servant to begin serving the meal to everyone present. "We have heard that some mighty warrior bested the Princess in training combat."

He nodded at Irinl. "It appears that this is true. We would decorate such a warrior for all to see, as such a happening is rare and deserves recognition."

Irinl sat straight. "What manner of decoration, Prince?"

Princess Nandau held out her hand. An orange ring decorated with an ornate inlay of blue lay in her palm. "First Warrior. The same as that which you wear, Sister."

Irinl leaped to her feet. "I would bestow this honor!" She stalked around the table and snatched the ring from her sister's hand.

"Of course," agreed Nandau.

Irinl returned to her place, grabbed Frahn's right hand and tapped his third finger. "Wear it here." She slipped the ring on as he held out the indicated finger.

"It self-adjusts," she said. She dropped into her

chair and looked at her sister and at Helf. "The Prince Warrior Frahn did it." She dragged over a steaming vessel and dumped some of the contents on her plate and then on Frahn's. And began to eat.

Helf jerked back in his seat and stared at Frahn. "You did that?"

Frahn winced and nodded. And said, carefully, very softly. "We were training." He looked at the table top. "She wanted to do that, train." Now he knew that he was in deep trouble. He had battered The Second Princess.

Helf banged down his cup and laughed and laughed. "I like you Frahn. You are truly your father's son. A Noble Prince, a shrewd businessman, and a mighty warrior." He threw his arm over Nandau's shoulders and hugged her.

She kissed his cheek. And smiled warmly at Frahn, then at Je'leel and Eulin. "We are many honored to have such guests. Much has come from a simple search for armor and a weapon."

Then they sat and talked about inconsequential things and enjoyed the meal.

Frahn noticed, every now and then, that Irinl did wear one of those rings on her right hand. He hadn't noticed it before.

Over dessert, Irinl looked around the table and announced, "As soon as Prince Frahn's armor and weapon are ready, we shall leave to fetch back the relic."

Helf's eyes popped wide. Nandau nudged him under the table.

It would be two days before everything was ready for the expedition.

Chapter Four

A New Princess

Lelty. Not Exactly A Beautiful Spot.

Sansmod Arttle and his men blew a hole in the wall and crashed into the treasure room. They managed to kill all but one of the Gray Orz guarding the room and its contents. The survivor flew out through the remains of the north wall.

The men hastily scooped everything that even vaguely looked valuable into large sacks and ran outside, eager to leave before reinforcements arrived.

They were gone before Gray Orz swarmed around and into the shattered building.

Growling curses, they began to clean the room, remove the bodies, and make a list of the stolen goods. In one cycle they would hire a hunter to find the thieves and to recover their treasures.

Hamplanam. Deep Green. Moist.

Gurgling wetly, it read the commission and tapped one deep red, curved talon against a fang. This would add a great amount to a badly depleted account. There was only one thing of use in the documentation listing all the things taken, a unique artifact. That thing would be the point of origin for the search.

Shuddering its eyes, Szerul thought, and agreed. Provided that a certain sum was provided first.

It was.

Szerul left its home and began.

Lelty. Not Exactly A Beautiful Spot.

"That was not your treasure, you ugly lump of pilda glur!"

They stood in the mostly repaired treasure room. Four of the Gray Orz stood with them. One had just explained what had happened. And thanked her for her compliment.

Irinl glared up at the speaker.

The Gray Orz was twice as tall and twice as wide as Frahn. The demons were covered in grey platelets. Glowing green eyes stared down at her.

"This is a demon elseplace," hissed Eulin to Je'leel.

"Yes," agreed Je'leel "It is."

"It was taken from us," said the speaker, deciding it was a useless debate to argue over things not currently owned. "We have taken steps."

"Do you know who did it?" asked Frahn.

"No," said the speaker, wondering whether he could bargain for one of the pair standing near the door. They looked pot ready. "We have taken steps."

"Thinking hungry thoughts," said Je'leel to

Eulin.

Eulin shrugged. Her motion started the speaker's mouth to drooling.

"What steps?" demanded Irinl. Her foot began to tap a slow, steady rhythm.

The speaker looked down, licked its lips and swallowed loudly. "We have hired a hunter."

"Does it have a name, this hunter?"

"Yes. It does."

"What?" asked Frahn. "Is this hunter's name?"

"Secret," replied the speaker.

Eulin walked over to the group. "May we buy this secret?"

"Slurgs always tell secrets," stated the speaker. "NO!"

"Mind your manners, beast!" snapped Irinl.

The speaker burped. "My manners are impeccable, small lulick."

She kicked it on the side of one massive foot as her hand grabbed the hilt of her sword, ready to slice the thing into ribbons. "Piz ta!"

The speaker looked down, then at Frahn. "Is this before meal taste tickle your pet?"

Frahn pursed his lips and nodded, fighting to suppress his smile. "Yes. Why?"

"It must be hard to train and to house break."

Frahn choked back his laughter. "Yes. Very hard. Why?"

Irinl gurgled a curse under her breath and set her

stance.

"Curious. Nice ears though." Hephira ears were somewhat long and somewhat pointed. So were those of the Gray Orz. The speaker nudged Frahn. "Sexy ears. I will for it pay top cash."

"Not for sale."

"Why?"

This time Frahn did smile. And hoped that Princess Irinl wouldn't attack this thing.

The speaker gasped. "That is not nice!"

"Oh." Frahn forced his face into a blank expression. "Sorry."

"Why?" repeated the speaker, rolling one eye at Irinl.

"Very rare, hard to find."

The speaker gurgled. "We understand rare, hard to find." He patted Irinl on top of the head, buckling her knees. "Bet that it tastes good." And rolled the other eye at Frahn.

"I, ummm, haven't tasted it yet." Frahn couldn't look in her direction at all. "Ahhhh, time for us to go." He stepped back, tugging her with him.

Je'leel stepped between the Gray Orz and them. "Tell me the secret's name, handsome," she said.

The speaker stepped close to her and sniffed and snorted and sniffed again. Then it stared at her and frowned, furrowing its brows, snout, cheek pouches, and neck. "You are one of them?"

"I am my mother's daughter," stated Je'leel.

"Her name?"

"Dat," whispered Je'leel.

The speakers eyes popped wide and flared blue green. "Lovely fangs, beautiful purple eyes?"

"Mother," sighed Je'leel.

Irinl looked at Frahn, very puzzled by what she was hearing. "Shhhhh," he whispered. "I will explain later."

The speaker leaned even closer to Je'leel. "The secret's name is Szerul the Glizan of Hamplanam. A noted hunter seeker."

"Many thanks," said Je'leel, rubbing the speaker on its protruding stomach.

"Oooooo," moaned the speaker.

She stepped back. "We are leaving now." And nodded at Eulin.

They faded away.

"Could have left that small untrained pet for our collection," grumbled the speaker to the others, wiping its lips, heading for the door.

Doth Lamex. The Land of Pleasure.

They sat on the grass in their assigned area. Eulin had brought them here. It was the safest elseplace in all the universe of elseplaces. And the most comfortable for every creature that was. It was also the most private. She thought that they could plan what to do next in comfort.

They sat on the grass, three of them. The fourth

member of their party still stood and glared at Frahn, hands jammed on her hips, one foot tapping.

"PET!" she snarled at him. "I am nothing's pet, Prince Frahn! Certainly not YOUR'S!"

Eulin winked at Je'leel and murmured, "He will never get a taste that way."

"Shhhh," hissed Je'leel.

"Ummm," said Frahn, one corner of his mouth twisting, wanting to smile.

"Speak!" demanded Irinl.

"Umm." The smile refused to stay away.

"Say it!" she demanded. "Now!"

"Hard to train and not house-broke." He started to laugh, scrambling backward at the same time.

"Youuuuuuuuuuu . . . plis plit!" She lunged for him."

"NOT ALLOWED!" boomed something from somewhere.

Irinl jerked her hand away from the sword hilt, eyes darting here and there.

"Doth Lamex Guardian," explained Eulin.

"They are lovely," said Frahn.

"Doth Lamex Guardians?" asked Irinl, looking puzzled, checking their area, wondering where it was hiding.

"Your ears, Princess."

She nodded at him. "I didn't think that you noticed. Ears. Prince."

He frowned at her.

She stalked over and tapped him on one knee. "Tell me about fangs and purple eyes."

He nodded. "Please sit down and then I will tell you about my sisters."

She sat. So he did. He told her about Je'leel's mother, Dat the indjinn, who had deep purple eyes, long canines, and claws. The claws were not too noticeable as she kept them clipped short because she lived in his father's elseplace. Then he told her about Sa'ar, The Heart of the Vander, The Purple Mage, Eulin's mother. And what Eulin's training had been and why she was now a Dragon Master.

Irinl stared at him. Her large azure eyes seemed to be even larger than before.

"Princess?"

"And your mother?"

"Just a Princess. And nothing more. Other than Queen of her new lands." He smiled. "A warrior like you."

"Demons will always tell things to indjinns," explained Je'leel. "The speaker could smell my indjinn nature even though I am formed like my father's folk."

"Let's away for food," said Eulin, beckoning Je'leel to come with her. They headed out of their area to arrange things.

He looked at her, brows furrowing. "Princess?"

She shook her head. "Nothing! It is nothing, Prince."

"You have a really strange look on your face."

"It . . . is . . . nothing."

He nodded and stood. And began to unfasten his armor, walked away, and to stacked it under a tall tree. Then he leaned his weapon on the neat pile.

"What are you doing?"

"This is a safe place and I would be comfortable."

She shrugged. "I am comfortable."

He nodded. And shrugged, walked back, and sat, his back against a tree.

She jumped to her feet, stomped away, and began to yank off her armor and set it next to his, resting her sword on top of the two stacks. And turned and stared at him. And walked past, very slowly, all the way around the tree.

"Princess?"

"Tell me of your lands and why you are still un-mated."

Frahn moved so the warm sun could bath him in its heat and did, eyes unfocusing, staring into nowhere.

". . . and that is all. Oh!"

She was sitting right in front of him, legs crossed, elbows on her knees, head resting in her hands, staring into his face. He hadn't noticed her do that.

"You must come for a visit," he added. "I believe Mother would enjoy meeting you. Warrior to warrior."

She frowned at him. "You left out some, Prince."

"I did?"

"Yes. Why are you still un-mated?"

He sighed. "I suppose for the same reason that you are, Princess. I didn't, don't, find any of the other Royals very attractive."

"Not the same," she snapped. "For I am not pleasing to the eyes of the Royal Males."

"Ummmm, hard to believe that."

She glowered at him. "I am a little tall. My skin is dark. My body is hard warrior, not so rounded as Hephira values demands in a Princess. And my manner is dagger sharp. Everything not pleasing to those Princes of our lands."

He nodded. "Every elseplace has their own ideas and values. It is probably why we do quest wander, to understand that, and the many ways of seeing."

"I have been to few elseplaces."

He smiled. "I suspect one may see many before we find your relic." He stood. "Stand up. Please?"

She did, eyes watching him carefully.

He held out his hand, palm to the ground, near the top of her head. "Not a little taller," he said, smiling broadly. "But, a little short. Your skin," he held his hand next to her bare forearm, "is a lovely tawny golden fair color, not dark at all."

His eyes danced over her under-armor garments, the soft clinging , Hephira silk-smooth cloth. He cleared his throat. "Your, ahh, form is, um, not so hard looking." He smiled warmly. "And I find your manner straight and true."

He sat. "So, you see, to one of my lands you look

different than what your Royals see."

She turned and walked far across their clearing and sat under one of the tall trees, large azure eyes staring at him from the distance.

Frahn looked down at the grass, then the other way, and saw his sisters returning, talking gaily about something. And wondered exactly how many of the Hephira cultural taboos he had just bend and broken speaking to her the way he did. It dawned on him that he didn't know anything about her culture at all, just a few vague tales.

His sisters sat near him and asked why he was looking so strange.

"We were talking," he explained. And told them of his conversation.

Eulin shrugged. "We ordered food. And I sent tiny blue-greens to search for this creature mentioned by the Gray Orz." She smiled. "They will also search for the Hephira artifact."

A table oozed up from somewhere, stabilized itself, and was covered with serving dishes and everything else they might need.

"Let's eat," said Eulin.

As they began to eat, Irinl slowly walked over and joined them.

Je'leel looked at the side of her head. "You are almost healed. It is the nature of this place."

"True?" Irinl looked at Frahn.

He looked at the side of her head, carefully

moving her hair aside. "Yes. There is only a tiny mark now."

Then Eulin explained Doth Lamex. And how it had come into existence as a place of rest and healing and safety. And how it was now so many protected that no-one, no-thing, could affect it.

"We shall have several days to visit," said Eulin. "The seeking dragons will probably take that long."

"I would go elsewhere," announced Irinl. She rose to her feet, walked over to the tree where their armor was stacked and began to put her's on.

"Um," said Frahn, hurrying over and doing the same. As soon as they were done, Eulin and Je'leel joined them.

"Where?" asked Eulin.

Irinl looked at Frahn. "I would visit his lands."

"Ummm?" said Frahn, trying to not look startled.

"Sure," said Eulin, leading them to the entry field, taking them out.

Hahn Dohr Kahn. A Bright and Sunny Day.

They came down in a large area paved with smooth black stone. It was at least one hundred yards square. Along one side stood a row of houses made of wood. A number of streets passed from the pavement into the town at this edge of the gigantic square. On the opposite side reared an enormous structure still under construction.

The central section of it appeared complete. The

massive wings on either side were partially completed.

Folk hurried in and out of the great wooden doors in the central portion.

One of the two empty sides of the square edged vast fields stretching into the distance The other side opened to the not too distant river.

"This is new," said Frahn, staring at it all. "It wasn't here when I left. Wonder what it is. Stay here."

He hurried toward, and stopped, the first person he met. They could see that the conversation was animated, very lively.

Frahn walked back to them looking very puzzled. "It seems that this," he waved his arm at the structure, "is home."

He turned and led them toward the great doors, mumbling, "I really do not understand."

Inside, he asked for directions and was directed up, and up, and up. And into a large room whose windows looked out over the great square and the adjoining town.

He pointed out the quay stretching into the sea at the river's mouth. And other structures he recognized. And told them about the great bridge leaping over the river joining the two kingdoms.

Someone thumped into the room, causing them all to spin around. She was filthy, her clothes sweat stained. Her heavy boots were grimy.

She grinned and hurried to them, wrapping Frahn is a great hug. "Welcome home, My Prince. You have grown into a very handsome man." She released him.

"With very handsome traveling companions."

He nodded. And bowed. "It is good to be home, Mother Queen."

She laughed. "Such formality." And plucked at her clothes. "I was working next door when I was told of your arrival." And smiled at the others. "Not very queenly."

"Ummmm," said Frahn. "You know Eulin and Je'leel, my sisters."

"Of course. Most welcome, daughters."

Frahn's face flushed. "OH!" Then he gently laid his hand on Irinl's shoulder. "May I introduce The Princess Nadarl ca Irinl. She is the sister of the Hephira Queen. Ummm, when she was younger, she fought in the great battle that released you from captivity."

The Queen bowed to Irinl. "Doubly welcome then, most beautiful Princess."

Irinl bowed. "Majesty."

The Queen smiled warmly at her. "You may call me Lurin. What shall I call you, Lovely Warrior?"

"Irinl."

Lurin beckoned. "Come with me while I get clean, Irinl. You may tell me all about that armor and how my son comes to wear such as well." She pointed to a side door. "Your rooms are in through there."

The Queen and her guest disappeared through a different door.

Eulin looked at Frahn. "Your mother was working? Doing physical labor."

He nodded as they headed into the adjoining rooms. "Yes. She believes that all in the realm must do their share for the good of the kingdom."

Lurin looked at Irinl. The Queen's head poked above the mass of frothy bubbles in the huge tub, and began to scrub her face clean.

"Our Prince is neither wed nor bound to anyone," she stated.

"He told that it was so."

Lurin ducked, popped up, and swiped her hair back from her forehead and wiped the water from her face.

"Our King, Frahn's father," she said, "is not Royal yet is greater than any King there is."

"Prince Helf, my sister's King, told me of him, what he knew." Irinl edged closer to the tub. "And Frahn's sisters told me more. Some."

Lurin smiled. "There is much that I do not know." She told Irinl all that she knew. And then began to ask probing questions about the Hephira.

Irinl answered all that she knew.

Lurin reached out and lightly touched Irinl's hand. "Our Son, the Future King, may chose or be chosen by anyone, royal or not. He may ask only."

Irinl nodded. "I do not think that he is ready to chose or be chosen, or to ask."

Lurin's head snapped up, her eyes boring into Irinl's eyes. "My son will ask someone soon, ready or not. We have a kingdom to insure. Succession must be obvious to all. And he does know this to be most true."

Irinl felt the command in that statement and the iron will, all fierce warrior, and knew that Frahn would soon have a Queen by his side, however she was selected.

Someone soft-knocked on the door and said, "Meal is ready, Highness. How many places shall be set?"

"Five," replied the Queen. "We have Royal company."

"Royal?" gasped the voice. They heard footsteps hurrying away, running footsteps.

"Would thee, Warrior Princess, fetch Us great towel?"

"Of course." Irinl stood and grabbed one of the towels from the stack, shook it open and waited. As Lurin stood and stepped out of the tub, Irinl gasped.

"I am so ugly?" laughed Lurin.

"Those scars."

"A clumsy dragon," explained Lurin. "Healed by some of Our King's women." She shrugged. "Otherwise I would be dead." She wrapped the towel around herself. "And a small accident while building the Great Span."

Irinl wondered at the casual manner in which this Queen dismissed injuries from dragons and construction accidents.

She led Irinl into the Queen's Private Chambers. As Lurin dressed, she said, "We both are warrior trained. We know how to accept injury and pain, and death, if it comes."

Irinl nodded. "That is so."

Lurin plucked at her shirt. "Would you dress in Our Kingdom's colors?"

"I will. If it pleases you, your Majesty."

"It does that." Lurin hurried to door and shouted orders to someone. And turned back to her guest. "The proper size is on the way."

She watched Irinl unbuckle her armor and then slip from her under-armor garments. "A terrible wound." The scar ran from the edge of Irinl's left arm pit down the outside of her ribs and twisted across her mid-section.

Irinl nodded. "Received in the great battle when we freed you. I would have died. Your King's magical one's cast healing on all. My Captain, in whose arms I was gushing blood and lay dying, found it hard to believe when I stopped leaking all over him and stayed alive."

"It seems that we both owe them much, my son's Father and his, ahh, companions."

A female servant ran into the room and handed Irinl a stack of clothes and rushed away, anxious to tell the other servants of The Queen's exotic visitor.

Irinl quickly dressed.

"I will have your other clothes taken to your room."

Irinl nodded. "These clothes are very comfortable."

Lurin laughed. "We are happy to hear that."

As they entered the dining room, servants rushed away, having quickly reset everything as would suit feeding Royal guests. Frahn rose to his feet and stared.

Eulin nudged him. "Your mouth is hanging open."

Lurin and Irinl were both wearing the pale rose shirts with the black dragon embroidered over the left breast. Their black trousers draped gently over soft tan boots. It was the Royal garb of the kingdom. Irinl's braid hung past her neck, over her shoulder, brushing against her right arm.

"That shirt certainly accents things," observed Eulin. "Especially the placement of that dragon design."

Je'leel nodded and sat as Lurin and Irinl did. So did Eulin. Suddenly Frahn jerked and gasped, "Oh." And sat down, his face flushing.

Lurin leaned over and whispered to Irinl, "It appears Our Prince was surprised." The Queen made a slight gesture. The servants quickly began serving. And whispered among themselves wondering who this Princess was and from what part of the other kingdoms she had come from. By morning, the kingdom would be abuzz as the tale swept through every household, all talking about the exotic Royal visiting their Queen.

During dinner Lurin explained the palace. The Grand Council had insisted upon it. They had felt that the kingdom must have such a structure as a symbol of the kingdom's strength and wealth.

Lurin had argued that it was a waste of time and money and manpower as the kingdom was still building itself. The time and effort could be better spent in other pursuits. But she had finally conceded the argument. She had been the lone dissenter.

"Even The First Lord said that it must be so." She smiled. "If I had not agreed, the entire kingdom would have been unhappy." She nodded at Frahn. "A lesson, Our Prince. There are times when even the ruler must accept that which they might not agree with."

"Ummm," agreed Frahn. "Yes, I can see that." He began to worry about his mother's last comment. It sounded to him as if she was saying something not too subtle about future wives.

Lurin sat straighter in her chair and rapped on her glass with a knife. Servants leaped forward and filled large mugs with the local beverage. "We hope thee truly do, Prince Frahn, for hear Us now and obey without argument!"

Frahn's eyes popped wide. He straightened up in his chair. "As thee command, so shall it be," he stated formally, firmly.

Lurin stared at him, and stated firmly, "For Our Kingdom and its Future King, it is necessary that Our

Noble Son does choose a Queen."

Frahn nodded. The blood began to drain from his face. This was not good.

"This fact and event has been known for long and long, yet a decision has not come forth."

He nodded again. His stomach gurgled, small wrinkles formed on his forehead.

"As a decision has not been made, a decision that is long overdue, therefore, in this matter, The Queen has decided."

Sweat ran off his forehead and down the sides of his face. "No," he gasped.

Lurin sat even straighter and glared across the table at him. "Thee would dare argue with Us on this matter?"

He gulped. "No, Majesty." And managed to shove himself into a straighter position. He was doomed.

She pointed toward the window. "There, in the Great Square, when the sun sits directly above, on the morrow, there will be a Royal Wedding for all Our folk to see."

He blinked. His mind raced, trying to think of something, anything that he could do to affect this event.

"On the next day from this," she stated, firmly Royal, daring him to disagree.

Fighting to control the quiver in his voice, he answered. "Yes, Majesty. It shall be so." He wondered how she could do things this fast? It must have been planned long before he had returned home. Which kingdom had been chosen to supply the Princess? What had his mother done to secure this marriage? Could he get out it? What, what, what?

"Who?" he rasped, not daring to look at anyone else seated around the table.

"Thee will wed Our Choice! Willingly! Will thee not?"

"Yes," he stated. "Who is it?" Then he leaped to his feet. "NO!"

"WHAT?" snarled Lurin.

Frahn leaned both fists on the table top and frowned at her. "I will not marry anyone who does not willingly agree, kingdom allegiance or no, Mother!"

Lurin smiled at him. "We are agreed on that, Son. Sit!"

"Oh." He sat down. And sighed. "Who is this person?" He wondered if he had ever met her, what few he had already met. There were numbers of kingdoms.

"A true Princess."

He nodded. There were dozens of kingdoms, in the Old Kingdoms, and dozens and dozens of true Princesses out there.

"Fierce and loyal."

He nodded. And tried to think of anyone that he had heard about that would fit that description. Fahn Bahn Trahn had a reputation for great warriors. But he couldn't remembers how many, if any, young woman that King had raised.

"Exotically beautiful."

He slumped and sighed. She must have selected someone from one of the far edge kingdoms, from one of the small Old Kingdoms located at the extreme borders, near the great seas. It must be a Princess from that small population of hardly ever heard about or met folk. Those folk hardly ever traveled to the Royal City. And they never traveled on the great waters.

"Would thee peer pon this beauty before thee do wed her, Our Prince?"

Frahn cleared throat, and nodded, once again, ready to face, literally, the inevitable. "Yes," he rasped. "Yes, I would." He sighed and hoped that she would at least be pleasant to look upon. His eyes jumped around the room, searching for anyone that had slipped ever so quietly into the chamber while this discussion had been going on.

"Then close thy eyes most firm and We will make it so!"

He frowned. But did as ordered. He listened intently for a door to open or to close, for soft footsteps to approach. But whoever it was they were being extremely quiet.

Lurin beckoned over a servant who set a wooden box on the table in front of her. Undoing the small latches, she opened the box and lifted out a glittering headband, all soft silver filigree and pale green gem stones. Shoving back her chair, she stood, stepped behind Irinl and settled the headband in place, making small adjustments to Irinl's hair until she was satisfied.

"Stand up, Princess," she whispered.

Irinl did.

Lurin stepped behind her and set her hands on Irinl's shoulders and smiled over the top of her head at Eulin and Je'leel who were staring wide eyed at her.

"Unshutter thy eyes, Our Prince and Future King," commanded Lurin. "It is time for thee to gaze upon the future Queen of this Our Kingdom."

Frahn carefully did, and squinted down the table. He leaped to his feet and gasped. "You?" His eyes jumped from face to face. "Mother? Princess Irinl?" He wobbled.

Eulin tapped his leg with her hand. "Better sit down."

He dropped into his chair and stared at Irinl and the sparkling headband.

Lurin smiled at him. "Our Son," she said gently, "in this matter thee may refuse, as we did so say."

He cleared his throat. "I may?"

"Indeed. As We did agree pon no forced joining."

A smile wobbled into place. "I bow to your choice, Majesty, and to my fate." He looked at Irinl. "You really want to do this?"

Her head jerked, up and down, once. "Yes. I will be your's, your Queen." The great azure eyes enveloped his. "If you agree."

He bounced to his feet. "Indeed! Pon my oath as Prince of the Realm."

"Then it will be so," stated Lurin. "And you know our customs. Leave us now."

He stood, bowed to them. And hurried from the room.

Lurin hugged Irinl. "He may no longer gaze upon thy loveliness until he do thee wed." She laughed loudly. "T'will be only the next day. For Our Mother it was a full five days after many weeks of courtship."

Carpenter craftsmen worked all night preparing the high platform. Messengers hurried around the town, across the Great Span, telling one and all of the coming event. And when the sun was directly overhead, the pair stood on the high platform, in plain view of the surrounding crowds.

Lurin the Queen smiled and waved happily to everyone below. Her brother, Frinda and his Queen, Sook, did the same thing, although Sook was much more restrained as this type of behavior was little done by witches. She, however, had brought the other Royals from their elseplace.

Prince Helf grinned at Frahn and said, in an almost whisper, "We really didn't believe she would ever be wed. We are very happy for both of you."

Princess Nandau hugged her sister. And murmured into her ear. "He most be very special. For a non-Hephira."

Irinl patted her sister's back. "I believe so."

"ATTEND ME ALL!" boomed The First Lord, silencing the crowds.

And into the silence, the brief ceremonial words were spoken. And the two new kingdoms saw the Prince take his Princess in his arms and proclaim her as his, forever and forever and forever.

Then the celebration started as the carpenter craftsmen began to dismantle the platform as fast as people got down from it, taking the wood back to the construction site from where they had borrowed it. The wood would be needed there soon.

"Now," said Frahn, his arm around Irinl's shoulders. "Now we must walk all over town and join in the celebration, for this is our custom."

And so they did. Toasting, drinking, eating, in this place and that, buffeted from spot to spot. The long day wandered into night. The celebrations slowly growing louder.

"Are we alone?" she murmured.

He sat and leaned back against one of the tall pilings at the far end of The Great Quay. The sea vessels creaked and mumbled against their moorings. She was sprawled in his lap, leaning against his chest, wrapped in his arms.

"Yes. The folk are staying off the quay."

Far down the quay, coming from the town, they could hear the ongoing noise of the ongoing celebration. It was the first wedding holiday and the first real holiday that the kingdom had since the first settling and all were determined to enjoy it as much as possible.

The other Royal party had gotten trapped in *The Wet Way Inn* and were being delayed by the countless toasts by the sea folk crowd. It was their inn, the place where they gathered when not at sea.

"Brother," shouted Lurin in Frinda's ear. "We have to find a way out of here as the Hephira are tilting at bad angles."

Frinda grinned and leaned close and whispered in Sook's ear.

Slowly they faded away.

And into the Royal Chambers.

Lurin hugged Sook. "Well done. I will show our guests their rooms and return shortly." She tapped Helf on the shoulder. "This way, Prince and Princess." And led them away.

"We were always told that Hephira were dir dit," said Sook. "But they are not."

Frinda laughed. "They are very nice and are very shrewd traders and extremely fierce warriors." He threw his arms around her. "What do you think my sister wants this time?"

A sea folk peered at them with his far seer and told his companion that their Prince had slipped the shirt off his Princess. His companion slammed him on top of the head and called him a sneak peek.

Then they walked back inside the inn and told

everyone.

Irinl sighed happily. "Let's go to our rooms."

He kissed her again. "Lovely, lovely, lovely," he murmured.

"Is it proper in your lands," she laughed softly, "for a Prince to tear the clothes off his Princess in public?"

"Way out here no-one can see." His fingers traced gentle patterns across golden skin.

"Did your Mother, the Queen, upset you?"

He grinned. "I thought that I was doomed." And ran one finger over her mid-section.

She had explained that scar.

"I was afraid to ask you, you know. Afraid that you would say no."

"Prince, mate," she growled. "Let us go to our rooms."

He handed back her shirt, a somewhat crumpled shirt. "Here." And sighed. "It will be sunrise before we make it that far."

Shrugging on her shirt, she stuffed it into her trousers. "Into the battle, My Prince." She stood. "Was I correct?" She glowered at him.

"About?"

"Am I as beautiful without my clothes."

He laughed, a very happy laugh. "I had no doubt. None." He stood, reached over and fastened her shirt. "Into the battle, My Princess."

They strolled down the quay and into town. And

were dragged into *The Wet Way Inn* where the happy sea folk winked lewdly at him and at her and bought food and drink.

Eventually the pair broke free and headed up the long main road toward the royal quarters.

He was wrong.

The sun was quite high and pouring light into their rooms by the time they stumbled in.

Irinl aimed her badly tilting Prince at the gigantic bed and shoved.

Frahn hit the edge of the bed and crashed down. Then he crawled further in and around and flopped onto his back, squinting at the ceiling. "We made it, right?"

Irinl crawled up to him and peered down into his face. "Yes," she mumbled. And laid on his chest and fell asleep.

He was already asleep.

Chapter Five

And The Hunt Is On

Quetl. A Bustling Metropolis.

He ran for his life did Sansmod Arttle. Harder than he had ever run before. He wobbled as he ran, clenching a large orange sack, bulging with money, in one hand, a strange looking wand, sword large, in the other.

He hurtled down narrow alleyways and skidded around corners, dancing through this intersection and that. Then he twisted to one side and leaped into the node. And was gone.

Szerul splashed to a halt, snarling angry sounds. And glared at the node. The target could be anywhere, could have gone to any elseplace in the universe of universes of elseplaces. This was going to take longer than originally thought. It stepped into the node and went to a place where certain kinds of information always came.

High on a stone wall the tiny blue-green dragon clung to the rough surface noting everything. Then it darted into the node. Dragons could follow anything, anywhere. The tiny blue-green dragons were especially adept at this. This skill was a closely guarded bit of knowledge known to few beings other than dragons.

Ism Zamin. Large. Urban.

He knew where to buy what he needed. So he set off to do just that. Lodgings. Food. Drink. Protection. In that order.

But he was careful. The lodging place was selected because it had nine doors on the ground level, six corridors, and three sets of stairs leading up and down.

He hired a servant and ordered food and drink. Then he sent the servant to a certain place with a message and instructions to lead back whoever responded.

The tiny blue-green dragon clung to the outside of the wall and ate a small hole into it just big enough to slip into and through. Peeking out, it watched Sansmod. He still had the artifact.

Hahn Dohr Kahn. A Relaxed Day.

They were eating breakfast, Eulin and Je'leel. No one else was awake. Yet. Or, if they were, they had chosen to stay in bed. Outside, a few of the folk who had celebrated less hard were beginning to go about their daily work. The primary topic of conversation among the folk as they worked was the previous day's events. Many told each other of eating or drinking or even touching one or more of the Royals.

The Hephira were an even bigger topic of conversation. But the general feeling was that they were a nice looking folk even if they had somewhat long and somewhat pointed ears, and even if they had enormous eyes. But all concurred that they must be fine folk as their Prince had wedded one.

The tiny blue-green appeared, perched on Eulin's shoulder and chirped into her ear. And disappeared.

Eulin smiled. "Found it. Now when everyone is ready to travel, we can go and fetch that Hephira artifact back to its rightful owners."

49.24.01.84, MDQ. In Ship's Notation.

He stood among the rubble of the crater pocked landscape and beamed happily at the destruction. Popping open the visor on his helmet, he sniffed the acrid air. "Ahhhhhhhhh." It was a wonderful smell. It smelled of death.

Turning to the silver woman standing by his side, he leaned forward and kissed her. "We find anything? Valuable?"

She shook her head. "Little." She handed him a thick book. "This is their journal of business. They were just a moment ago bargaining for some strange device and were willing to pay great sums for it."

His eyes twinkled. "Does it say who or what they were bargaining with?"

She smiled at him. "Yes. The Society of Narzt. On

Mindsight." She nodded. "Ship is checking."

He waved at their surroundings. "Gyre my own, if these, these removed things dealt with this Society of Narzt then that Society must be as evil as what used to live here. I propose that we visit them and see what this strange device is all about."

"It must be a powerful thing."

He nodded. "Not something that should fall into the hands of folk like that." He pointed at the rubble. And slid an arm around her. "It should fall into my hands."

"They are nice hands."

"Let us get comfortable."

She had Ship take them up.

Dol Spar. Monetary Control Headquarters.

The General steepled his fingers and looked over the top of them.

She glowered.

"This assignment requires your skills."

"Skills-schmills," she grumbled loudly. "Send Abernak."

"He would probably get killed."

"Good. He's a pest." She smiled.

He winced. And sighed. He recognized the signs all too well. She was angling to get something. And wouldn't budge until he gave her whatever it was.

"All right," he said, hoping to speed up the process, "what do you want?"

"Nothing." She leaned back, stretching out her legs, now draped across one corner of her large desk.

He nodded. And admired her legs. Even if they were covered in the golden material of a Monetary Control uniform.

She nodded back, and watched him admiring her legs.

"Take the job," he growled.

"I'll need help."

Ah, ha, he said to himself. "Of course," he said to her.

"My assistants."

"You do not need me to make them go with you."

"For this job, they are underpaid."

Double ah ha, he thought. "What?"

"Pay raise one full grade. Promotion one full grade."

He jerked upright.

"We can afford it," she said, swinging her legs down, sitting upright.

"All right."

"Full control." Her eyes glittered. Hob-goblin eyes.

He winced. But agreed.

"Vunderbar." She rubbed her hands together and leaned forward on her forearms and smiled. It was ghastly. "Got any hints?"

Cence Uses. Green and Golden.

He stumbled along the narrow path, lurching, wobbling. Hoping to make it back to their lodgings before he collapsed. His clothes were stained by great sweat patches and were tattered and torn by magical blasts.

She walked behind him, a long dagger fastened to her belt in the small of her back. In the diffused light seeping through the thick overgrowth, her skin appeared to be a faint green color.

The path was much too narrow for them to walk side by side.

She watched him carefully. And hoped that he would be able to stay on his feet long enough. He had gained some weight during training and would be hard to drag. And then she saw the last curve in the path, just ahead.

He stumbled, corrected his aim, and staggered into the small meadow and into their cabin.

She looked around the outside, from habit.

By the time she entered, he was sound asleep, flat on his back, mostly on their bed. His legs still hung over the side. Sitting on the floor she yanked off his boots and socks and then stood and heaved him around until he was more or less properly situated. Bringing in a bowl of water she gently washed his face and hands, cleaning the bulk of the grime off. He could take a proper bath when he awoke. Satisfied that she had done well, done all she could for the moment, she slipped outside and walked into the middle of the grass covered meadow. And practiced.

The dagger flashed and glittered as she turned and twisted, leapt and spun. It didn't look like much, this fluid dance, all balletic poise and soft skill.

In a final whirl she popped the long dagger into its sheath and strode over to the small spring fed pond, bent and washed the sweat sheen from her face.

Then she strolled back to the cabin and stretched out on the bed next to him and fell asleep dagger and sheath lying next to her free side.

The instance his eyes opened, she sat up, twisted around and kissed him.

He wrapped his arms around her. "Just tired. That was the last lesson. For this time. Training with Grandfather is hard."

"Rest."

"Certainly. We may lounge around here as long as we wish."

She nodded. And sat up and began to unbutton his shirt. "Bath need."

He grinned at her. "That warm pool is big enough for two." And tugged her shirt loose.

"This is a nice spot." He admired the meadow, the pool that they were in, and the sky. And her, especially her. Then he sighed.

"Grandfather has given me a task to do." He

knew he would never be able to dissuade her from coming along. So he told her all that he had been told.

She slipped close and lightly rubbed her hand over his chest. "I am Ta," she whispered. "I am Tajaar."

He held her close and whispered back, "I know." Then his hands slid down her rib cage.

"We will stay here for a few more days."

"You must rest."

"We will do that. Also."

Grandeville. Tinker's Place.

She slipped into the large living room, a thing of silence, and stood and looked into the midnight dark. The moon was low in the sky casting some pale light into the room from one its thinner states of being. He stood in front of one of the large windows staring out. He was as motionless as the air outside.

Then she stood next to him, touching him, waiting for his awareness to acknowledge her presence. Her breathing was slow, silent. She knew there was nothing out there of concern. Had there been, Smoke would have alerted all. So she stood, a gray shadow in the gray light.

"What are you doing up?"

"I felt your restlessness." She gently rested her hand on one of his.

He grunted.

She leaned against his side. "Tell me what dares disturb you so and I will kill it." Deep below something rumbled, a deep bass note mostly felt rather than heard.

Slipping his hand free, he draped that arm around her shoulders. "That's the problem. I don't know. I am just feeling restless." He kissed her on the temple. "Hair smells nice."

"The Princess bought some special hair washing potion."

"I didn't mean to wake you up."

She slipped her hand inside his robe and under his pajama top. "You didn't." A small half-smile formed. "I think that you are losing weight."

"I don't think that you are."

"Hum hum," she murmured, pushing him gently toward one of the couches, the largest couch.

In the morning, all slipped silently around the sleeping pair.

Chicken stopped and pulled the comforter higher, giving it a tuck here and there. Then she joined Smoke and Chantal in the kitchen. "Most sound asleep."

"Smoke," asked Chantal, "what's going on?"

Smoke shrugged a shoulder. "Nothing. She has the ring."

"Not what I meant," snapped Chantal, whipping the bowl of eggs viciously with the wire whisk. "And you damn well know it."

Smoke peered around Chantal into the large mixing bowl. "I think that the eggs are innocent." And gave her an ever so gentle pinch. "I don't know what it is. He is worrying, down deep. All I can see is vague unease about his children."

Fair Morn wandered in, filled a coffee cup, and smiled. "Oh boy, baby dutch."

"Put your top on, show off," grumbled Chantal as she checked the oven temperature.

"Just us babes here." Fair Morn filled another cup and handed it to Chantal. "Here."

Then Messenger bubbled in, leaving wet foot prints. She had just come from the shower room and was wearing one of the thick white robes, a towel wrapped around her head. "Morning morning morning. Oh boy, baby dutch." She gave Chantal a friendly pat as she slipped by to stand in the doorway to the dining room. "Yum yum yum yum yum."

"Breakfast?" grumbled Chantal. "Or my butt?"

"Both. Grump." She looked at Fair Morn. "Where's your top?"

"Who is a grump?" Sha'gar peered over the top of Messenger's head into the kitchen. "Why are they on the couch? And why isn't she wearing her top?"

"Nobody knows. Chantal is," explained Messenger, slipping around Sha'gar to begin setting the table, singing softly, mostly to herself, "Grump, grump grump, grump. Fair Morn is a show-off, off, off, off."

"Sgenn has the ring. And I am not!"

Chantal banged her wooden spoon on the edge of one of the cast iron skillets. "One track minds." Then she began to pour the correct amount of egg mixture into each. "I know that she has the ring. I gave it to her. And I am not bothered about where or how or with whom he wants to . . . "

"First Light," said Szart, slipping into the kitchen, interrupting any further description of his activities. "Have I eaten that before?"

"Don't think so," replied Chantal, finishing the last skillet. "Where's your top?"

"Not wearable. I used it last day to wash the insides of the windows."

Smoke handed Szart a cup. "We have a big supply of rags for things like that."

Szart nod and sipped.

"Witches," observed Sha'gar, "are exhibitionists."

"Magicians," suggested Szart, "are pak tak."

Fair Morn refilled Chantal's cup. "I just think that it is more comfortable."

Chantal slipped the last skillet into the oven and closed the door. "Maybe Sgenn knows. How about someone slicing some melon?"

"Breakfast is almost ready." She began to tickle him gently.

"I suppose." He tickled her in return.

"We can shower after the meal."

"O.K."

"And a long soak in the tub."

"Sure."

She sat up and patted his stomach. "You have lost weight."

"Must be all the hard labor I do around here."

In the kitchen, Chantal snorted as she began removing the skillets from the oven. "Never heard it called that before."

Then they all settled around the dining room table and smiled at Sgenn and Tinker as they joined the rest for breakfast.

Szart and Fair Morn wore their tops.

Ism Zamin. Large. Urban.

They were eating a meal sometime around mid-day, Sansmod Arttle and his hired protection.

It had been a number of weeks and Sansmod had finally located a potential buyer for the artifact. This individual was a very wealthy buyer. He was the type that was always interested in the rare cultural artifact from someone else's culture. This buyer was so wealthy that Sansmod was seriously thinking of retiring, doing something else, less hazardous.

It was a good thought.

It was a good thought interrupted.

The door blew in and shattered against the opposite wall along with pieces of the door frame and wall fragments that the door had been anchored to.

Sansmod jumped one way, toward the corner where the artifact was kept. His protection leaped the other way, towards where the door had been.

Szerul the Gilzan slithered into the room and sliced the protection into several parts. Then it looked over at Sansmod who stood, staring at this apparition, at the parts of his protection. He held the artifact in one hand. Gurgling wetly, Szerul slipped toward him.

Screaming wildly, half-crazed from fear, half-mad from fear of losing everything he had worked so long and so hard for, Sansmod did something he had never done before.

He attacked.

He leaped.

He swung the artifact.

It sliced through the monster with no apparent resistance at all.

"WANDO!" Sansmod leaped away and stared at the mess. He stood, shaking, staring at the creature as it wetly gurgled something at him and died. Sansmod held up the artifact and peered at it. It didn't seem to have a sharp edge. What exactly was this thing? He had thought it merely some strangely shaped relic of a religious nature, always valued by the folk who bought exotic items from other cultures.

Then he stared at the bodies on floor and the horrible wound that he had caused in the creature, whatever that creature might be. Then he decided that it would be best to get a long way from here. Now. He didn't think that he could concoct a good enough story to stay out of the local lockup. Running to the chest, he yanked it open, grabbed the sack of money, and spun for the door.

The weapon belched and blew a hole through his chest, dropping him where he stood.

The man stepped over, ripped the wand from the limp hand, shot Sansmod once more, for luck, just for the fun of it, and ran from the room.

Across the street they shimmered in. And stared at the gathering crowd. Irinl pointed. At the sizable hole in the building where a door should have been.

"I will go look," said Je'leel, stepping into the street and into the edge of the ever gathering crowd. In a few moments she stood inside the room.

"You are not allowed," stated a burly man. He gestured at another equally large fellow.

"Outside, outside," said this one.

Je'leel nodded and hurried away.

"It was not there," she told them. "Just four dead bodies. Three men, one demon."

"Glurfrik!" snapped Irinl, foot starting to tap.

Eulin shrugged. "I am sure that the blue-green will follow your artifact. So we will have to wait some more."

Frahn looked at their surroundings. "Has anyone been here before?"

"No."

"No."

"Nope."

"Then I propose we stay here and visit this

elseplace." He looked at Eulin.

"The blue-green will find me wherever I am."

So, they found lodgings and wandered around.

36.36.21.09, XTB. In Ship's Notation.

They stood and looked at the image swelling and filling the screen.

The planet was vaguely green with large yellow patches. That was the land. The sea was blue.

"Mindsight," announced Gyre. "Small sensor is down searching for the Society of Narzt headquarters."

His eyes danced from spot to spot as one of the large cities filled the screen. "Not a very friendly place." His finger tapped here and there. "Weapon. Weapon. Weapon. Weapon. Weapon."

"Heavily armed."

"Ho, ho, ho, ho, ho, ho, ho." He adjusted the screen. "I'll take the Sparkling Tigers. They can use the exercise."

Off to one side of the screen a small bright yellow dot began to blink.

"The headquarters," stated Gyre.

He nodded. "Time to get dressed for visiting." They walked arm in arm to the armory.

The great space craft made slight adjustments in its position above the selected target area. She helped him dress and checked everything carefully.

"Voice control on the red missiles. For me." He smiled. The was absolutely no warmth or humor in that smile. It was his business smile. "The first shot down there and you take out every weapon site. Use the yellow missiles. They leave nice craters."

She kissed him.

He snapped his visor down and told the Sparkling Tigers to come to the portal room.

The Trakar of the Society of Narzt looked around and smiled happily. Everything had proceeded as smooth as smooth. He slowly walked around the black table and carefully examined the thing. In the hazy light favored by the Narzt, it still glittered soft golden tones.

It was a strange looking thing thought the Trakar. He wondered why it was worth so much to obtain. And then he wondered whether they ought to deliver it after all. It warranted some thought, their bargain.

One of the Ratlar charged into the room, jerking to a halt nearby. "Trakar, they are no more."

"Who?"

"The Fallgician. One went to deliver your message. They are gone. Dead. Rubble. Something devastated their entire domain."

The Trakar smiled. "Oh. That is most unfortunate." Now the object was rightly their's. Now they could find out what it was. And why it was so valuable.

As he and Gyre waited in front of the portal, the

Sparkling Tigers arrived, sharp claws clattering on the steel floor plates. They were as large as a pair of very large horses, all flashing bright light shafts and vague shapes inside. They warbled greetings to Macabre and Gyre and jostled up to the portal waiting to be taken through.

The portal crackled and hissed. The fire snakes writhed around the edges. The surface beyond the portal shimmered in the heat haze of the opening. It was the last portal in existence.

Nothing could be seen on the other side.

Macabre hugged Gyre and gave her a friendly pat. "Watch carefully."

She nodded. And Ship told portal where to take them.

Macabre stepped through followed by the Sparkling Tigers.

Without a sound, they shimmered in. Four of them.

Two of women stepped one way. The two wearing glittering gold scale armor stepped toward the table.

"HALT!" commanded the Trakar.

"The wand," hissed Irinl.

"Where did you get that?" demanded Frahn, pointing at the object lying on the table with the tip of his sword.

"Took it," replied the Trakar. "Primitive." He

fired.

The blast snapped through Frahn's chest. Gold scales blew in all directions as he was thrown staggering backward.

Irinl leaped at the Trakar, screaming rage war cry. His second shot threw her into the air.

Eulin called. And pointed.

The orange dragon, with black and green patches on its flanks, spit at the Trakar as he turned toward her and Je'leel. The acid ball splashed across his chest.

His howling ended. Suddenly. The Ratlar hurtled from the room, screaming for help.

"Quickly," said Eulin. "We must get them to my home. I cast quick heal on them but they need much, much more than that."

Je'leel nodded grabbed Eulin's hand as Eulin cast.

They were gone.

The four of them.

The Ratlarian rushed back into the room, many strong. And stopped. And stared. There were only the remains of the Trakar, steaming, to be seen. No one else.

"They were here," stated the one. He carefully walked over and looked at what was left of the Trakar.

"My, my," said someone. "What happened to him?"

The Ratlarian whirled around and stared.

Macabre walked over to the table. "So that is the thing? Doesn't look like much to me." He picked up the artifact in his left hand, an ugly weapon suddenly in his right hand And fired.

The Ratlar near the remains stumbled backward He had started to reach for his weapon.

"Slow," observed Macabre.

The Ratlarian charged. And were overwhelmed by the Sparkling Tigers.

The ground shuddered. The first of the missiles impacted weapon installations on the surface.

"Ho, ho, ho, ho, ho, ho, ho." Macabre wandered out of the room, casually firing at anything that moved.

In a few moments the Sparkling Tigers came clattering from the room and caught up with him. Back inside the room there were only a few tatters of cloth and some stains on the floor.

"Take us up, Gyre. I think we will just erase this place from ship and have a snack of some of those confections made in John's elseplace while we do."

Magevern. Deep Below The Surface.

They whirled in, startling Cazor and Bant. The pair had been practicing spell casting.

Cazor, The Spell Master, had been training Bant. For a moment the air crackled with spell anger before they recognized Eulin

"Imdar, Xarx, here quickly," ordered Eulin.

The pair ran in separate directions to fetch their Healer and her assistant.

Je'leel looked at her half-sister. "Call Mother. The

Royals are both very messy."

Imdar, The Healer, ran up to them followed by Marl, The Seeker, Tinlee, The Adept, and Moonda. As they gathered the limp forms in their arms, Xarx, Imdar's assistant, hurtled along the corridor toward them carrying two large jars. Wrenching them open, one after the other, she dribbled the contents into the horrible wounds. Then she looked at Imdar.

"Maybe," said Imdar. She directed them to her quarters.

They hurried down the corridor. Dat appeared behind Eulin and Je'leel.

"Who did that to his son, your brother?" Eulin had called her. Then she told Dat how to find the place where they had seen the artifact and what had happened there.

Dat was gone.

"What is she going to do?"

Je'leel shrugged. "I have no idea. Mother never said anything about fighting and things like that while she was training me. Indjinns have no need. Very few things can affect them."

Dat was there. She grabbed Eulin. "What did you do to that elseplace?"

"Nothing, Mother. I cast quick heal on them and we came here right away. I was afraid that they would die if we didn't. One of the dragons spit on the one who did that to them."

"Mother?" asked Je'leel.

Dat released Eulin and looked at Je'leel. "That elseplace is nothing but smoking rubble."

"What?"

"How?" asked Eulin.

"I do not know."

Je'leel pointed down the hall. "Hurry, mother. They need your help."

49.32.25.55, BDB. In Ship's Notation.

The great vessel was drifting slowly in a fairly empty sector of space.

Macabre hadn't decided where they ought to go next. He was considering home. They hadn't recovered much this trip. Not much to realize for the last few jobs. Other than that strange looking artifact.

They sat watching the stars drift across the view screen. He had one arm around her. The other hand was holding a doughnut. So far, Ship's data banks hadn't found any information on that thing, that long thing with the cross piece inside a circle that decorated the one end.

"Only one more," said Gyre.

"Is that necessary."

"We would have you live as long as possible."

"No fun if you are unable to do what you enjoy."

"Two then."

"Hephira," stated a wall speaker.

"It is the object," explained Gyre. "An ancient artifact called a Cross-Star Wand."

"Good for what?" He looked at the second and last doughnut in his free hand. And took a big bite.

"No data," said Gyre and the wall speaker. Then she leaned close and whispered in his ear. "There is something alive in Ship that does not belong here."

"What?" He suddenly held a small hand weapon instead of a doughnut. One cheek bulged large. "Where?"

"Very small. Very strange. It keeps flicking in and out."

He pulled his arm free and sat up, chewing the doughnut remnant. "Flicking in and out?" Crumbs flew here and there.

"We have never encountered anything like this before."

He swallowed noisily. "Can it be isolated?"

"No."

He stood. "Does this small visitor favor any place in particular?"

She rose and stood next to him. "The room where you put that artifact."

He walked over and tapped on a console. And carefully studied the image of the room. "Where?"

Gyre touched the screen. "Just there."

"Magnify." The image expanded and expanded. "Well," he said, "there it is. What is it?"

"Checking."

Ship's main brain began to scan all the images in its vast data banks.

Magevern. Deep Below the Surface.

"Him first," said Eulin.

Imdar and Xarx stepped aside as Dat moved up and looked down at Frahn. "Very messy," she said.

"Mother?"

"Yes." She ripped his clothes open and reached into the gaping wound. And began to rebuild. "He was fortunate to have his sisters along. Otherwise he would be beyond repair."

And, after awhile, she stepped back, and turned and carefully began to inspect Irinl. "One of those folk."

Dat peeled open the remains of the armor and then the under-garments. And nodded. "Not too bad. For one of them."

"Mother," cautioned Je'leel as Dat's hands began to run over Irinl's torso, the uninjured portions. Then she began to rebuild everything that she felt needed rebuilding.

Je'leel stepped closer. "Irinl is a Warrior Princess," she cautioned.

"All right." Dat carefully altered what she had been crafting. Then she threw her arm around Je'leel's waist. "Very beautiful, don't you think? She is repaired."

Eulin looked over their shoulders at Irinl's body, at what Dat had been doing. "Very nice." She smiled. "Our Brother will be surprised."

"So will she," added Je'leel.

Imdar and Xarx urged them all from the room.

Eulin led Dat and Je'leel to the wash area.

Grandeville. Tinker's Place.

Winter had passed and Spring had arrived.

They were out back. On, or near, the rear deck. They were "goofing off" today. At least that is what they told him. In reality, they were keeping an eye on him. And working on the flower beds, checking this, checking that, and watching him, ever so carefully.

He sat at one of the wooden tables working, editing a large manuscript.

Sgenn sat close, silent, still.

Chantal came stomping down the deck, dropped heavily onto the bench next to him. "O.K., stud butt," she growled. "Enough of that silent worrying. What the hell is going on with you?"

He made a small mark on a page, dropped the pen, and looked over at her. "What?"

She frowned darkly at him. "We want to know what is bothering you? Because you are bothering us with your bother. And we do not want to be bothered."

"That way," added Sgenn.

He laughed. "Whole lot of bothers, huh?"

Chantal glared at him. "Answer . . . the . . . question!" Her hands balled into fists.

He sighed, heavily he sighed. "O.K. It is the kids. I feel like something is going on out there that is not right."

"So, how do we find out, John? It has been a

number of weeks and we haven't received a call for help or anything."

He nodded. "I know."

Chantal looked at Sgenn. "Anyway you can find out?"

Sgenn nodded slowly. "Which child?"

"All of them," said Tinker.

Sgenn stood and walked out into the first pasture. Everyone could hear the deep down mumbling. And watched as black things lifted up in front of her, seeping up from the deep below. She said something to them. And they flicked away, one by one. Then she walked back and sat near Tinker again and looked at Chantal. "Now we wait." No-one asked her what she had sent.

He looked around. "Where's Dat?"

Magevern. Deep Below the Surface.

Eulin kissed Je'leel and rearranged the blankets on the bed. "Found it."

"What?"

"The Hephira artifact."

"Where?"

Eulin shook her head. "Strange. It is in some kind of metal room that keeps moving."

"Can you take us there?"

"Of course. As long as the small one is there." She smiled at Je'leel. "And as soon as they are ready to travel."

49.26.36.08, QBC. In Ship's Notation.

"Whatever it is, it appears to be harmless. So far."

Macabre had relocated the wand a number of times, from room to room. And each time their tiny visitor had reappeared where ever they had placed the strange artifact.

"There is no record of it in our data banks. It is unknown."

"Not surprised," grunted Macabre. He was doing the exercises she had prescribed some time ago. "Anything that can pass that easily through Ship's shields could stay out of sight if it wished to do so." He finished and wiped the sweat from his face. "Any idea why it stays by that Hephira object?"

"No." She rubbed his back. "The creature is not native to the Hephira region."

"Maybe we should just store that artifact on some dead rock, leave our tiny visitor hanging in space."

"It has been harmless."

"So far. So far." He pondered which weapon to try on it.

Suddenly blast doors began slamming shut throughout Ship.

"Intruders, intruders, intruders," chanted Ship from the ceiling speakers.

Macabre leaned toward the wall and yanked down something big, black, ugly, and wonderfully lethal. "Where? What?"

Gyre changed the view screen. Four people stood in the room with the strange artifact.

Macabre ran down the appropriate corridor, Gyre by his side.

"It is an all metal room." Je'leel looked around.

Irinl snatched up the Hephira artifact. "I have it."

Frahn slowly turned, searching the room. "But where are we? And how did it get here?"

Eulin shrugged.

A door hissed open.

A large man slipped inside.

He was pointing something at them. "You are on Ship," he said, ever so calmly. "And I brought it here."

Cold, blank eyes watched each of them. "And, you are as strange a group of thieves or pirates as I have ever seen." Two were obviously warriors of some sort, one of them Hephira. Warriors he understood. But the other two looked too unperturbed for his comfort level. "How did you enter my ship?"

"We are not thieves," snapped Irinl, one foot beginning to tap. She glared up at the large man holding the strange thing which he kept pointed at them. "This is our wand, taken from us a long time ago."

"Ho, ho, ho, ho, ho, ho, ho. Perhaps we can come to some small agreement on that?"

Irinl slipped toward this large and very rude person dressed in the strange garb.

"Careful," said Je'leel. "That weapon looks like Mother's. If he fires, Mother won't be able to do anything."

Macabre stared at her, ignoring the glaring Hephira. "Who has a strange weapon just like this one?" He waggled the tip at her.

"One of my mothers."

Eulin scratched under the the chin of the tiny blue-green and told it that it had done a good job. It chirped happily.

"Name me your names." Macabre flicked several levers on the side of the weapon. "That thing your beast?"

"Prince Frahn."

"Princess Irinl."

"Eulin. Yes, the tiny one is mine."

"Je'leel."

He nodded. "I am Macabre."

"Gyre," said the silver woman. She waved at their surroundings. "Ship."

Je'leel looked at him and smiled. "You are Macabre?"

"I am what I am."

Je'leel nodded. "Father told me about you."

Eulin nudged her. "He knows this?"

"Yes. They are friends."

Irinl looked up at Frahn. "Husband Prince?"

Frahn shook his head. "I do not know. He didn't tell anything like this."

"Me either," said Eulin.

"Who exactly are you?" Macabre's finger tightened just enough on one of the triggers.

Gyre readied herself to yank him back through the doorway into the other room. One shot and the emptiness of space would suck this room and all its contents away."

"John Tinker's children," replied Je'leel. "Irinl, Frahn's Princess Wife."

"How do I know that?"

"You gave Fair Morn one of those." Je'leel pointed at the thing Macabre held. "I recognized it."

"Name me his . . . associates."

"Smoke, the Princess Chicken, Fair Morn, Sha'gar, Sgenn, Szart, Messenger, Chantal." Je'leel watched him. "R-Bar died. Some of them you have never met."

He handed the space cannon to Gyre. "Come, let us go sit in comfort and talk. For once, I am surprised."

Gyre released all the sealed doors. Ship prepared refreshments in the room toward which Macabre was headed.

They all followed Macabre as he headed down the corridor, swaying from side to side, leading them to one of the several lounges. Je'leel thought that he must have badly damaged his legs long ago to have such a gait.

Eulin sent the tiny dragon back to its home.

Grandeville. Tinker's Place.

Sgenn nudged him.

"What?"

"Sedeem is all right. Rorx is fine." Her fingers dug into his forearm.

"WHAT?"

All eyes snapped in his direction.

"Frahn, Eulin, Je'leel, and Irinl are sitting around talking with persons named Macabre and Gyre."

Smoke shoved the appropriate memories around.

Sgenn nodded. So did Sha'gar and Szart.

"Who's Irinl," asked Tinker. "Everyone's all right?"

"Very healthy," said Sgenn. A half-smile tugged at her mouth. "Irinl is Frahn's . . . Princess Wife."

"Holy cow," said Tinker.

"Guess you can stop worrying," grumbled Chantal. "Worry butt."

They all felt him relax.

"Damn worry wart," mumbled Chantal.

Sgenn sent her servants away. They were done.

"A Princess." Chicken smiled.

Dat appeared. "Beautiful."

"Where have you been?" growled Tinker.

So Dat told him, what she thought he ought to know. After all, he was her Great Master. Even if he forgot it most of the time.

Chapter Six

Just A Local Agitation

Grandeville. Tinker's Place.

He sprawled on one of the couches and looked at them all. One of his arms was draped over Je'leel's shoulders. She was slumping also. Just so he could.

It had been a week or since she had returned. And she had told them everything about what had happened. Well, almost everything. And how Macabre had sent lrinl and Frahn to the Hephira Kingdom to return their artifact. And then how she and Eulin had left the giant space vessel as Eulin sent them to their respective homes.

So, he sprawled and looked happy around the room. The cats, all six of them, were being petted and tickled, and fed tidbits of bread and cheese. Everyone was eating brunch, sitting on the floor. Or had just finished. He had just finished.

Dat sat by his other side, basking in the delight of being big. She had dressed in the same type of clothes as all the rest. Corduroy shirt, blue jeans. She had even buttoned the three lower buttons of her shirt.

He sighed. It was a very happy sigh.

"Bout time!" grumbled Chantal, scratching the calico, under the chin. The calico purred and crossed her eyes in pure cat joy.

He smiled at her and the happy cat. "Sounds just like Smoke, that cat."

"I don't drool. Or cross my eyes when I am happy." Smoke leaned over the back of the couch and ruffled his hair. "But I could spit a little, if you wish."

"Sorry I said anything."

"Heh heh heh." She attacked his hair again.

He slipped his arm from Je'leel and slumped lower. "Get away, get away!" And looked over at Chantal. "For what?"

"That you stopped being such a worry wart!"

He finally managed to grab one of Smoke's wrists. And laughed. "What? Me worry?"

They somehow managed to wind up on the floor. Tinker, Dat, and Smoke. Je'leel had slipped sideways as Smoke had toppled over the back of the couch in a fluid controlled movement.

Smoke purred loudly at him.

"If you spit on me, I will thump your butt."

"Sounds indecent to me," commented Chantal.

"Only in public." Smoke peered down into his face, crossing her eyes. "We can use my room." She laughed. "I will even let you scratch me under my chin."

He sighed. "Kin I get up?" He rolled his head

around. "Get off, Dat."

She sat up. "You dragged me down here."

"I did not. It was this great lump."

Smoke sat up. "I am not a lump." She poked him in the stomach with one fingertip. "Fatty deposit."

Sha'gar joined them, looking over Smoke's shoulder to peer at his stomach. "Hum," she said. She leaned further and gave him a poke.

"Wait a minute," he snapped.

Szart sat next to Smoke. And did the same thing. "Hum hum," she said.

"All right! Knock it of!"

Chantal stood behind Sha'gar and Szart. "What's that you're carrying around, Cowboy?"

"OUCH!"

Smoke had given him another jab in the gut.

He lurched upright frowning darkly at her.

She batted her eyes at him. "MindMate?"

He sighed. "Never mind."

"Looks like you need more exercise," observed Chantal, staring pointedly at his stomach.

"I am not getting fat. I do not need exercise." He stood and stepped past Dat. "And I do . . . not have that problem."

"Meaning what?" Chantal glowered at him.

Chicken banged into his back, wrapping her arms around him. "We do be most svelte." And kissed the back of his neck. "Me'Lord."

The others stood and crowded around.

"Right," agreed Smoke. "Skinny." She gave Chicken a little poke.

"You guys are making me nervous," said he. They mobbed him.

Merde," grumbled someone from the bottom of the pile. "Again."

Je'leel knelt next to them. "Father?"

"What?"

"What are you doing to them?"

Someone started to laugh.

From the bottom of the pile.

"Nothing," said the voice.

"EEEEEEK!" squeaked Fair Morn. "He is playing with my fatty deposits."

"Father!" gasped Je'leel.

"Boogle," he said.

"Actually," laughed Fair Morn. "It is more like a massage."

"Damn grabby," snarled Chantal, squirming free. She stood. "Come on, daughter. Let's go make some cocoa. It is not proper to watch him assaulting your mothers." She winked.

Je'leel went with her to the kitchen.

"I am not," he grumbled, "assaulting anyone. It is the other way around."

Messenger giggled. And twitched. "Stop! Stop! Stop!"

"Not doing anything."

"Princess!" gasped Messenger.

"How about this," he said, shoving at someone. "I will just slide free and watch you assault each other."

"Nay assault, Me'Lord. Mere friendly a'carress. EEEEEK!"

"Heh heh heh," said Messenger. "What you get!"

"Off. Off. Off," he announced.

"Flee," laughed Fair Morn, rolling away. "The vile clutcher has released me." She sat up and peered inside her shirt. "I bet he left finger prints on my fatty deposits."

The loud sigh was Tinker as they unpiled. "Goofy, goofy, goofy," he mumbled as he stood.

Messenger tugged her shirt back into order and stuck her tongue out at Chicken. "Grabby fingers."

Chicken danced around and hid behind him. "Most pleasant a'grab. Think thee not, Fair Prince?"

"Sure." He had decided that it was best to be agreeable. It was safest direction in the chaos he felt rapidly approaching. He reached back and pinched her.

"Eeeeeek."

"What you get," stated Messenger, heading for the kitchen to see how the cocoa was coming along.

"Most vile," hissed Chicken, tickling his ribs.

"At least he didn't grab your fatty deposits," observed Fair Morn. "What there are of them."

"Winged wench," snarled Chicken. She blew warm on the back of his neck.

"Hum hum hum, " said Szart slipping close to

him. She poked him in the gut with one fingertip.

"Hey!"

"Forsooth, Our Heart?" laughed Chicken. "Be thee wobbly scarecrow of Oz?"

"O.K.," he sighed. "What is it with you guys? This time?"

Szart began to unbutton his shirt.

"Stop that."

"Checking," she said.

"For what?"

"Straw." Sha'gar, stepped up behind Szart.

Chicken stood on her tiptoes and peered over his shoulder. "Nay hay."

Szart ran her fingertip over his stomach, making circles around his navel. "No dead grass."

"Or straw," observed Sha'gar.

Fair Morn joined the group and grinned at him over the top of Sha'gar's head. She was taller than anyone else. "Maybe we ought to check a little further?"

He batted at Chicken's hand. She had reached around his waist and was fumbling with his belt buckle. "Stop that! Stop it, stop it." He spun away, glaring at one and all. And headed for the kitchen, fastening his shirt.

"Hi, grump." Chantal gave the cocoa one last stir. "Get a cup. It's ready."

"I made it," announced Dat. She smiled proudly, canines protruding over her lower lip.

Messenger dropped a marshmallow into his cup.

"And one for you," she cooed. "Certainly are. And we didn't do anything either."

"What?" He stared at her, and licked the brown line from his upper lip.

"Grump, grump, grump, grump, grump, grump," she sang, heading for the living room with the marshmallow bag.

"HUMBUG!" he yelled at her back.

Fair Morn bumped up against his back and carefully wrapped her arms around him. She didn't want to jostle his cup.

"Da da, da da, da da, dum," she sang.

"Now what?"

"Theme music." She tightened her arms.

"For?"

"The Winged Warrior," she intoned. "Defender of the Young and Innocent, that's us all, swoops down and prepares to carry away the vile humbug yelling nasty buggel. That's you."

"I am not."

"You did, you did," stated Messenger, poking her head into the kitchen from the dining room doorway. She smiled at Fair Morn. "Haul that yucko nasty creep bug thingee away."

"Goofy," he mumbled. "Let go."

"Heh, heh, heh," cackled Fair Morn. "Do the crime, do the time."

"Let go."

Fair Morn looked at Chantal. "Should I read him

his rights?"

Chantal shrugged.

"Yes," he said.

"Creep bug thingees don't have any," stated Messenger. "Haul him away."

Chicken looked over Messenger's shoulder. "Looks dangerous a'Us."

"Ugly expression," observed Sha'gar. She threw an arm around Sgenn.

Sgenn nodded. "Hum."

"All right." He sighed, resigned to whatever they were up to this time. "What exactly is going on? This time? Huh?"

Chicken stepped around and batted her eyes at him. "Naught." And filled her cup. Messenger gave her a marshmallow.

"Oh?"

"Right," agreed Fair Morn. "That is because The Winged Warrior has the horrid beast pinioned in place. Heh heh heh."

"Immobilized," said Smoke.

"Definitely," agreed Chantal.

"Maybe," suggested Szart, taking another marshmallow and eating it. "He is angry because he is now unable to clench her fatty deposit or deposits?"

"Mega-goofy," hissed Tinker. "Let go. I need to get a net."

"Gotta promise. First," stated Fair Morn firmly.

"What?"

"That you'll lighten up," said Chantal.

He gasped. "Me?" And grumbled. "Who got jumped upon again? More than once. Who is being accused of all manner of strange behavior? Again? Me!"

He sighed. "O.K. You are safe. I will keep at least two feet of empty space between us at all times."

"One extreme to the other," stated Chantal. She stepped over and tossed her arm over Smoke's shoulders. "How about we toss this one away and go get another? More pleasant."

"Weeeellllllllllll," said Smoke, grinning broadly, emptying her cup, looking at him. Then she sighed dramatically. "Fraid we are stuck with him."

"Heh heh heh," chortled Fair Morn, releasing him. "You are free."

"Oh boy." He carefully looked from face to face.

"Oh, oh." Messenger began backing up, pushing at Sha'gar and Sgenn.

"Flee," yelled Chicken. "For safety of thy deposits fatty." She dashed for the living room.

They all scattered. Except for Dat and Je'leel.

Dat smiled at him.

Je'leel filled his cup.

"Well?" he asked.

"Daughters are safe," stated Dat. "But, as you are my Great Master, I have no choice but to wait and be abused." She began to unbutton her shirt, the last three buttons.

"Dat," he hissed.

"Great Master?"

"Forget it."

"My f.d.'s are beautiful."

"Yah, I know." He looked at Je'leel. "Any idea as to what is going on?"

"Father?"

"Yes?"

"I think they want you to chase them."

They heard several doors slamming.

"Outside." Dat yawned. "Think that I will take a little nap." She headed for the living room.

Je'leel stepped close. "Don't tell."

"O.K."

"I think that they think that you have been sitting around doing nothing for long enough."

He nodded. "That's it, huh?"

"Yep. I am going up to my room and read." She turned away and headed for the hallway.

He slipped out the back door, around the garage and generator shed, headed for the barn from the back side.

Then he slowly worked his way up the outside ladder, taking great caution to make no sound. At the top, he looked back toward the house and the garage. He was high enough to look down on the some of the roofs. Turning, he carefully peered through the upper window of the barn. And ever so carefully, he eased it open and slipped inside, stepping silently along the nearest joist into a dark shadowed corner. He perched there, breathing slow. And stared down at nothing, down between the joists, down at the floor, twelve feet below, allowing his eyes to soak up the details.

Time passed, things down there moved. A chicken wandered in. Then a mouse. And then his prey.

She slipped out of her hiding place to watch the door to the chicken coop. It was creaking open, slowly creaking open.

Messenger eased inside.

"Go away," hissed Szart from the top of the stacked hay bales.

"Oooops." Messenger ducked back and hurried away seeking some other spot.

And in those few moments, he had stepped silently from joist to joist to joist to stand directly above her. One hand touched a cross-brace, one foot dangled free. He dropped.

"PTAR TAK!" she cursed as he landed, grabbing her, dragging her into the hollow on top of the stack, the hollow space that she had carefully constructed between some of the bales.

"Gotcha," he whispered.

"Hum hum hum," she replied.

"Gosh," said Messenger to Chantal. "He got her." It was considered fair to notify the others when someone got caught.

"We better split up," replied Chantal. She carefully, gently eased open the door of the small garden tool shed and peeked out at the yard, searching for anything that might indicate that he was lurking about.

Finally she let out her breath. "Looks all right, safe enough." And slipped outside, closed the door, and slipped into the thick screen of bushes that separated some of the flower beds from the first pasture. Keeping low, she worked her way toward the end of the house.

Then she hurried along one edge of the swimming pool.

He surged straight up and dragged her in.

"Damn!"

"Heh, heh, heh," he whispered into her ear, toppling her over. They were in the shallow end of the pool.

After a while, he left his second victim to dry out on the rear deck and clumped loudly toward the driveway end of the deck. Then he eased along the garage and back around the generator shed and up onto its roof. The shed was a steeper-roofed addition to the garage, a two story structure. Slowly he inched sideways until he could lean over and peer around and up. She was sleeping on her back, great butterfly wings spread, soaking up the heat. Still where he had seen her from the barn.

He made his move.

"Sleeping on the job won't do." He grabbed her.

"You are wet." Fair Morn smiled at him. "And awfully friendly." She curled her wings up and over them.

Sometime later, she joined Chantal and Szart on the rear deck. "At least I wasn't the first."

"He's damned sneaky," grumbled Chantal.

"Farp tar," snarled Sha'gar as strong hands grabbed her by the ankles, and pulled.

They stared down at the deck. There was a crawl space underneath it.

"Number four," said Fair Morn.

"Heh heh heh," cackled Szart.

Two bodies splashed into the swimming pool. Sha'gar had moved them there as they were fairly dusty from below the deck.

Chantal stood. "I'll get some more towels."

"Yum yum yum," he said, bobbling in front of her.

"Hum," replied Sha'gar.

"Certainly are," he said. And paddled to the deep end of the pool and climbed up the ladder. He slipped across the flower beds and into the brush screen.

Chantal stood on the edge of the deck. "I put towels on the table."

Sha'gar heaved herself from the pool and walked over and grabbed one.

"EEEEEEEEK!" screeched Messenger from inside the tool shed. "Eeeeeeek, eeeeeek, eeeeek."

"Hum hum," said Szart.

"Hum hum," agreed Sha'gar, tossing the towel on the table top. "Cocoa?"

"I'll get it." Fair Morn stood and headed for the kitchen.

He walked onto the rear deck with the body of his victim slung over one shoulder. "Hi there." And dumped her into the hammock and walked into the house.

Messenger giggled. "Forgot to keep my eyes closed."

The door to the walk-in closet in the tub room swung inward and thumped softly against the wall. And after a long quiet period, she peeked up and over the top of the laundry bags stuffed with the heavy white robes and towels. He charged inside, slamming the door shut.

"S'blood!" gasped Chicken as she was tumbled into the sacks.

"Gotcha!"

"Oh, indeed," she laughed. "Thee certainly do that." And squirmed. "Cease thy tickling a'Us."

"Heh heh heh." Leaving her sprawling on towels and robes, he eased the door open. "Everyone's on the rear deck." He took off his shoes and socks and emptied his pockets of anything that might make a noise. And top-toed soundlessly into the hall.

"Hi, Princess," said Messenger as Chicken walked out onto the deck.

Soft as night he passed through the living room and along the connecting corridor to Corporate Headquarters and into the main room. Sinking into one dim corner, he sat and waited, listening intently.

Finally he eased into the supply room on silent toes, to the other end, and ever so slowly pulled that door open, just a crack, just enough to take a peek.

All in one movement he flipped the door wide and sprang inside. She rolled. They tumbled off the far edge of the bed.

"OOOOF!"

Smoke smiled down into his face. "I must be getting old." He had wound up on the bottom again.

He shoved her off, onto her side. "Look just fine to me."

She smiled. "Not ticklish."

"I know."

She purred.

He gave her a little nip. "One to go."

She winked. "Happy hunting, MindMate." And stretched. And watched him slip from the room.

Throwing the door open, he clumped into his bedroom and began to bang open and shut the drawers in the chest of drawers, all the time watching his bed. Several of the comforters from the living room had been tossed into a heap on top of it. Then he slammed the last drawer shut, walked over and slammed the door closed, and on silent feet tip-toed over to his bed, knelt down and shoved one arm and hand under the mound. He slithered under. "Surprise."

"Sulda." Sgenn, laughed a soft laugh.

"I think that he will be awhile," said Smoke as

she joined the others on the rear deck.

Fair Morn handed her a cup of cocoa. Messenger dropped a marshmallow into the cup. "Here, mom."

Je'leel walked from the house. "I could smell the cocoa from my room." She looked around. "Where's Father? And why isn't anyone wearing a shirt?"

"Occupied," said Smoke.

"He stole them," explained Messenger.

"He is the occupier," stated Fair Morn. "Maybe we ought to make something to eat. If we take our time we should finish by the time they are, um, ready for lunch." She stood and headed back toward the kitchen, Messenger with her. Fair Morn threw a comradely arm over the much shorter young woman's shoulders. "Maybe next time."

"Hum hum hum," said Sgenn, nuzzling his neck. Then she kissed him. And gave him a little poke in the side.

He rolled toward her. "Nice grey eyes." He gave her a little poke in return. "The rest is pretty nice also." He tickled here and there. She smiled, a soft half-smile. And hitched closer.

Visitors, said Smoke in their minds.

"Mik tpar tpar," grumbled Sgenn.

"Don't grump." He hooked his arm around her waist.

Frahn and his wife, said Smoke. *Father*. She laughed.

Sgenn rolled away and sat up. As she stood, she

kicked the comforters off the bed, and waited for him while she dressed.

He yanked on his clothes and kissed her. "Let's go." They strolled out the side door.

"Hephira." Tinker looked at her.

Frahn smiled. "Father, this is Princess Irinl, Queen Nandau's sister."

Helf's babe, explained Chantal to those that did not know about the Hephira.

As Tinker walked over, Irinl bowed and dropped to one knee. "Mighty Lord, Son Husband's Father."

"Ummmmmm? What?" His eyes jumped from face to face, looking for some idea of what to do now.

Chicken stepped to his side. "Rise, Princess. And welcome. We do be most proud and happy do thee Our Own Noble Son wed."

Irinl stood and smiled.

Tinker reached around and patted Chicken on the hip. "We certainly are." He smiled at Frahn and Irinl And wondered how his gang had managed to get their shirts back on in time. "Can you stay for a few days?"

"Yes," said Frahn.

Tinker smiled and introduced everyone.

Irinl bowed properly to each. And hugged Je'leel.

Dat wandered from the house and looked over Tinker's shoulder. "Very nice, don't you think?"

"Yep," agreed Tinker. And said to Frahn and Irinl. "We were just about to eat. Join us? Relax."

Everyone grabbed dishes and began to serve

themselves. Frahn told Irinl what they were doing and about the different foods.

"I made her even more beautiful," whispered Dat into Tinker's ear. "Indjinn beautiful."

"What?"

So Dat told him about that.

He pulled her to one side of the deck. "Does she know what you did to her? To her body?"

Dat shrugged. "I didn't get a chance to explain." She smiled. "They must have figured it out by now. I just made things nicer."

"Things?"

"Yes." Dat nodded. "Do you want to eat? Or play with my things?"

"Let's eat. And behave."

"I am always well behaved," grumbled Dat. She walked away to get a cup of cocoa.

Tinker got in line with the rest of them.

Chicken nudged him as he sat next to her. "A very beautiful Princess, My Lord."

"Yep." He took a bite from a thick sandwich. "Certainly is," he mumbled.

She leaned close. "Our sons do follow their father, do they not?"

"Sure," he mumbled, just to be agreeable. And wondered what she was up to this time.

But lunch passed rather quietly, for them.

And he relaxed. Again.

Chapter Seven

Small Plans

Winl Fzar. The Land of the Hephira. Long At Night.

They shimmered into existence.

The two of them.

Throwing back the hood of his black garb, he looked around the room. And saw it.

Gleaming soft golden sheen. Lying inside the ornate display case.

She carefully, silently, checked the room. Guarding while he walked over and tapped the clear top of the case with a short scarlet wand with a glowing blue tip.

The cover disappeared. He reached inside, removed the object, now much reduced in size, and dropped it into his pocket. Then he stepped quickly, silently over to his companion. Gently taking her by the arm, he nodded.

They shimmered away.

Grandeville. Tinker's Place.

The days had passed in quiet, some more

peaceful than others. Mostly in relaxation.

Messenger and Chicken had altered one of Messenger's swim suits and had convinced Irinl to wear it and to try out the swimming pool.

Now everyone was lounging on the rear deck. Frahn walked over and sat next to Tinker.

"Father?"

"Ummmm?" His eyes popped open.

"Mother thinks that you should visit."

"Ummm?"

Chantal stepped over and shoved a cup of coffee into Tinker's hand. "Here." And winked at Frahn. "Wait a bit. He was sound asleep."

Frahn nodded and watched his father take a sip from his beverage, eyes still closed.

Chantal headed into the house. To make a phone call.

And, after a while, his eyes opened and he looked at Frahn. "What?"

Frahn smiled. "Mother thinks that you should come for a visit." He leaned close. "She wants to show you the town of Spa where the hot springs are."

Smoke glanced over at Tinker and slowly licked her lips. Tinker ignored her.

Frahn grinned. "And I would show you the Dragon Fang Wing. They built our other new town. And it is only a short trip from Spa to Wurm."

"Wurm?"

Frahn laughed. "Named after The Great Black

Dragon."

Tinker smiled. "I see. What did the dragon think?"

"She thought that it was nice. Dragons do not seem to have much of a sense of humor."

"I suppose."

"The two main streets of Wurm are extra wide so she can visit without damaging anything."

Tinker smiled and sipped from his cup. "Well, that is certainly different."

Frahn nodded. "You could come for The Dragon Festival. We are inviting all of Bahn Duhr Tohr to come." He smiled. "Mother thinks that this will make us ever so so much money. The Black Dragon agreed to be the theme for the three days."

Tinker laughed. "Lurin is becoming quite an entrepreneur."

"What?"

"Business person."

Frahn nodded. "The Kingdom requires a lot of money to build roads and towns."

"You going to leave anything undeveloped?"

Frahn sat straighter and frowned, just a little. "M'Ban's Mount, three quar along the Marhn River." He relaxed and shrugged. "Of the north and middle lands we know little. Nor much of the coast line."

His eyes shifted as he watched Irinl climb from the swimming pool to sit next to Messenger. Then he looked back at his father.

"What?"

"We did not properly thank Dat. We would be dead if she hadn't helped."

"I do not require thanks," said Dat, walking over to the pair, stretching and yawning. She sat next to Tinker. "It is good to take a little nap, now and then."

"A little nap?" Tinker nudged her. "It has been four days."

Dat nodded. "A little indjinn nap."

"Oh."

Dat smiled at Frahn. "She is beautiful."

He blinked. "Who?"

"Hephira Princess Irinl."

He nodded. "Wonderfully so."

Dat smiled at Tinker. "I'll bet that he really likes playing with her body."

Frahn gasped. And blushed.

"Knock it off," growled Tinker.

"Gimble, gimble, gimble," grumbled Dat.

"Change the subject."

"May I go with you?"

"What?"

"When you go to Hahn Dohr Kahn to play with Queen Lurin's body."

Tinker glowered, fumed, and grumbled at her. "You are gonna be back inside that ring if you don't stop."

"Perl pin pin!" mumbled Dat.

"MOTHER!" snapped Je'leel, stepping up behind

Tinker's chair. "That is very bad."

"What is?" asked Tinker.

Frahn hurried away. Irinl had beckoned him to come over to her and Messenger.

"What she said," explained Je'leel. She sat in the chair just vacated.

"Oh?"

"He was picking on me," explained Dat. "Just because I wanted to know if he . . . "

"DAT!"

"See," said Dat to Je'leel.

Messenger patted Frahn's hand. "Don't mind Dat. Indjinns just seem to have really narrow conversational interests."

"I told Messenger that we must return and make preparations for the exploratory trip." Irinl kissed Messenger on the cheek. "So, everyone understands."

"Of course," said Messenger. She hugged Irinl and smiled at Frahn. "We will come and visit you." She grinned at Frahn. "And your mother."

Chapter Eight

Just Another Witch Thing

Grandeville. Tinker's Place.

Things were not going well.

Not at all.

Not even a little bit.

He glared at the computer screen. And leaned back in his swivel chair. Leaning back didn't help. That paragraph still didn't make sense. He frowned at it. The paragraph didn't mind at all.

Downstairs there were a number of hurried conversations, all carefully kept away from him.

"Badly bothered," hissed Szart. R-Bar hadn't told her about things like this.

"Draw straws?" suggested Messenger.

Sgenn stood. "I will go." Nothing frightened her. She headed down the hall, into the Chamber, and up the stairs. Toward his office. She stopped outside the door, listened intently. Something was grumbling on the other side of the closed door. She carefully pushed the door open and peeked into the jumble and mess that was his work space.

He was now glowering at a pad of paper.

"Coffee?" she asked, all soft voice. Theurgist proper.

"Huh?" He spun around, his chair squealing loudly.

"Coffee? And cookie?" Stepping slightly to one side, she beckoned. A coffee pot, two cups, and a line of cookies floated into the room, summoned from the kitchen. "Szart sent."

"O.K." He nodded and laughed at the aerial parade. "Thanks." Then looked at her, still standing next to the door. "What?"

"May I enter?"

"Of course." He scraped one of the other two chairs clean, adding to the general clutter on the floor. "Here."

She walked in, and sat. On his lap.

"Oof!"

The pot filled a cup. She handed it to him. And a cookie. Before taking a cup and cookie for herself. "I am not heavy."

"Ooof of surprise. Chantal has a lot of green."

"What?"

"In her eyes. But your's are just pure smoky grey."

"Theurgist grey."

"Pretty nice." He took a sip and reached for another of the cookies. And glanced over at the clock on the wall. "Kinna early for coffee and cookies, cookie."

"Nervous nervous."

"Nervous?"

She nodded. "Your bother anger frustration stress felt tak tak danger hazard."

"Oh . . . sorry." He held his cup out and watched the pot refill it. "Someone should have said something."

She shook her head. "None felt . . . safe."

"Safe?"

She nodded.

He laughed. "Safe!" And laughed and laughed.

"Not nice," she hissed into his laughter.

He choked it off. "I am the least dangerous person in this house."

"Badly bothered witch mates-for-life are im tik. None dare resist."

"Really?"

She nodded.

"How come you are here?"

"Someone had to come."

He set his cup on the desk top in the only clear spot. "You sure that you are safe?" He slid his hand across her waist.

She nodded, watching his face carefully, and plucked at his shirt buttons with two fingers.

In the kitchen, Sha'gar looked at Szart. "Theurgists are devious and sly."

"Hum hum," replied Szart.

Chantal laughed. "Well, he won't be worrying about that paragraph for awhile."

"Indeed." Chicken started another pot of coffee. "They do keep pot and cups."

Chantal tapped Sha'gar on the shoulder. "You can help me clean the barn." She walked out on the back porch to where all the rubber boots were kept.

"Ptar prak," grumbled Sha'gar, following her. Cleaning the barn was not one of the things she liked doing. "Im dim dik dik tar."

As the door closed behind the pair, Szart nodded. "Most coarse. Even for a magician."

Fair Morn grinned at her. "You can help me clean the hot tub."

"Ptar ptar rak tak!"

"All we have to do is scrub it." She threw a comradely arm around the shoulders of the short witch. "Better than getting covered with itchy hay stuff."

Messenger beamed at Chicken and Smoke.

"Kitten?" asked Smoke.

"Weeding."

Chicken smiled. And punched Smoke gently on her shoulder. "Tis most warm and sunny a'day."

"Yep," agreed Smoke, beginning to unbutton her shirt.

By the time the two of them had made it to the rear deck, they had shed their shirts. Dropping them on one of the large wooden tables, they stepped down into a flower bed and set to work. Messenger told them what needed to be done and where. The flower beds were her's.

Out on the front lawn they came down. Not too lightly.

"BOOOOF!" she gasped.

He looked at her.

"Not-light ground hitting sound," she explained.

"Ah." He walked over to the front deck. And stepped up. And tripped. "Pretty quiet. Wonder if they went into town." He opened the front door and stepped inside, calling, "UNCLE! AUNTS!"

She headed for the kitchen to find something to eat for him. He headed for the back side of the house, the rear deck.

He sighed. A very happy sigh. And gave her a tickle. Just a little tickle. "Wasn't going to get anything accomplished anyway." And laughed. He was lying on his back, staring up at the ceiling, one arm thrown loosely across her back. He thought that it was a very nice back. So, he tickled her.

She was resting, more or less, on top of him. She tickled him back.

"I didn't know you could do that."

She lifted up and peered into his face, a soft half-smile tugging at one side of her mouth. "It was not all that different. I am a body formed standard female of your kind."

"Not what I meant. Coffee pot, cups, cookies."

"Szart sent. As I did so say."

"Oh. Right!"

"You should not do that," she said sternly.

"What?" It was a very cautious question. He stopped sliding a finger up and down her backbone.

"Anger frustration stress pak tak." She shook her head. "All get fear fear much worry."

He smiled, finding it hard to believe that any of them would be afraid of him. "Like I said. I am the least dangerous person in this house."

"Not true, love mate center. All fear great injury when you are near wild."

"Humbug." He didn't believe it.

"NO!" She lurched upright. And glared down at him. Deep down things rumbled.

"Hear that rumbling?"

"Of course."

"How could I injure you with those things always around?"

She stared at him, just stared. "Know you not?"

"What?"

"There is no witch defense to the mate-for-life. All know this."

He sighed. "They do?"

She nodded.

"True?"

She nodded.

"Just the witches?"

She shook her head. "No longer. Once."

"I don't believe it."

"Im dik dik." She frowned down at him.

"Chantal would shoot me. After punching me

first. Fair Morn is twice, or more, as strong as I am. Probably much more. Smoke is all predator swift."

She shook her head. "It has spread through our collective being. All are one. From the first. With R-Bar."

"She never said anything. Nor did Ran. Or anyone else."

"It is true."

"Ummmmmmm."

She nodded. "It is true."

He snapped upright, shoved her onto her back and punched. It was a killing blow. Nothing happened. No dark monstrosity stopped him. None of the automatic Theurgist defenses snapped into existence.

"It is true," she said, looking up at him.

His fist, just lightly touching the edge of her throat, snapped back. He shuddered. And blinked. "I always thought all that running away was just a game." He reached down and gently slid a finger over her cheek. "Why didn't anyone say anything?" A tear meandered down his face. "I wouldn't hurt any of you for anything. Ever!"

She held his hand and kissed it. "Most running away is fun play."

"Isn't there anything we can do about that? Fear?"

"No," she said. "It is the way it is."

"GAZOOKS!" cried Chicken. "Tis Shem!"

"OH!" gasped Shem, whirling around, face

flaming red, staring at the wall of the house. "Sorry Aunts."

Tajaar ran around the corner of the house and down the deck toward them. She held a large sandwich in one hand. "True-mate?" She stopped and stared at them. "Aunts of Shem?"

"Toss our shirts down here," said Smoke. "He can't stand there staring at the wall while you eat."

Tajaar handed the sandwich to Shem and pelted them with their shirts.

"Thee may turn thyself, Our Nephew. And sit."

Messenger giggled. "Really red, really really." She finished stuffing her shirt into her trousers and clambered up onto the deck. "That sandwich looks good."

Tajaar nodded. "Dead nice-cooked bird in your cold box."

Smoke headed for the kitchen. "I will make a bunch. Everyone is headed this way. Him too."

Chicken strolled after her. "We will thee help."

Messenger ran after them. "Me too, me too."

Fair Morn and Szart stepped from the side door. "Somebody say something about food?" Fair Morn smiled at their visitors. "Just get here?"

Shem nodded.

Fair Morn and Szart set their buckets down and sat at the table. "Hot tub is clean and refilling."

By the time Tinker came banging out the side door, everyone had gathered around the large wooden table. On the table top sat several platters of sandwiches. Sgenn walked from the house and sat at the table.

"O.K., everyone, we need to talk. OH! Shem, Tajaar. When'd you get here?"

"After lunch," suggested Chantal, grabbing a sandwich.

"Just a little bit ago," said Shem, his face flashing red again.

Chicken made room next to herself so Tinker could sit next to her.

"What have you guys been doing? This time?" His eyes flicked at Shem.

"Naught." Chicken shoved over one of the platters. "Most well behaved."

"Working our butts off," grumbled Chantal around a mouthful of sandwich.

"Yah," agreed Messenger.

"Itchy tak ptar rak," grumbled Sha'gar.

"Even," agreed Chantal. Then she leaned closer to Sha'gar. "We will shower and soak after lunch."

"Ummmmm," said Shem. "Thanks for the lunch, but we have to go."

Tajaar grabbed another sandwich just as they faded away.

"Most strange," observed Szart.

"O.K.," said Tinker. "Now we can talk."

"Pon?" Chicken slathered mustard on another sandwich.

"How come you guys didn't tell me about this, ahhhhhh, mate hazard whatever stuff." He looked grumpy at them.

Everyone looked elsewhere.

"You should know better," he grumbled. "All of you."

"We do, Me'Lord, we do."

"Witch flight protection," explained Szart.

"Huh?"

"Save save run," stated Szart.

"Sure," he said. "What?"

Chantal's fist thumped on the table top. "Pay attention, Cowboy! And stop that grumping, it is making us all nervous."

"What?"

Chantal sat back. "Apparently way back in their history in an older, more, ahhhhh, primitive times, their mates could kill them with impunity. And did. Some of the survivors developed a protective reaction. As soon as they felt their mates approaching a certain level of agitation, they fled, literally running for their lives. It has become automatic now. Like breathing. All the witch clan magic users."

He looked at her. "Even if they know better?"

"Yah. It is instinctual. It is irrational. So cool it."

"Merde," he mumbled. And sighed heavily. Slowly he looked around the table. From face to face to face to face. And sighed again. And looked at Smoke. "Can't you do anything?"

She shook her head. "Tried." And smiled at him. "We are at your mercy."

"Double merde."

Eyes jumped everywhere, looking for a safety route.

He sucked in a deep breath and slowly exhaled, calming himself.

They all settled down.

He stared around the table. "This been going on since R-Bar?"

"Not exactly," stated Smoke.

"Ahhhhh?"

She looked at Chantal.

"Critical mass, John. From what I can tell we got a small dose from R-Bar. Then Ran. Then Szart finally overdosed the system. It seems to have taken some time to become a full-blown problem. You, somehow, brought it to a head this morning. Before that, but post Szart, it was a vague uneasiness. But no longer. Now it is pure panic."

"So," he asked. "How come when we are facing bug uglies and mean nasties you guys weren't fleeing every which way?" He frowned. "Isn't the stress level way up there then?"

"Fiercely protective," said Szart.

"Mate save," added Sha'gar.

"Strong strong." Sgenn nodded.

He sagged. "All of you? Got that too?"

Chantal leaned on her forearms. "That too,

babe-magnet."

He lurched to his feet. "We ain't going anywhere till we figure this thing out." He stomped inside the house. "EVER!" All eyes watched him.

"Damn well better calm down," snarled Chantal. "Or I am going to lace his diet with Valium." She glared at the magic users. "You guys are a real pain in the butt." And stared at the table top as tears blurred her vision.

Messenger slipped close to her and slipped an arm around her waist. "Don't cry, Cowgirl. Please?" She blinked back her own tears. "Please?"

Chantal jerked upright, wiped her eyes with her shirt sleeve and yanked out her handkerchief and blew her nose. "O.K., kitten." And wrapped her arms around Messenger and hugged her. And stared at the magic users.

Black eyes stared back.

"How come none of you ever said anything? It is like marrying someone and then finding out that they have gave given you a horrible disease."

"Rar ptar tar," snapped Szart.

"It is not talked about," said Sha'gar as she leaned forward. "It is passed female to female, this knowledge. None dare tell the males. Much fear, much terror." Her eyes flicked toward the house. "He is the first to know."

"Many would try to kill him if they knew that he knew," stated Szart.

"Damn the elseplaces to hell and gone," grumbled Chantal. She looked at them. "I know, I know."

Reaching out, she lightly touched his mind. "Let's go in and sit in the living room and see if we can come up with something." She stood and headed inside.

"He is calm enough." She tossed an arm around Sgenn as she passed and tugged her. "Come on, Quiet. Let's get the cookie jar and grab a couch. After Sha'gar and I have a quick shower."

They all gathered together and talked. But all that they accomplished, several hours later, was to demolish the cookies.

And then.

He wandered in.

And flopped into one of the couches. Causing Messenger to bounce a little, and Chantal to grumble, a little.

"Well," he said, looking around. "Anyone care to get beat up?"

"Not funny," snapped Chantal.

"Figure anything out?"

"Nay, Sweet Prince. Tis conundrum fierce."

He nodded. And looked over to where Sha'gar and Szart sat. "Isn't there some super sneaky spell one of you knows?"

"No," said Sha'gar.

Szart hissed. "If we knew that, every witch clan in all the elseplaces would owe us debt."

Sgenn nodded.

"Ummmm," he said. And looked at Smoke.

"MindMate?"

"If I shut off from all of you, do you still feel it?"

She shrugged. "Can only try it and see." She looked at Fair Morn. "Let's have an early dinner." And headed for the kitchen, beckoning Chantal to come along with them.

He hugged Messenger. "We will find a way, kitten. We always do. Somehow. In spite of everything."

She nodded. "It is really terrible, really really."

"Many many generations," said Szart.

Sometime after they finished dinner, they relaxed in the large living room doing various relaxing things. Each in their own fashion.

He was reading a spy novel.

And she walked into the house. From somewhere.

"My, my, my," she said. "We are all lovely, aren't we?"

Heads popped up all around and all stared at this person.

"What?" He stared at her even harder.

She smiled warmly, very warmly at him. "I think that I will like being part of you, Sweet John."

He jerked upright. "What? What are you talking about?"

"I," she stated very firmly, "am going to be part of you!"

"NO! YOU ARE NOT!"

"Of course I am."

He leaped to his feet and pointed at the front door. "OUT! Get out of my house!"

She stepped over and glared at him. "I will not. And you can't make me." She slapped him.

With the flat of both hands he sent her stumbling backwards. Back toward the door. And did it again.

"Out!"

Twisting around, she slipped back into the room. "Can't make me," she snarled.

Everyone felt it. He was starting to slip, anger boiling up, adrenaline surging.

Eyes started checking the shortest distance out of the room.

The woman slapped him again. "You will do what I tell you to do!"

"That does it," he growled, and slipped forward, right fist clenching tightly.

Szart bolted for the hall.

Smoke ran into the room from the hall. "Clamp your mind shut," she demanded. "Now, MindMate, now!" Sha'gar slipped away, into the dining room.

He reacted instantly to Smoke's command.

The woman was gone.

Szart peeked into the room from the hall doorway. And whispered, all harsh rasp. "It worked." She carefully watched him.

Smoke hugged him. "Don't release until you

calm down, MindMate." And kissed him

They all crowded around. Smiling, all trying to hug Smoke.

"Gosh." Messenger dabbed at her eyes with her shirt tail. "I thought that she was real. Really really."

Smoke threw her arm around her. "I put all my energies into it, kitten."

Fair Morn hugged him. "That was a surprise."

"OOOOOOF!"

She released him and kissed the back of his neck. "Forgot." And sat on the nearest couch.

Chicken brought in a loaded tray. "Glasses for one and all." And tossed the empty tray into the dining room as soon as all the glasses was taken. They were brimming with brandy. She held up her glass. "To Our Most clever Dark Sister. And Our Verra Own Prince." She tossed the liquid down her throat.

"Gazooks, tis fiery stuff." She grabbed the bottle from a nearby table where she had set it, and began to refill the glasses.

Chantal looked at him over the rim of her glass. "Peek-a-boo."

"Oh." He released.

"Not bad, Cowboy." She hugged Smoke. "Sneaky clever."

Smoke hugged her back. "That's us predators."

Chicken refilled the glasses.

"Good thing we already ate dinner." He dropped into a couch, next to Fair Morn. "At this rate we are all gonna have to crawl to bed."

"I'll tuck you in." She kissed his cheek.

Szart sat by his other side. "Have I ever had this stuff before?"

"Don't think so."

"Nice flavor. Reminds me of sismo." She took a big swallow.

"Slow down. Sismo?"

"Yesssssssssssssssssss." She squinted at him. "Bottled by the Imhin on Adv Eace." And unbuttoned her shirt. "Warm."

"BOOP, boop de do dah," sang Messenger dropping into his lap, waving her empty glass to whatever melody she was hearing. "Gosh Szart, you look funny."

She waggled her hand. "Boop, boop, boop! Do bop do DAH!" She hiccuped. And leaned against his chest. "MyTinker, I think that she is trying to dissolve our bones."

"Who?"

"Pincers Bottle," gurgled Messenger.

"It is her way," he whispered. "How she releases stress."

Chicken lurched over, glass in one hand, bottle clenched in the other. "Hail, Great LoveLord." She began to refill everyone's glasses. "T'was a'mighty deed thee do do do." Leaning forward, she squinted at him, smiling a very crooked smile. "Most relaxed we do be, one and t'all."

Messenger hiccuped.

"Our kitten do be fou."

"Fee fou de do," giggled Messenger, beaming up at her.

"This crowd is getting wrecked." Chantal looked around the room.

"Yep." Smoke walked over and picked up Szart. "One for bed."

"Hum," mumbled Szart.

Sgenn stood, grabbed Sha'gar by the collar and headed for the hall and the Chamber. Towing the floating magician along.

Messenger slowly toppled over, giggling as she sprawled across his lap and Fair Morn's.

"You going to take advantage of my weakened condition?"

"Nope."

"Boooooooooooooo . . ." She fell asleep.

Fair Morn stood, cradling Messenger in her arms. And leered at him. "I'll be back."

"Sure thing, Arnold." He lurched up, walked over, and hooked an arm around Chicken.

"Me'Lorp?" She leaned against him.

"Drunker than skunks, one and all."

"Let's away to Mine Own Bedroom, Sweet Prince, a'go" Her smile was even more lopsided. "We do require, We do, some guidance we do."

"O.K." *Fair Morn, go to bed. Or whatever.*

"Jolly good." Chicken tugged him into motion.

"Thee has Us and We do have bottle mostly full. Some."

Sgenn wobbled into the living room and dropped into a couch. "Sha'gar sleeps deep," she said to no-one in particular. And sagged sideways over onto the cushions.

Chantal hoisted Sgenn to her feet. "Come on, Quiet, no sense sleeping on the couch."

Sgenn rolled her head and looked at Chantal. "That was a very powerful potion that she offered us."

"Certainly was. Everyone got pretty numb, pretty fast." She started them down the hall, one arm around Sgenn's waist. "Must have been an after effect of Smoke's little test."

As they entered the Chamber, Sgenn lurched. "Sleep with me? I feel comfort need?"

Chantal laughed. "Sure. Your place or mine?"

Chapter Nine

Exploration and Discovery

Hahn Dohr Kahn. A New Season Starting.

Ice Time had finally melted into First Growth, releasing the exploring parties into the unknown.

Queen Lurin had taken two ships east along the coast to map and describe everything beyond their knowledge in that direction. She intended to push as far and as fast as she could, anxious to at least understand the full extent of her new lands.

The First Lord was to push the Edgewater Road along the southern coast in the same direction as fast as possible as well as to improve the roads to the interior towns.

Prince Frahn and Princess Irinl had started due north from their newest town, Wurm, built by The Dragon Fang Wing of the Silver Rangers. They intended their exploration party to shoot straight ahead until they ran out of land or something in the environment stopped them. At that point they would veer sharply to the east and what they assumed would bring them to the coast in that direction.

The plan, such as it was, was to link up with Lurin's ships. and then sail back to the castle city. If that failed, then they would retrace their route.

If all went well, they would have produced a map showing the extreme edge of their kingdom's lands. And all expected to be back in time for the first Dragon Fest. Fast ships had been sent to the Old Kingdoms with materials to lure visitors to the Great Fest.

Frahn and Irinl slowly worked their way northward, accompanied by one Order of Blade, six Silver Rangers. All shared in packing their supplies and marking their trail. Two map makers made sketches and wrote page after page of description.

And, every now and then, a supply team caught up with them, refitting the small group and taking all the notes and drawings and sketches away.

They had been walking many, many days and had finally left the forest behind them. Now it was tall grass and scattered clumps of bushes with a few trees.

And now, these many, many days later, leaving Wurm, the little expeditionary force was very informal and relaxed with each other.

Everyone felt like they were back in shape after the long period of Ice Time and the usual limited opportunities for physical exercise.

Out here, they found openness and little else. First it had been dense forest, now it was open grasslands. They had seen little else. Other than the creatures that lived in these environments.

Frahn had pointed out to the rest of the party that the plants and the animals were much the same as those in the lands of The Old Kingdoms.

And so it went.

Day after day after day after day.

Steadily trending north.

Stacking stone monuments twice a day.

For all but the map makers this was the major event, this was the major event in their existence.

Then one day Frahn looked south. M'Ban's Mount was a small cone sitting on the horizon. And of the forest, nothing could be seen.

One of the map makers announced when Frahn pointed this out that it appeared that the lands north of Wurm were, so far, three times the distance as the distance from that town to their southern coast. And in the far north, it looked as if there might be some mountains, a slight bump here and there, crowded with clouds.

"Stay in the inner channel, Ship Master, and let us see whether this be bay or mere narrow passage."

Lurin stood on the high rear deck with the Ship Master next to a large table. Anchored to the table top was the map. It was updated at short intervals as they sailed along. The crew were free to come up and look, just to see where they had been and how the land was shaping up.

So far, their expedition had found a few small rivers and four small bays. The bays were well sketched but the rivers nothing but openings leading somewhere. Lurin had decided that these could be explored at some other time.

Now they were sailing north between the coast and what were turning out to be a chain of islands. It was a jumble cluster of islands. All sizes, All shapes. A few with mountains high enough to gather clouds around their peaks.

For two days the passage had been just that, a passage. Sometimes narrow, sometimes wide.

Lurin had laughed and thumped the Senior Map Maker on the shoulders, telling him to not worry about filling in every little bit. This was a preliminary map after all. And then she asked him whether he knew of other folk with his skills in The Old Kingdoms. It was going to take many to adequately map rivers and islands and who knew what else in the vast interior mostly blank on their map.

The next day they sailed out into open water, the islands falling behind them.

"A vast land, Majesty," said The Ship Master.

Lurin nodded. And smiled. She tapped the map with one fingertip. "We do believe that these lands are greater in extent than any kingdom in all of Bahn Duhr Tohr. It will be of great interest to see how Mine Own Brother's holdings do compare."

Frinda had pushed straight up his side of the great River Marhn and was surprised when it began a slow curve to the west. On the east side of the river, cliffs rose, their river edges steep cliffs. And far beyond the hills rose the gigantic cone of M'Ban Mount.

By the end of the next day, it became apparent that this river was much larger than anyone had thought. As they sat eating their meal in the gathering dusk, he laughed, "This river favors My Sister for it does continue more and more into our side."

Sook filled his plate. "Your lands are vast."

"All our lands are vast. These Kingdoms have greater territory than any five or six of The Old Kingdoms put together."

"Husband?"

"Erm?"

"You and Queen Lurin will have to make may Lords and Princes happy."

"Why?"

"Your fortunes are great, your populations are small. Strong temptation."

He frowned. "The Kingdoms do not war upon the other. Not for some times past. Ever since My Mother formed them into a single union." He grabbed one of her hands. "None would dare attack us." Then he laughed.

"It is funny?"

"No. But I just realized how powerful a kingdom that is just over there pon far river bank."

"Your sister's?"

He reclined against the thick cushions that littered the floor of their small tent. "My sister has the greatest force in all of Bahn Duhr Tohr."

Sook moved around and nudged a few cushions into place so she could join him.

"She has," explained Frinda, "the great black dragon, that Wing of the Silver Rangers, and her King. If the dragon didn't eat the attackers first, the Rangers would kill them. They could call upon all the Silver Rangers for help plus the Hephira armies from the lands of Frahn's Princess. And then there is her husband. And his cohort. They would certainly destroy anything that would think to bring harm to her. And your mother would absolutely get involved because Mother and Father would."

He rolled her way and wrapped his arms around her. "Even the dullest of the dull would know better than attempt such a foolish venture. And we are widely separated from the Old Kingdoms by vast water."

"Hum hum," replied Sook as she ran her hands through his hair before dragging him down.

It was a few many days later when they noticed far to their left a new thing. The land was beginning to slope downward to the west. And in that direction there was a gray-green that sparkled wet.

Frahn halted their party and set up camp. Then they all set upon the usual task, building a stone pillar.

On the next day they would take a small side trip just to see what that gray-green was.

And that is exactly what they did.

It stretched out of sight, into the west. And to the north and to the south.

It was a gigantic swamp, all marsh meadow and meandering water courses. The higher patches of ground had trees and brush on them.

"We are not going down into that," stated Frahn. He looked at the map makers. "Just sketch it in as you see it. In the morning we will head back to the marker and start north again."

Irinl slipped an arm around his waist. "A foul appearing place down there, My Prince."

He nodded. "Mapping that can be a job for someone else. More well prepared than we."

They made camp.

She stared at the map. They were still sailing in a general northward direction, still following the coast. Two river mouths had been added to the map, a few more islands.

Now the forest on the shore had thinned and had become mostly grassy plain. There were fewer areas along the shore with sandy beaches and more areas of vertical cliffs as the land undulated in gentle waves ever higher.

Everyone on board the ship was stopping and checking the map now as their excitement built. This land just seemed to stretch further and further to the north.

It was a topic of conversation among the crew. Small bets were being made as to how far it would be before they finally could swing to the west across the top of this huge island.

Ahead of them, in the distance, they could see them. Large mountains, stretching away to the east and to the west. The grass plain had been rising with great wide plains, a slow gentle incline, rising steadily to become the edge of the suddenly up thrusting rock teeth, all sharp ridges broken by narrow canyon splits. The taller peaks shown white in the sun of summer.

"Rugged lands there," said one of the Silver Rangers.

Frahn pointed at a narrow gap. "We will camp just there, close to that brownish yellow patch. And wait for the resupply unit. I don't think we want to proceed further until we are fully supplied."

And soon, they met one of the small streams flowing southward, small streams that disappeared into the soil of the plain. The water was carefully sampled and found to be fresh, clear, and quite good.

Then, there they were, not far from their chosen camp site, standing and staring.

At it.

The totally unexpected.

The Ship Master pointed. Far ahead. On the edge of their sight.

"Mountains?"

"Most certainly so, Majesty."

Lurin looked at the map. A long straight line headed straight up from Wurm. It was the route that the Prince and Princess should be following. She wondered if these great rock giants stretched that far to the west. And whether the interior party would push into them or turn and travel toward the eastern coast to be met there. She frowned. And wondered.

Frinda looked at the map. And hugged Sook with the arm thrown around her shoulders.

"This great river bends back towards Lurin's lands. It makes a great curve."

They stood in the gathering dark, the small cluster of tents making soft sounds in the slight breeze.

The grass stretched ahead of them and to all sides. Except on the far side of the river. Over there it was dense forest. The land was flat, apparently over there as well, with the exception of a few low hills.

"If there were reason for it, we could easily sail this far." He laughed. "We must think of some clever and pleasing gift for my sister. If it wasn't for her desire to see over the horizon, I would be stuck doing some boring thing, forever and forever, back there in The Old Kingdoms." He sucked in a deep breath. "This is ever much more fun." And wrapped her in his arms. "Don't you agree?"

"Hum." She kissed him.

Grandeville. The Burger and Bowl.

"Not bad." Green started on his second hamburger.

"Partner?" Red waved at the passing waitress and ordered a couple more pitchers to wash down their meal.

"We got waxed in the first game, but we are ahead in the second by five pins."

"I think that they were showing off in that first game. Now they're gonna let us win so we won't sulk." Red licked his fingertips and wiped his hands on a napkin. It was their turn to bowl.

Their opponents walked up to the table and dropped into their chairs, beaming happily at the two gigantic men.

"Your turn, guys," said Janine, grabbing some fries from Green's heap and dipping them into the catsup on her plate.

Green rolled his eyes at her and nudged Red. They headed for their lanes as Green said loudly, "Never could understand how anyone could treat french tries that way."

The two women watched the pair amble down to the floor of the bowling alley.

"Was that a grump?"

"Nope," replied Sandy. "That was a Green."

Janine dumped more catsup on her plate. "What I thought. Think we won too big in the first game?"

Sandy laughed. "Nah, it was good for them. After all, they are winning this game."

"Only because we are letting them." Janine bit into her hamburger.

"Shhhhhhh," hissed her friend. "They'll hear."

"Too loud in here," mumbled Janine around her mouthful.

Sandy shook her head. "They are very good at reading lips."

"OOOOOOP."

"They weren't looking this way."

"Learn something new every day."

Green looked at his partner as they started back to the table. "If we got good at this, think they'd still want to come?"

"Hadn't thought of that."

"I did."

"That why you are doing so badly?"

"Yep."

Red laughed all the way back to the table, and kissed his wife. "Just because, babe."

"Good. Now get out of the way, moose. It's our turn."

"Weird game," said Red, when Sandy and Janine were out of earshot.

"Why?"

"Those two lady jocks are trying as hard as they

can to let us win in spite of our ineptitude, and you are trying to bowl as badly as you can."

Green finished his second hamburger. And picked up the third one. "Keeps them happy. Besides, everyone's having fun."

"Me too," said Red.

"Being happy?"

"Bowling poorly on purpose."

"Thought so."

"Let's go to Big Darlene's and get some chili afterwards."

"Good idea."

"Thought so."

When Janine and Sandy returned, after ensuring that the game was properly close, Red smiled. And asked, "What do you think about us asking Tinker and one of his babes to join us? Ummmm, one of these days?"

Sandy looked at Janine.

They both said, "Chantal."

"I'll ask," said Sandy.

The game proceeded.

Hahn Dohr Kahn.

"Ruins."

The small group stood and stared at them.

"Perhaps, Prince, a decaying jumble of rock," suggested one of the Silver Rangers.

"Looks like ruins to me." Frahn started that way.

"HALT!" It was The First of the Order. He ran past Frahn and spun around to face him.

"Prince, Princess, if that jumble is truly a ruin then we shall proceed you. Ruins may have unfriendly dwellers in them."

The Order hurried past, great swords slithering from sheaths, gleaming in the sun.

Frahn nodded. "They appear ancient. But do as you will."

The Silver Rangers fanned out and strolled toward the jumble of rock. Frahn and Irinl walked behind them, more or less in the center of the line. Irinl frowned at the backs of the guard.

Frahn decided not to say anything.

But as they approached the pile it became obvious that it was indeed the ruins of a number of structures, not just some strange natural formation. And soon they realized that it had once been a large central structure surrounded by smaller buildings clustered around the central one. These other buildings were mostly heaps and piles of the strange yellow-brown stone. The central structure was less deteriorated, as if the outer ones had protected it.

"A strange place." Irinl fingered hilt of her sword.

"Double strange. Three times strange." Frahn looked at her. "We have no record, in any library of The Old Kingdom of such a place, nor have we seen rock of this sort yet in these new lands." He smiled, then frowned. "And Mother has never mentioned reading anything in the ancient records that would have led her to believe such a place existed or that some population once lived in these lands. She would have cautioned us to watch for such a thing."

He lightly touched his sword hilt. "I wonder who, or what manner of being, they were?"

"Certainly can't travel that way."

A rather wide tributary cut diagonally across their path and into the main stem of the river. On the far side of the water they could see the glint of water interspersed with solid land.

"Stretches into your sister's lands," said Sook.

"Indeed it does." Frahn pointed. "It does appear that the two kingdoms be separated from each by great swamp. Let us proceed up the river bank and see whether there is somewhere a route to the east. A dry route."

One day of continuous mountains plunging into the sea and they hit open water as far as the eye could see, stretching to the north and to the east and to the west. This mountain range seemed to head more or less west.

The two vessels swung about and were soon headed in a general northwest direction, following this new coast line. The ships held well off-shore. Yet even this far out they could all hear the roar of waves crashing against the steep, rocky flanks of shear cliffs.

But, now and then, there appeared a dark gap where some river punched an entryway to the sea.

"Map Maker," said Lurin. "When we cross Our Son's northern course, I would turn and seek the closest gap in those stone fangs."

He nodded and beckoned over the Ship Master.

"Majesty," said the Ship Master. "When we attempt that I would have the other vessel stay well behind. It would not do us well to founder both on unseen rock."

She nodded. "As you wish."

Every day they hiked to the ruins and explored. The map makers made sketch after sketch, and now, four days later, they had a vague map of the place.

It had been, originally, a rough square with a taller area more or less in the center. And all agreed that it was a strange place. No one had ever seen anything, anywhere, like it.

They had finally crawled up and over the rumble, following a route carefully mapped that took them into the central structure. Stepping through what would have been a second story window they found that the stone floor was remarkably intact, given the state of the rest of the ruins. And eventually they found a place where a stairway led down.

Two days of clearing rubble and they were inside, standing on the ground level floor of a large open room. Light shafted down through fissures in the ceiling. Remnants of wall paintings could still be seen. But, by and large, it was an empty room. The floor was rubble strewn, most seeming to be pieces of the overhead structure. In the center of each wall there was an opening.

These openings had bowed sides. All were the same. The remnant window upstairs had been the same shape.

Irinl nudged Frahn. "We are leaving the only footprints."

"Ummmm." He looked around. "Nothing comes down here, it seems."

"Prince, Princess?"

It was the First of the Order. "Which door?"

Frahn pointed. "That one. It appears to be headed toward the center. Perhaps?"

"We will go first." The First pointed, taking two of the others with him. The remaining three stood and waited, swords drawn.

And shortly came an echoing hollow call, "It is a long hall. With another opening. Another room."

"Interesting place." Frahn smiled at Irinl. "This trip was getting pretty dull."

Then they heard them. Heavy footfalls thudding in their direction.

Irinl yanked her sword free as she leaped away from Frahn's side.

The Silver Rangers stepped to either side of the

opening.

And he charged into the room. "PRINCE! PRINCESS!" It was one of the Silver Rangers. "Come quickly." He spun on his heels and hurried back into the hall.

Five very puzzled people followed him. And burst into the room at the other end.

Light poured down from a diagonal shaft built into the ceiling, illuminating the figure pinned to the far wall.

"PARDAK!" Irinl stared at it.

The figure, arms and legs thrown wide, making a grotesque X, had shafts driven through hands and feet, anchoring the body to the wall. A weapon of some sort had been rammed through the mid-section.

"Horrible," gulped Frahn. He looked at Irinl. "Who is it?'"

It was obvious that the person was an Hephira, a female Hephira, dressed in deep blue armor comprised of strangely shaped scales. A ruby pendant hung from around her neck. Her hair had been gathered into a long rope and tied to a protrusion on the wall. It keep her head from falling forward.

"I do not know," whispered Irinl. "I have never seen armor like that."

Below the body some sort of ornate structure protruded from the wall.

The First was carefully examining it. He heard them approach and straightened up, banging his head into one of the corpse's feet. "OUCH." He reached over and touched it.

"Stone! This is a statue."

Then each of them touched it. It was a statue, artfully carved, and skillfully painted. Even standing very close it was hard to tell that it was only stone rather than flesh.

Irinl spun away and snapped, her foot starting to tap. "I want this chamber thrice searched." She pointed. "Clean that floor. Put everything over against those walls."

The Order scattered around the room and carefully began checking everything. And then everyone started moving the rubble, clearing the floor.

"A double question," said Frahn, stepping close to Irinl. "This ruin." He nodded at the wall. "And her."

"Princess," called one of the Silver Rangers, kneeling near the entrance. "See here." He had cleaned a large patch of the floor just inside the space in front of the entryway.

Irinl and Frahn hurried over.

The exposed floor had the beginnings of something showing. The floor was inlaid stones, mostly a soft blue-grey color. Exactly centered on the middle point, the axis of the hall, was a patch of brown, a bar of brown inlaid stones. It appeared to bisect the room. It was aimed right at the statue.

"Two more days," said Frahn. "Then we must leave and push northward. We have a Queen to meet.

Next summer we shall send a large company to this place and fully investigate these ruins." He began to clean the floor, following the brown pattern. And smiled at Irinil.

"Mother will certainly be surprised when she hears about this."

Frinda stood and slowly looked around them and then at the map spread on the ground, held open by a map maker. "This watery arm descends from these great mountains just ahead of us, it seems. That great bog swamp divides the lands and feeds the great river. All this water must flow from many such streams and rivers. Unless out there are many, many springs."

He straightened up and tossed an arm over her shoulders. "Can you take us home? And mark this spot so we may return back to it?"

Sook nodded. "Place a mark on your map, map maker." And gestured. A tall orange rod appeared, anchored deep in the ground. "Just to tell all where they are on the map."

Frinda laughed. And watched the camp as everything was packed away. He strolled along holding her hand. "I would wallow in soft luxury with a certain black-eyed beauty before getting all from the three map portions and adding them to The Great Map. I wonder what my Queen Sister has seen?"

"Hum hum hum," replied Sook. "Soft luxury."

"And wallowing," laughed Frinda.

Winl Fzar.

Helf stalked back and forth and glared at the three guards. The three carefully held themselves in absolute rigidity and wondered what was going to happen to them. They had never seen The First Prince in such a state of anger.

The First Princess watched her husband carefully. However it had happened, she didn't believe that this trio were at fault.

"It was there last Sun Fall?" growled Helf.

"Yes," stated the First Guard of the Chamber of The Relic.

"And," snapped Helf, "this pair heard nothing? At all?"

"No. Ah, yes, they heard nothing."

"And they were alert, not sleeping?"

"On my honor."

Helf whirled away and stomped off. Then he spun around and jabbed a finger at them.

The pair jerked. Slightly.

"Then," hissed Helf. "You two will journey to the Princess and tell her what has happened."

This time the pair jerked visibly. The Princess Irinl was known to have a Training Master's zeal in thumping guards who deviated slightly from their duties. How she would behave when she heard this news they didn't wish to experience.

"GO!" Helf watched the pair run from the room. His eyes slid over the First Guard.

"Take a selected group and visit the Grey Orz just in case they have had something to do with this."

The First Guard nodded. "Right away." And ran from the room.

Nandau stepped close and slipped an arm around his waist. "A strange thing, husband."

He nodded. And hugged her. "That pair looked sturdy enough. They will probably survive your sister's rage."

She nodded. Then bumped him with her hip. "I would walk on the upper walls. Now."

He laughed. "And calm down your Prince?"

"Yes." She towed him toward a side door.

Hahn Dohr Kahn.

The First Lord sat and smiled at his pair of visitors. They were in his meeting room.

"You may as well relax. The Queen is sailing in unknown waters and the Prince and Princess are walking somewhere on their own." He laughed gently. "Urgent or not, this business will wait until they return." He stood. "Sometime before Ice Time."

He urged them through a door. "No more than forty or sixty days from now." The First Lord beckoned over a gaily dressed young woman. "Show them to comfortable quarters and make sure that they are told the instance that the Prince and the Princess return."

"Come, Warriors." The young woman walked off and wondered what this Hephira pair were so excited about.

Chapter Ten

Adventures, Such As They Are, Begin.

Grandeville. Tinker's Place.

"All right, all right, all right, all right."

It was mid-afternoon and he came bursting out of the side door and onto the rear deck. They were relaxing in the warmth of a late summer almost fall day.

Everyone, from early morning on, had been working, preparing everything that needed preparing for what ever winter might bring. This time they had started early.

Chantal had just returned from the valley after seeing a number of patients: three horses, two cows, and one llama. And had immediately headed for the shower room.

"Me'Lord?" Chicken peeked up over the edge of the swimming pool. And brushed water from her face.

"Well," he said, dropping into a chair, "if we are going to visit Frahn and see his Silver Rangers, shouldn't we be packing?"

"Most sudden a'decision." Chicken stared up at him.

"Certainly is." Szart sat in his lap and gently felt his forehead with one hand. "Hum."

"Yah." Messenger dragged her chair over, sat, and leaned close to peer into his face. "Really really."

"I feel fine," he grumbled. Szart quickly yanked away her hand.

Chantal walked out and sat on a bench. She was wearing one of the thick white robes, a towel wrapped around her hair. "Don't start that grumbling, Cowboy." She nudged Fair Morn who was making sandwiches and stacking them on several platters. "Must have gotten a sudden urge to visit Lurin."

"Insatiable." Fair Morn looked around the rear deck. "Lunch is almost ready," she announced to one and all.

"Ha ha." He tickled Szart. "I thought that everyone wanted to do that?"

"We could visit Mother," said Szart. "Also." She twitched. "And my sister."

Chicken surged from the pool. "And Mine Verra Own Brother." She walked over, bent and kissed him.

"Next day," mumbled Sha'gar, pushing another pillow under her head. She was sprawled in the hammock. Smoke had dragged her into the barn for a general reorganization of everything in there. Again. And she was tired.

Smoke returned from the kitchen and handed

her a cold can. "Here." Then she walked over and ruffled his hair and admired the sandwiches. "Tomorrow is soon enough." She walked over to the table.

Fair Morn slapped her hand. "I am not done yet."

"Quality control." Smoke took a big bite and chewed thoughtfully. "Not too bad. Where's the pickles?"

Sgenn joined them carrying a tray laden with jars. "Here."

"Soup's on," called Fair Morn.

"Where?" Chantal stood and looked at the lunch.

"Generic announcement." Fair Morn bit into a sandwich. "Better than not too bad," she mumbled as she shoved a platter over to Chicken. "So, how was your day?"

Je'leel and Dat joined them. "Both living rooms are clean and neat." Je'leel sat next to Chicken and took a sandwich.

Dat sat next to her and took a pickle and waggled it. "These are a unique food stuff to this elseplace." She smiled at Tinker as he, Szart, and Messenger sat down on the opposite side of the table.

"Kosher dill," said Fair Morn.

Sgenn peeked inside her sandwich. She didn't like mayo.

"It is dry," said Fair Morn. She pointed. "These have mustard and these have mayo and those have mustard and mayo and these are just plain old roast beef slapped between two pieces of bread."

"Yum yum, yum." Smoke took another.

Sgenn took a plate over to Sha'gar and set it on her stomach. Two sandwiches and a pile of pickles. Then she walked back, tapped Szart on the shoulder and sat next to Tinker and nudged him gently with an elbow.

"Hi, Quiet. What's up?"

She tilted her head back. "Clouds." And nudged him again. "Hum hum."

He reached for another sandwich. "Want some chips?" And laughed and threw his arm around her shoulders.

"Mother is taking a trip with J.C."

He choked and grabbed something to drink. "WHAT?" All eyes jumped in his direction.

"To some strange place with Doc and Badnews."

"Oh." He sighed. "I thought you meant out there."

"Lon Don," she said.

"Probably London. Doc has a friend who lives there."

She took a drink, making sure that he saw the ornate ring she was wearing on her finger.

Everyone relaxed, feeling him relax.

Grandeville. Doc's Place. A Few Minutes Earlier.

Doc burst into the library. "Change of plans, J.C.

Pack a bag, we are headed for London. Ask Reep to come along, it will be a treat for her. I've ordered tickets. Badnews is bringing the car around. Where is she?"

J.C. looked up at his friend and employer. He had been working on this project for six days and was pretty involved in it.

Doc yanked over a chair and sat.

"J. C."

J. C. blinked.

"J. C."

J. C. frowned.

And then Doc saw his eyes focus.

"Hi, Doc. Been here long?"

Reep slipped into the library. And over to J. C. "What is this London elseplace?" asked the softest of soft shadows.

"Winnie," said Doc, "an old friend of mine wants us to come and visit." Doc's eyes twinkled. "He has found some kind of artifact and wants our advice on it. Apparently it is a rather unusual find."

J. C. sat up, tugging Reep close. "Not another pseudo-monster?"

Doc laughed. "Not at all, J. C. This came right out of his back yard, so to speak." He bounced to his feet. "Shower, eat, and pack." And laughed again. "Winnie is paying for everything. Ta, ta." The door banged shut behind him.

"You coming?"

Reep nodded.

"Well then, let's shower, eat, etc."

They hurried up the circular staircase to their rooms.

Grandeville. The Home of Red and Sandy.

"Surprise, babe." He was eating dinner. She was eating breakfast. It was morning. He had just gotten off work. She was just getting ready to go to work.

She refilled their coffee cups and looked lawyer suspicious at him across the table. "What surprise?"

He grinned. "Green and I have been such good boys that the Chief gave us the day off."

"In the middle of the week?"

"Uh huh." Red took another helping of the stew and dumped some hot sauce on top of it.

"Well," she said, "what are you going to do with your windfall?"

"Depends."

"On?"

"Whether some lawyer babe and her secretary babe need to work today."

She peered at him over the top of her cup. "Depends."

"On?"

"What you and Green have on your minds relative to those babes."

"Good stuff." He finished the stew. "Thought that we could all go up to Tinker's, give him a surprise visit. And talk him into taking Chantal bowling with us next Saturday cause Green and I have that weekend off also."

He grinned. "Make it a day of surprises. Been quite a while since we visited him and his harem."

She yanked a gigantic briefcase around and fished out her planner and flipped it open. "Can we be back by three?"

"Right." He reached down the phone and shoved it at her. "You call Janine and then I'll call Green. We can take a nap later."

Hahn Dohr Kahn.

Frahn pointed. "Look!"

The small party stood at the end of the wide hanging valley. Not far from where they stood one of the many streams shot into the air and fell down, down, down, pluming into feather mist before it reached the water below.

A long, narrow bay stretched before them, sided by other mountain slopes. They could see a small beach and meadow area. The water stretched out of sight as it curled around the bend of the narrow fiord.

A ship was anchored near the shore meadow. There were three tents pitched on the only open space. Tiny specks moved around them.

"It must be Mother. We are very lucky." He pointed. "We can surprise them. Let's head over to that side. The slope looks less steep." And laughed. "And our discovery will be another surprise."

A sailor ran over to the table where she sat talking with the map makers and pointed. "Highness, up there, a line of figures are coming down that slope." And after some squinting and finger pointing everyone in camp spotted the small group of slowly descending dots.

Lurin sent a sailor running to the ship with instructions for the cook. Then she sat and watched the group coming lower and lower. She felt a great worry fade away.

They had been camped here for a hand of days and she had been debating whether they should sent a party into the interior to search for them. Or whether they ought to just sail back and wait for the overland party to turn up on foot.

All through the meal, the feeling was festive, although the food served was plain, Lurin watched her son's eyes sparkle and knew that he was bursting to tell about something but was restraining himself until the proper time.

Finally the meal was over, the table cleaned. Lurin had her maps brought out and spread, on the table top and pointed out the features of the coast line that they had seen.

"It is truly a vast land and will take many times to fill in all the empty spaces. Now show us your map, Our Prince."

Frahn nodded and one of his map makers carefully unrolled their map on top of Lurin's.

"A swamp?"

"Yes, Mother. It appears to stretch from here to here, and far into the west. If we project these northern mountains, it seems that this swamp divides the two kingdoms."

Lurin nodded and touched one finger lightly on a strange mark. "And what is this?"

"A great mystery." Frahn smiled broadly and had all the sketches and drawings flattened out on the table.

As Lurin looked through the many drawings of the figure on the wall, she gasped. "An evil mystery." And stared at Irinl. "Princess?"

Irinl shook her head. "I have never seen armor of such construction." She reached over and grasped one of Frahn's hands. "We will have to go back and search the histories in our libraries. Something horrid lived in that place at some time."

She tapped a drawing. "That thing looks like our ancient artifact."

Lurin nodded. "As soon as we get home." She dropped the sketches she held onto the pile and stood. "We will break camp immediately and sail as soon as possible."

Bahn Duhr Tohr. The Quarters of the Royal Advisors.

The beast from the jungles of Krantal held her

immobilized, multi-arms wrapped tight. It took a small nip, here and there, checking the tastier parts. She struggled weakly, but knew that it was no use. It tightened its deadly embrace.

"Knock, knock, knock," said a disembodied voice.

"Im pik tar," she snarled. "Ptar ptar."

"That is vile" said the voice.

"Sounds like our youngest," said Hanred, no longer the beast, releasing her.

"Plak plak," she grumbled, waving on her blouse. "Enter."

In a swirl of dense dark, they did. Szart thought that swirling dark was a nice effect.

"Fancy touch," grumbled Ripple.

"Hayou, Mother, Father," said Szart, being all witch formal. Hanred winked at her.

Then they all gathered and greeted Ripple and Hanred as Hanred filled mugs for one and all, handing Ripple the first one.

"We came to visit Lurin, but everyone is out exploring somewhere," explained Tinker.

"They have the newest kingdoms in all the lands," said Hanred. "Her and her brother, Frinda."

Ripple stepped close to her daughter. "You look happy well."

Szart nodded. "Most true."

"Hum."

"It was R-Bar done."

"I know," said Ripple, softly, very un-witch. "I miss her most greatly."

"And to visit Our Bonny Prince Frahn," added Chicken, smiling at Hanred as he handed around the rest of the mugs.

Hanred drop into a chair next to the table and stared at her.

Ripple whipped around. "Husband?"

"Did you know that?" He took a sip from his mug.

"What?" hissed Ripple.

"Prince Frahn is their son, ahhhhh, his son."

"Be something a'miss?" asked Chicken.

"Now what?" grumbled Tinker, wondering what sort of disaster they were walking into this time.

"Princess Lurin," mumbled Hanred.

"Queen Lurin," interjected Ripple.

Hanred refilled his mug and took a swallow. "Told one and all that her King was from another elseplace. He had great wealth and a greater wrath did any folk attempt ill-conceived actions against the new lands. And that this Mighty Lord had commanded the great black dragon, M'Ban, to serve her well."

Ripple stared at Tinker. "You?"

Tinker sighed.

"Relax," hissed Chantal.

Sha'gar looked from Hanred to Ripple. "Does someone make trouble?" Red flickered deep in her eyes.

Sgenn slid her hands into the wide sleeves of her

grey robe.

"Calm, fierce ones, calm," ordered Ripple. "It is a surprise. Your news was a surprise to me, to us." She touched Hanred lightly. "There is nothing here to threaten anyone."

"Very surprised," said Hanred. "The Princess, ah, the Queen, apparently felt it, erb, best to, ah, keep you a secret." He grinned at Tinker.

Who grumbled, "Not what she told us."

"Cool it, Cowboy," snapped Chantal. "She must have had a good reason."

"Indeed," agreed Chicken. "Praps do We speak most gently with Our Own Brother, We might find what do be a'foot?"

Umm," umm'd Tinker. "O.K., go ahead."

Chicken hurried from the room.

"Let's go shopping," bubbled Messenger.

Fair Morn smiled at her. "Why not?"

Chantal stood, walked over, and tapped Tinker on the shoulder. "Come on, grumble butt, we are going shopping."

As the door closed behind them, as they herded Tinker down the hall, Hanred looked at Ripple.

"Hum," she said.

"Any witchy idea why Lurin did that?"

Ripple shrugged and beckoned him over to the couch. "She always wanted her private business to be private."

She waited until he got properly settled. "Now,"

she purred. "What was that terrible beast about to do?"

It grabbed her.

Grandeville. Tinker's Place.

The large car glided to a halt next to the large van and they piled out. Red and Green from the front sea. Sandy and Janine from the rear.

They had taken three steps toward the rear deck, where they assumed everyone was probably lounging, when they jolted to a halt.

It was the scream that did it.

Someone, just down the slope from where they stood, had just screamed terror.

Red and Green whirled, ran back to their car. Red popped open the trunk, reached in and grabbed out two shotguns, handed one to Green. They both jacked in cartridges.

Then walked over and stared down the slope toward the county road.

A single figure was charging up the narrow driveway, long legs pumping hard, hair streaming in brown waves behind her head.

"See anything?" asked Red.

"Nope. Just that California babe." Green's eyes were slowly tracking back and forth. Nothing else down there was moving, just the solitary figure rapidly approaching. "Must be from Southern California."

Sandy and Janine stood on the edge of the rear deck so they could see past two huge men who were watching something.

Red walked back to the car, unloaded the shotgun and placed it back in the trunk. "Don't think that I will need this."

The woman hurtled into the parking area, shot past Green and then Red, just giving them a fast glance in passing, and jolted to a halt in front of Sandy and Janine, chest heaving as she sucked in deep breaths.

Green joined Red at the trunk of the car. "Nothing down there. Wonder where she came from?" He set his shotgun, now unloaded next to the other one.

"Or escaped from?" suggested Green.

The woman stared up at Janine, who still stood on the porch steps. "I, we, help us. Kandto!"

Janine nodded. "You want me to help you? My name is Janine."

The woman blinked.

Janine and Sandy carefully stepped down, trying not to frighten her.

"My name is Sandy. What is your name?"

I, me, Mar ae Soal, The Gentle Eyes, us, Kandto."

"Bug nuts," said Red softly as he grabbed a blanket from the trunk.

Green shrugged.

The pair carefully walked up behind her.

"Here." Red slipped the blanket over her shoulders and flipped the sides around. His eyes looked over the woman's head and into Sandy's. "Tinker's babes will loan her some clothes. Let's go into the house."

"Kandto Janine." Mar looked at Sandy.

"Ahhhhh, Sandy. I am Sandy." She waved one hand at the house. "Shall we go inside."

"Kandto Sandy. I, me, escape from Argar, us." She thrust out her arms showing her wrists.

Red scooped up the blanket. And stepped around and gently examined the marks. And nodded. "Look like rope marks." And handed her the blanket. "Here. This Argar live around here?"

Mar frowned and looked at Janine. "Kandto, I, me, lost, us. Ppple, us, threw. I, me, safety run, us. I, me, Ppple helped, us."

Green stared past the top of Mar's head at Janine and lightly touched the side is head with one finger. "Inside. Into some clothes."

"Don't radio in it yet. Please?" Sandy's eyes jumped from Green's face to Red's.

Green shrugged. Red nodded.

Sandy smiled and gently took one of Mar's hands in her's and tugged her up onto and then down the deck. "Let's go inside. Mar."

Janine looked at the two cops as Sandy and Mar walked down the deck. "Where did she come from?"

"She was halfway up the driveway when she screamed."

"And there was nothing else there," added Red. "I'll go down and see if her clothes are lying around." He turned and headed down the driveway.

Janine and Green walked up and along the rear deck.

Je'leel walked out of the side door holding a book in one hand. She smiled at them, her eyes rapidly scanning over Mar. "Father and the Mothers are not here. They went to visit Lurin and Frahn. Where's her clothes?"

"We don't know," said Sandy.

"Think they will mind if we, un, borrow some?" Janine smiled at Je'leel.

"No. I will tell them when they return."

Mar stared at the young woman.

"I am Je'leel. You are safe here."

"I, me, Mar ae Soal, The Gentle Eyes, us."

"Come on," said Sandy. "Let's get you into some clothes." She and Janine took Mar inside.

"Would you like some coffee?" asked Je'leel.

"Sure." Green smiled at her. "Red is here also."

Je'leel nodded and hurried toward the kitchen. Green walked back down the deck and out past the driveway to peer down the slope to see whether Red had found anything and watched him trudge back up.

"Well, partner?"

Red shook his head, and pointed. "Her footprints start just there, in the dirt, next to the driveway. No sign of anything else around, including her clothes."

Green nodded. "Pretty strange."

They started walking back up to the house.

"I don't think that she is crazy," said Red.

"Me too."

"Nobody around here talks like that."

"From this world . . . "

"What I thought."

"Me too. Je'leel is making some coffee."

Red cast a sideways glance at Green. "Wonder what Tinker is up to?"

"Bet that babe would have been a surprise."

Red nodded. "Wonder what gentle eyes means?"

Green shrugged as they sat at one of the tables where Je'leel had set a pot and a number of cups. Then they drank coffee and chatted with Je'leel. And waited for the others to join them.

Chapter Eleven

So, It's A Puzzle.

Lelty. Grey. And Dusty.

They stood in a small group. Talking. A tall slim man, dressed in jeans, shirt, and boots. A slightly shorter woman dressed much the same way with the exception of a large blade, shorter than a sword, larger than a dagger, hanging at an angel in the middle of her back from a sturdy green belt. And four tall, wide, thick, lumpy beings known as the Grey Orz.

The discussion had been going on for some time with neither side agreeing to agree. On anything.

The man frowned and wondered what to do now. The Grey Orz nodded to each other. The woman thought of yanking out her blade.

He huffed out a breath of air and scuffed one boot in the ashy grey softness and wondered why his Grandfather had insisted that he had to come here and do this.

"You must do as I say," insisted Shem.

"None tell the Grey Orz must do anything," snarled the spokesman, peering down at him. "Ugly creature."

"I didn't want to have to do this." He looked

over at the long stone building and told it to go away.

It did. In an explosion of rock, dust, and something else. But it all blew away from them.

"Now," he said. "When they come to you, you can truly say that there is nothing here to see." He grabbed Tajaar's hand and faded them somewhere else.

The Grey Orz snarled and growled at each other and argued about who's stubborness was responsible for that.

Uata. Land of Traders.

Argar raged through the dwelling. He roared through the entire vast cluster. It took days.

But there was no sign of her. There was no trace of her. Not a wisp. Not a fog trickle.

Where Argar was, the inhabitants fled in other directions, rattling and banging every which way.

But, finally, order settled back. Argar had returned to the One Dwelling. And there he made a decision he didn't want to make. But. He had no choice. Not if he wanted her back. So, he did it. He sent an emissary to them. And sat and sweat beads of fear.

Grandeville. Tinker's Place.

She plucked at her clothes and looked from Sandy to Janine and then at her new clothes.

"You look fine," said Janine, gently.

Mar looked at her. "I, me, dress proper, us, Kandto?" Janine smiled.

"Very proper," said Sandy. "Let's go back outside and talk."

As they settled along the benches at the table where Red and Green sat talking with Je'leel, Dat wandered out the side door, yawning and stretching.

Je'leel frowned at her. So Dat ordered on a shirt. She was already wearing jeans. Then she called on sandals.

Sandy smiled at her, past Red and Green. Their backs were to the house.

Dat sat next to Green.

Mar stared at Dat.

"I am Dat."

"My mother," explained Je'leel.

"Mar ae Soal, the Gentle Eyes, I, me, us."

"I will make cocoa." Je'leel stood and headed for the kitchen. Dat went with her.

Green looked at Mar. "Where did you come from? You are not from around here, are you?"

Mar looked at Sandy. "Kandto?"

Green's eyes flicked to Sandy and back to Mar. Sandy gently held one of Mar's hands in her's. "What does that mean, Mar? Kandto?"

Mar stared at her.

"Please?"

"Great Protector. One of the Naml. I, me, beg help, us, Kandto."

Janine silently mouthed her question at Sandy when Sandy glanced at her past Mar.

"How do you know we are that?"

Mar hastily stifled her grin. "You have Qawl, you."

"Qawl?"

Mar nodded and indicated Red and Green. "Kandto Sandy Qawl. Kandto Janine Qawl. Most Karta Qawl, me, seen, us."

Red nudged Green. "Think The Chief'll give us a raise, me and you being Qawl and all."

Green shrugged.

Janine frowned at him.

Green shrugged at her.

"Mar," said Sandy, "tell us where your home is."

"Fic Rth, Kandto."

"Told you," said Green to Red.

"That the place you escaped from?"

Mar's eyes popped wide. "Nable, Kandto. I, me, from Uata escaped, us. To Entob. I, we, thrown here by Pple, us. Argar, I, me, taken from Fic Rth, us." Mar blinked away a stray tear.

"She's from out there," gasped Janine, clenching the edge of the table. Green started to stand. Janine shook her head. "I'll all right, Green. Just reminded me of all the things that I wish that I could forget." Green settled back.

Dat and Je'leel rejoined them. Dat carried a tray with cups. Je'leel a tray with two pots, one coffee and one cocoa. Je'leel pushed a cup of cocoa in front of Mar. "Try this. It is good."

Dat took a sip from her cup. It was one of the few food stuffs she bothered to eat with any regularity. She liked the taste of cocoa.

Sandy looked at Dat. "You ever hear of these terms? Kandto. Uata. Entob. Fic Rth."

"Fic Rth? That the gold and green place?"

Mar jerked, sloshing cocoa over the table top. "I, me, Fic Rth live home, us."

"Mother?" Je'leel looked at Dat.

"I do not know those other terms." Dat took another sip of her cocoa. "I only heard of Fic Rth from a Writtle. It said not to go there. So, I went to Unsat and took a nap. And was bought for my Great Master at the Witch Foregather on Hamtramick." She smiled at Je'leel. "Your father."

"I'm lost," said Green.

"Me too," said Red.

Mar grabbed Sandy's hand with both of her's. "Kandto, your enl, us, send Fic Rth, I, me. I, me, sell you, us."

"I am not an enl," grumbled Dat, refilling her cup. "And you are not nice for calling me one."

Green tapped his wrist watch with a finger.

Sandy nodded. "We have to get back to town." She gently freed her hand from Mar's.

"We will come back later. And visit." Then she hugged Mar.

Mar gasped. Kandto didn't do things like that.

"Enl are sneaky, mostly." Dat nodded at Je'leel.

"They are not nice, also."

Green and Red stood and headed for their car.

"Not going to say goodbye?" asked Red.

"Qawl don't do things like that," rumbled Green.

Red grunted. "Wonder what that really means?"

Green shrugged. "Thug of some kind."

Sandy promised Mar that they would return after dinner and told her that she was perfectly safe.

Je'leel assured Mar that it was so.

Dat grumbled, still unhappy at being called an enl.

Kazmar. Not a Nice Place To Visit.

The emissary stood in the room and tried not to quake.

The room was moderate in size, just large enough to be comfortable. A fire crackled in the fireplace. The heat removed and kept away the chill in the air.

This was the Grey Time.

The skies were grey.

The water surging against the nearby shore was grey.

The air was cold. And damp. It felt grey.

But it wasn't the chill in the air that caused the emissary to shiver. It was the couple sitting in the comfortable chairs, looking at him.

They were both dressed in identical garb. Loosely cut shirts with wide billowing sleeves.

His shirt ended just below his knees. Thick leg coverings with an ornate pattern of black interconnected lines ended just below his shirt.

Her shirt swirled around her ankles. Most of their garments were shades of blue, light and dark tones.

The pair looked perfectly innocent. The emissary knew better. He had been told that they were ageless, magic changed.

"Why have you come here?" asked the man.

"We do not like visitors," added the woman, lighting touching a large broach on her shirt.

The emissary's skin tingled.

He hastily blurted out his message. And knew that he was going to die. The man was laughing.

"Perhaps," said the woman, nodding at her companion, "we should visit this Argar person?"

"Do you think that we should?" He looked at the visibly quivering emissary. "He sent that! He must be even less brave."

The woman nodded. "Go away," she said. "And tell Argar to come here in person, if he dares. Maybe then we will consider what he has to say."

The emissary fled.

Hahn Dohr Kahn. Moderate Wind. Fair Sea.

The ship turned to the south.

Lurin indicated on the map where they were. "It will be many days before we reach home." Her eyes watched Irinl as she climbed up the lines, headed for the sailor's perch on the top of the main mast. "What do you think of that place?"

"An ancient place. An ancient place where evil lived. Whatever it was, it must have had a great hate for her ancestors. That statue was an Hephira. And even if she doesn't recognize the armor style, there is no other explanation." He watched his Princess as she climbed ever higher. "Unless there is another land of Hephira that are unknown to her folk. Have you ever heard of such?"

Lurin shook her head. "But We are not all that well schooled in the histories of the elseplaces. We think that you should confer with Our Mother's Dark Advisor, Ripple. That witch clan is widely scattered and may know something. But unless they are asked, they tend to remain silent. Make copies of the statue drawing and have them sent Ripple with suitable explanations."

She stared at nothing for some time. "Perhaps it is not ancient. Not if there is another Hephira world. We must tred carefully, My Prince. We are ill-prepared to stumble into some war on-going among other folk."

Frahn nodded. "I had not considered that."

"One must consider all possibilities, someday King."

"Yes, Mother." He looked at her. "But something that evil ought to be killed."

Lurin nodded. "But studied ever so carefully first." Her hand gently touched one of his. "Not something we wish to invite home."

Grandeville. Tinker's Place.

They sat on the rear deck eating breakfast, Mar and Je'leel. Dat sat sipping cocoa. Sandy and Janine had visited with them last night, just to assure Mar that she was safe.

So they sat and ate breakfast. A very quiet trio. Mar appeared content to be with them.

Her eyes looked at everything. This elseplace was very different from anything she had ever seen before. She wondered where Pple had thrown her. And how she would ever get home again. All the Kandto did was ask her questions. They seemed so disinterested in helping her that they left the Qwal behind last evening. Yet, she did feel safe here. This place was safe feeling.

So, she looked around at the flowers and the large rectangular water basin.

"Hello, Sister, Mother."

Mar stared. The young woman was suddenly there. Smiling happily.

"Eulin!" Je'leel smiled at her. "Do you want breakfast?"

"No." Eulin sat next to Dat and kissed her on the cheek. "First Greetings, Mother."

"This is Mar," said Je'leel. "Mar ae Soal. She is visiting."

Soft lavender eyes carefully examined Mar. "Hello, Mar. I am Eulin." Eulin cast protection over herself and Je'leel.

Mar stared at her. This lavender eyed one was a magic user. She had seen the slight pulse and wondered what had been done. It hadn't been directed at her as she hadn't felt anything.

"Who are you," asked Eulin, ever so gently. "Mar ae Soal?"

Mar blinked. "I, we, us, am me."

Eulin nodded. "And what did you just see?" The shadow dragon watched Mar carefully.

Mar jerked. "What are you doing." She looked at Je'leel. "What is your sister doing?"

"Being careful, I suspect. What are you doing?"

"Nothing," gasped Mar, looking at Je'leel, yanking her eyes from Eulin. "But she Eulin is a magic user."

Je'leel smiled. "Of course. She is Vander."

Mar's head snapped back. "Touch me not, Mage of The Purple. I, we, us, will not be handled." The muscles around her eyes tightened.

Eulin stared and stared at her. "What are you, Mar? I feel something more than I can see."

Je'leel looked at Dat. "Mother?"

"Never saw eyes like that before." Dat leaned sideways and twisted around so she could peer into Mar's eyes. "Certainly different."

Mar gasped. Dat's eyes were a solid purple color. For some reason she hadn't noticed that before. Dat leaned away.

Mar looked at the three of them. "Why did Kandto Sandy and Kandto Janine leave I, me with you, us?"

"Calm," ordered Eulin.

"We are not doing anything," added Je'leel.

"Tell us, Mar ae Soal, of yourself and we will tell you of ourselves." Eulin smiled, a soft gentle smile. "You did see something, did you not?"

Mar nodded, one short quick nod. "You magic did, twice. I, we, saw the pulse, us."

"Hum," said Eulin. "Is that all you saw?"

Mar blinked. "Yes. Who can see more?"

Eulin looked at Je'leel. "I wonder what Messenger would see?"

"They went to visit Lurin and Frahn."

Eulin pointed at the tree shadow stretching across the deck near where Mar sat. "What do you see there?"

Mar looked. "Crooked shadow."

Eulin nodded. "So, all you can see is the cast?"

"Cast?"

"The pulse. It must be the cast that you see. The magical surge."

"Oh." Mar nodded.

"If I cast on you, what do you see, what happens?"

Mar gasped, her eyes boring into Eulin's. The shadow dragon grabbed her, enveloping her in dense shadow.

"Sister?"

Eulin sagged. "She was draining it away. I could feel it. Draining is not a good term. Ummmm, more like dampening, or neutralizing. That person can somehow do that." She nodded at the black shape. "She is unharmed. Just wrapped."

"Release her."

Eulin nodded. And the black unfolded. "Do not do that again," she warned Mar.

Mar twisted around to stare at the shadow on the deck. "What do you do to I, me, us?"

"My question exactly," replied Eulin. "What did you do to us?"

Mar straightened up. "I, me, Mar ae Soal, The Gentle Eyes, us. One of the few."

"And you can see magic users using their powers?"

"It is so."

"How?"

Mar shrugged. "One of the few looks, thinks, wishes, feels the pulse to not be."

Eulin cast lightly over her.

Mar gasped.

"Small test." Eulin smiled gently. "Sorry. But I had to know." She looked at Je'leel. "Apparently she can stop casting but only before. She can't do anything to the cast itself."

She wiggled one finger slightly. The shadow dragon slipped away. Then she moved around and sat next to Mar. "You are safe from me, Mar, unless you mean harm to me or my sister or my mother."

"I, me, do not do that, us."

"Thought so. So, how come you are here in this elseplace?"

Bahn Duhr Tohr. Visitors Suite in the Royal Castle.

Tinker slumped in his chair and sighed. Sgenn poked him gently in the stomach as his lap had started disappearing. He yanked his legs back up. "Grump."

"What'sa matta, Simba Leader?" Chantal looked over from her chair. "Toots getting too heavy for you?"

"Let's go home. I am tired of shopping and visiting and sitting around."

"Me too," said Messenger. "Really really."

He looked to his left. "Szart, can you ask Sook to let us know when Lurin or Frahn finally get home?"

Szart nodded.

Chicken leaped to her feet. "Me'Lord, We will Ourselves say fond farewells to The Queen and The King." She hurried from the room.

Szart followed her. "I will tell Mother. And Father.

"I am not heavy," grumbled Sgenn.

"Nope. Just right." He looked at the rest of them. "Goes for the rest of you as well." He hoped that might stop that discussion before it got a chance to start.

London.

The car slipped silently along the crowded street. It was not silent outside, just inside. The car belonged to Winnie, Doc's friend, known to others as Sir Winfred Robson-Brown, the archaeologist, the rather stuffy chap.

Doc, J. C. and Reep occupied the rear seat, Badnews the jump seat. J. C. let Reep sit next to a window so she could look out. "London," he said.

She nodded. Other than large and crowded and strange in the way most large places were crowded and strange, she didn't think she could see anything of interest. But she looked out because J. C. thought that she might like to. This was not his first visit nor Doc's or Badnews' to London, only her's.

She was dressed in grey slacks and a soft beige blouse. J.C. had convinced her, telling her that it was a local custom. So she had shrugged and had done it, dressed as he had suggested. Witches did not worry much about things like that. At least, this witch didn't.

The car eased around a corner into a quiet neighborhood and down a driveway and into a large garage. Winnie burst from a door and beamed at them as they clambered out. The chauffeur opened the trunk and handed their luggage to the servants that had suddenly appeared.

"Well," said J. C., smiling broadly, "there's Doctor Watson."

Winnie laughed, a rolling hardy laugh. He looked exactly like that character from the old Sherlock

Holmes movies. And shook hands with Doc. "Jolly good, Doc, jolly good. Delighted that you came. Really quite a puzzle that thing, quite."

They were rapidly hurried down a hall into a large comfortable room. Heavy thick rugs, wood everything, floors, walls, ceiling. Plush overstuffed furniture, gigantic fireplace. Badnews slipped upstairs.

"Winnie," said Doc, smiling at his friend. "You remember J. C. This is his wife, Reep."

"Delighted," boomed Winnie, vigorously shaking J. C.'s hand and beaming at Reep.

Reep nodded at him.

"Well," said Winnie.

"Show us the artifact, Winnie." Doc recognized the carefully controlled impatience of their host.

Winnie smiled at him, stepped to a side door and led them down a hall and into his laboratory. Most of the tables were bare, not cluttered as they usually were when Winnie was working on an archaeological site, a dig. He led them over to a table near the window wall. A single artifact lay on the wooden table top, gleaming a soft gold in the light.

"Ummmmmmm," said Doc.

"Nope," said J.C.

Winnie stared at them. "Ummmmm? And nope?"

"Yep." J.C. grinned at him.

"J.C.," cautioned Doc. "Behave."

"Sure."

Reep reached out and carefully picked up the object. "Hum."

"What?" asked J.C.

"Hum?" echoed Winnie.

Doc gave a quick shake of his head to his friend. And watched Reep.

Sun beam soft whispered so only J.C. could hear, "Not this elseplace, this thing."

"Let's go talk." J.C. hurried her toward the door. He didn't want Doc or Winnie to hear anything she might have to say. So far, he had managed to keep Doc from finding out what she was.

Winnie leaned against the table, crossed his arms over his chest and watched them leave. As the door closed, he looked at Doc. "What was that all about?"

Doc shrugged. "No idea." He picked up the object and took a more careful look at it. "J.C. didn't recognize it." He guessed the thing to be about three-and-a-half feet long, maybe four. It was thin like a sword was thin. One end had a strange bulbous design. "Looks rather Celtic, doesn't it? Can't be, though."

"And?"

"That probably means several things if J.C. couldn't identify it. One, this artifact is unique. Two, the style doesn't link it to any other cultural grouping that has been described in the literature. Three, that means it is going to be quite difficult to figure out."

"What did she say to him?"

"I don't know. She is a very, very quiet person.

J.C. has never said anything about her origins and I have never been able to figure it out, either. Not from her vocal patterns. Not from her mannerisms. But she said that it wasn't local, I believe."

Winnie stared down his nose at his diminutive friend. "She is also an archaeologist?"

"No idea. J.C. is totally silent on everything about her. But, when she speaks to him, he always listens very carefully. And that means a lot because there are very few people that say anything that J.C. pays attention to. He doesn't have to. His mind remembers everything, it seems."

Doc ran a finger lightly down the shaft of the object. "Interesting, isn't it? Show me the drawings, photographs, etc., etc. I want to see it all and the place where you found it."

Grandeville. Tinker's Place.

In a swirl of dense dark they came down, onto the rear deck, in a clatter and a few loud thumps.

Three of the four occupants already there were unperturbed. The fourth screeched and leaped to her feet, ready to flee. Dat grabbed her by one arm and yanked her back down to the bench.

"It is just Father and the Mothers," explained Je'leel.

Then they crowded around the table, laughing and smiling. Eulin got hugged and kissed.

Tinker sat next to her. "Hi. Have you been here

very long?"

"Just a little while ago." She kissed his cheek. "First Greeting, Lord. I just came for a visit."

"Father," said Je'leel. "This is Mar ae Soal. She is staying with us for a bit."

"Oh." He looked over. "Hi there." And smiled at her.

Eulin nudged him. "She is from elsewhere."

"WHAT?"

Eight pair of eyes snapped around.

"Relax, damn it," snarled Chantal.

"From?" sighed Tinker.

"Fic Rth," said Dat.

"Let's go inside and talk," said Eulin softly as she stood.

"Oh, oh." Frowning darkly, he rose and followed her into the house.

Messenger whispered to Smoke. "Funny looking eyes."

"Look all right to me."

"They are different," whispered Messenger. "Really really."

"In what way?"

Messenger shrugged. "Just look different."

And then they all heard what Eulin told him.

"Gosh," gasped Messenger, staring at Mar. "We never met anyone like that before."

Mar's eyes were jerking left and right. She was trying to decide which way to run. There was something about the way they watched her that was frightening.

"Mar," said Je'leel, gently. "You are safe. These are my mothers. They would never do anything to you."

Sha'gar and Szart were watching Mar with cautious frowns.

Eulin and Tinker rejoined the group. He was looking very unhappy. And snarled at Sha'gar. "How did she get in? I thought that ward was supposed to keep everyone out?"

Sha'gar jerked. He was approaching a very dangerous level of agitation. And was glowering at her. "Not against plain folk, Mate'mer. Too many variables."

"Oh." He dropped onto a bench And looked across the table at Mar. "How about telling us how you got here and what you were doing before that?"

Then they all began to relax as he did as they all listened to her story.

Fic Rth. The Gold and Green Place.

In the elseplace called Fic Rth by the inhabitants, every once in a while, now and then, in some strange manner that no one understood, a young woman suddenly realized that she had it, a certain rare talent. And when that happened, she was sent to the town of Ain to The Place of Training.

There she met and lived with others like herself until her training was complete. When that happened she was free to do as she would. The talent had to be trained or the recipient would go mad, mostly from fright as her vision went strange. For reasons no-one understood, all the ones who had the gift were female, and all came from around the elseplace of Fic Rth.

Once trained there was no worry of mind failure. Each trained one who left The Place of Training could call herself The Gentle Eyes and wore a ring of plain white with two tiny stones of grey.

The Gentle Eyes were in great demand by those folk who feared the users of magic. So they were frequently hired by The Great Houses. But no one dared force them to work for them.

Argar, The Great Trader of Uata, hearing stories carried to his ever listening for bargains ears, legal or otherwise, by smaller traders seeking favors, sent emissaries to hire one for himself They were unsuccessful as none wished to wander that far from their elseplace. The Gentle Eyes hardly ever traveled out into the universe of universes. So Argar did what he always did. His motto was: If you can't deal, steal.

Dumping deep sleep powder into a local drink, they drugged Mar and carried her away. To The Hall of The Great Trader of Uata. Argar tied her wrists to the arm of the Viewing Chair, the chair Argar sat in while he was wheeling and dealing.

After two days, Argar said he would cut out her tongue if she didn't stop pleading for release. She could communicate by finger taps.

Days dragged into days but Mar never saw one pulse of magic. So Argar had her beat.

He was sure that some of his rivals were using magic while they made deals and believed that she was withholding that information.

Then one day, in the midst of a Small Trader riot, someone cut her free. And she ran. And luckily saw a node and dove into it, not caring where she came out.

She came out in Entob, frightening the inhabitants. Except for one elderly Thrint named Pple. The inhabitants were short, barely as tall as her waist. Short and wide and round and lumpy.

"With me come," said Pple in the hissing rasp that was the normal speech for the Thrint.

Few came to Entob. Few of anything came to Entob. There was nothing on Entob that anything wanted.

Pple was an anomaly for Thrint. He had gone elsewhere. He had traveled. He had seen two other elseplaces. And had returned. Not wealthier. But wiser.

In the deep underground that was his dwelling, Pple talked with Mar and put something soothing on the raw red wounds on her wrists. He didn't remark on her lack of clothes but only on her predicament. And what to do about it.

"This Argar will come seeking you. You must go elseplace safe, elseplace far unlikely. Come, we will go Up Top."

Pple led her from his home and up to the top of

a tall hill, up to the packed earth flat place defined by four tall stone columns. He pointed at the space and at the four columns. Then he dug a small hole in the center spot and pushed something into the hole and rapidly covered it.

At that moment, Argar's searchers poured from the node seeking her.

Pple shoved Mar between the pillars and did something. And Mar felt herself hurtled away.

To be there, bright sunshine, warm soil under her feet. She screamed. And ran up the slope toward the strange looking structure.

Grandeville. Tinker's Place.

"Merde," grumbled Tinker.

"Fear not, fair Mar. We will you protect from vile Argar." Chicken nodded. Her left hand clenched the hilt of her sword. They hadn't dumped their weapons yet.

"How could some little lump know about us?" He frowned at nothing in particular.

Fair Morn's finger brushed over the levers on her weapon's handle. They all heard the soft click.

"Gosh," said Messenger. Then she smiled at Mar. "That Argar wouldn't dare come here."

"Argar dares anything," replied Mar.

Sgenn looked at her. Somewhere, deep below, something grumbled all bass notes.

Mar lurched up from the bench and stared down at the deck.

"NO!" he snapped.

Sgenn looked at him and exhaled. Something was no longer there. Deep down.

"Sit down, flighty butt," snapped Chantal at Mar. "Nothing to worry about. Here."

After Mar carefully did, Tinker sighed. "Maybe if we, ummm, explain, ahh, a little, who we are, you will relax." He looked from Mar to Smoke.

"Very confused," said Smoke. "Feels safe. Feels frightened. Doesn't understand."

Mar twitched. That one knew how she felt yet there was no magic being used that she could see.

"You tell her, just enough." He stood. "I am going inside and lean this thing back in its corner." He headed into the house, the great black blade riding in its usual place across his back, the hilt sticking up past his left shoulder.

"I think that I will just keep my weapon for awhile," said Fair Morn. She stood and headed for the kitchen. "Anyone else want something to eat?"

"Me," said Smoke, sitting opposite Mar. She began to tell Mar what she felt she ought to know.

Chapter Twelve

Small Discoveries

Hahn Dohr Kahn. A Fairly Warm and Sunny Day.

The two warriors tried not to show what they felt. They felt like running for their lives.

They had trained with her before she had earned that ring she wore, the one that told one and all that she was a Master Sword, a First Warrior. At least, they thought, she wasn't armed although her expression told them that she wished that she was.

"And," she hissed at them, "how can an object just disappear from a room with only one door guarded by armed guards?"

"I do, I do, do not know, Princess," stammered the Sergeant.

"Unless," she snarled, eyes darting around the room, searching for something suitable to hit them with, "someone was sleeping or being elsewhere?"

"NEVER!" bellowed the Sergeant, momentarily forgetting his precarious position. Then he remembered why he was here. And hastily added, "Maybe it was magic." It was a desperation statement.

She froze in position. Then she looked at her Prince. The other guard shot a quick glance at the

Sergeant. He gave a slight shrug.

Frahn nodded. "My Mother's Mother's dark advisor could do that easily. So could Uncle's wife. Even Queen Sook. The Sergeant is most likely correct."

The Princess looked at the two warriors and snarled, "Go to your rooms."

They stared at her.

"Now!"

They hurried away, not quite running.

She looked at Frahn. "Magic'd?"

"Let us go across the river and ask Queen Sook."

Someone knocked gently on the outer door and peered carefully inside. "Prince, Princess, The Queen would see you in her chambers."

"Right away," replied Frahn. He took Irinl's hand as they started for the door. "Maybe Mother will have an idea."

Lurin spun around as they entered the room, she had been staring out the window, and frowned. "Our Husband, Your Father, came visiting while we did adventure and map. He and his returned to their lands after spending some time in the Central Kingdom."

She waggled a small scroll at them. "The Queen, My Mother, had this sent by fast ship."

"Bad news comes in clusters," grunted Frahn. Then he explained what the Hephira had told Irinl.

"Some of them are magic users," said Lurin. She looked at Irinl. "We think it should not be said elsewhere that thy artifact may have been taken by some magic folk. We will ask Queen Sook to send to them, asking them to come to us."

Irinl frowned, one foot beginning to tap. Frahn slipped an arm around her. "Mother?"

"Magic users stealing ancient artifacts is to worry about. Does this thing have special powers?"

Irinl shook her head. "None have ever said such a thing. It is very old with no written records. Perhaps when we search the Hephira library we will find something."

Lurin stepped close to them. "My only Prince, lovely Princess, tred carefully. What you found in our lands and this newly told event are bothering, deeply, troubling." She hugged them in turn.

"When they arrive, I will send them to the land of the Hephira. Go now, for I feel the need to not waste time."

She smiled at Irinl. "I will send those two guards deep into the interior to work with one of our road builder crews. They will have no-one to tell tales to that will listen."

Then she stepped back. And nodded. "Tred carefully. But arm yourselves well."

Frahn bowed. "Till we return, be well, Great Queen."

Grandeville. Tinker's Place.

They had been sitting on the rear deck discussing what to do. He was mumbling and they were gently teasing him in between agreeing to this or that. It was in the midst of the that, the that being the argument about killing, in the most gruesome manner possible, whatever had sent Mar here, when it happened.

Szart suddenly sat straighter, twisted and gasped. "Ric, ric, ric," she snarled angrily. "That sister is ptar tak tak." Sha'gar glowered at her. Sgenn just looked.

"What?" Tinker looked across the table.

"Sook," hissed Szart. "Sent a call. Hard." She relaxed a little. "Lurin wishes us to come. Now!"

"What?" he repeated.

Szart shrugged. "Sook did not say why. It was urgent, that call." She grumbled about it.

"Ummmmmm." He stared into nowhere.

"Me'Lord?" Chicken jabbed him in the side with a finger. "We do be most ready for to travel, we do."

"Oh?"

She nodded. "Most true."

"Mother and I will watch the house," said Je'leel. "Mar will be safe here."

"I, we, us, no not stay." Mar looked stricken eyes at them, staring, jaw dropping open. She lurched to her feet.

Chantal yanked her back down. "Cool it." And looked sideways at her. Mar sat and frowned at Chantal. She had never heard such a magical incantation like that before. She looked but didn't see anything.

One side of Tinker's mouth pulled down. "O.K., she comes along." He sighed "Might as well get your gear." He stood and headed into the house. "Someone fix her up."

"Come with me," said Smoke to Mar.

Eulin nudged Je'leel. "I will send a small blue-green with them." She grinned. "That way we will know whether they need any help. They will never notice. Ahhhhhh, most likely."

"Tell the Princess, just in case."

Eulin nodded. That is exactly what she did. During all the farewell hugs she whispered in Chicken's ear and told her. Chicken gave her an extra hug. "Most clever a'daughter. T'will be between thee and Us."

Then they walked out into the first pasture, waved goodbye to Je'leel and Eulin and swirled away in a cloud of whirling black.

The tiny dragon easily followed them.

Hahn Dohr Kahn. A Warm and Sunny Day.

Lurin's eyes popped wide as a black whirling cloud appeared in her room. The servant froze in place, face going white. And then, they were there.

"Our King," said Lurin, giving him a very proper bow, and indicating to the servant that he could leave and that all was well.

He rushed from the room, glad to be alive, and anxious to tell a certain maid what he had seen. Of course, during the telling of this tale he cut a more heroic figure, being more interested in impressing that certain maid than worrying about the exact truth.

And during the retelling later, that maid pointed out that their Queen was even mightier than anyone knew for she had a King who could do things like that.

After all the hugs and kisses, Tinker included, he cleared his throat and introduced Mar. "This is Mar, Gentle Eyes. We, ahhh, agreed to help her before we got your message."

He looked around the room. "Sook said urgent."

"A long story, Lord." Lurin smiled warmly at them, at him. "Come next door. It is better explained over maps and drawings."

Taking his arm, she led him in the proper direction. And in just a few moments, all stood around the large table and listened to the story as she explained the exploring of her new lands, shoving map after map at them. And finally she began to tell them of the strange ruins.

Slipping those drawings from a large folder, she laid them out and began recounting all that Frahn and Irinl had told her. She handed around the first drawing of the statue.

Mar took one look at it, screamed, and hurtled from the room.

"Merde," snarled Tinker as he turned and started to run after her. They skidded to a halt. This room had six doors. None standing open.

"Smoke?"

"All fear, terror, panic." She blinked and pointed. "That way."

And raced through that door, beckoning Fair Morn to follow. Between the two of them, Smoke and Fair Morn, they could stop and hold and control almost anything.

They ran through three rooms and out into a long hall, Smoke tracking Mar as she kept pushing at the panic in Mar's mind. Pushing, pushing, pushing, replacing it with calm.

"Just around that next corner," stated Smoke as she slowed to a walk. "We are lucky. She didn't run into anyone."

As they stepped around the corner, Smoke's minds grabbed Mar and held her in place, keeping her from bolting away.

Fair Morn wrapped her arms around the staring young woman and gently stroked her hair, murmuring gently to her, "You are safe, you are safe."

"You do not understand," hiccuped Mar, feeling something release her. "I, we, us, are all going to die, me, us."

"Nope," replied Fair Morn. "Not if you tell us what frightened you so." She felt Mar's muscles relaxing. "This have anything to do with that person that kidnaped you?"

"No," whispered Mar. "Worse. Horrid worse."

Fair Morn looked at Smoke.

"Calming down nicely. Sudden shock. Deep

down terror shock. Heavily guarded, protected."

Fair Morn hugged Mar gently. "Mar, what did you see?"

Smoke struggled to keep the terror from returning in Mar's mind.

"Xylinth Blade," gasped Mar. "It was a Xylinth Blade!"

"How do you know that?"

"The House has one many vaults deep. Only The Finished may see it. None may touch it. To tell another is to be hunted and killed." Mar sagged. And wept. "I, we, told you, us. Dead twenty times over, me, I, us."

"Nope." Fair Morn kissed the side of her face. "Wrong again." Releasing Mar, Fair Morn tugged her into motion. "Let's go back. You can tell Lurin about that thing or place. And then we will figure out what to do about it."

They walked slowly down the corridor.

"The Ones Who Are Not To Be Named made them," whispered Mar. "In time before time. The Warrior Princess, a'an Nald, The Swordpoint of The Victorious, drove them deep, taking the blades, using them. The House has only ever found the one."

She shuddered. "Those ruins must have been one of their spots. It is said that she, The Warrior Princess, was hated by her enemies above all things. And they hated much."

"Well," said Fair Morn as they turned the last corner, "that was long ago. Certainly nothing to worry about now."

Once they were all back inside the room, they convinced Mar to tell Lurin, and everyone, all about the blade, again.

Tinker frowned and stared at the drawing of the statue. And grumbled to himself as his eyes jumped from drawing to Mar and back again.

My Lord? asked Chicken, inside his mind, feeling his worry grow and grow.

Don't like this at all.

Most ancient a'history this.

"Ummmmm.," he said, agreeing with her. "Can't get too excited about ancient history, I guess."

The color had fully returned to Mar's face by the time they had finished their discussion of everything Lurin had told them and had shown them.

The Queen insisted on showing them to their quarters, shooing the servants away.

"Royal Guest's Rooms, Our King. Do stay some short while before following Our Son to the lands of Our Princess." Luring smiled slyly at him.

Giggling happily, Messenger handed her a large ornate ring. "I get it back."

"Suppose a few days or so won't matter," he mumbled.

Chantal laughed. *Big stud!* He frowned at her.

"Our People," pronounced Lurin, "would see Their King." She grinned at them all. "There are some who say that he does not exist and it is but mere fiction for some slight indiscretion on the part of a young Princess."

"We will here stay." Chicken bristled at the idea of a Queen being thought of that way.

Lurin threw her arm around Chicken's shoulders and smiled. "Majesty, We will so proclaim tomorrow a Fest Day." She beckoned over a servant that had appeared and sent him running to spread the word.

It would not reach the far towns but would spread rapidly through the central city and across the bridge to their sister city.

"Next day will be tiring for one and all. Our King must be dragged hither and yon."

"Sorta like a horse show," drawled Chantal, leering at Tinker.

"All right," he growled, trying to head off that discussion before it could get started.

"It do be Right and Proper for Our Lord to do so," pronounced Chicken in her most Royal tone of voice. She felt that if Queen Lurin said that it must be so, then that Royal wish would be served.

Mar watched Tinker.

Lurin slipped the ornate ring on one finger and smiled at Messenger.

Goggle eyes is staring at you, said Fair Morn.

Huh?

Fair Morn winked. *Mar.*

He glanced that way.

Mar jerked and hastily looked somewhere else.

She was more confused than ever. How could one man do this? That Queen was certainly ready to drag him away. And all these others didn't seem to be worried about it at all. And why did the short one give the Queen that fancy ring? The Queen had called him Lord and King. Mar looked at the Queen. There was no magic there.

"Lord King," purred Lurin, "wouldst stroll with Us and see all We have wrought since last thee were here?"

"Huh? What?" Tinker's eyes refocused. He had been wondering why Mar was acting so strange. They hadn't done anything. Yet? That he knew about. He stood and allowed himself to be led away, in the direction that Lurin wished to go.

"We will all sup together," said Lurin, loud enough for all to hear as she towed him into the hall. As soon as the door closed behind them she wrapped him in her arms.

"What?"

She laughed. "We would merely hold Our King and be held in return."

So he did. "Ummm?"

"You must visit more frequently as We do miss thee greatly."

"I'll talk to Chicken." He cleared his throat. "Let's stroll."

Lurin laughed and kissed him. "We will talk with that Queen, we Will. This be most Royal business." And frowned into his frown. "And does be naught business for a King."

He sighed. And was yanked into motion. Lurin's hand was gripping his. Tightly. She had a strong warrior's hand.

Grandeville. Tinker's Place.

Je'leel was sitting in the small living room, on the couch. Legs tucked up. Reading. Two of the cats had joined her. The large black male and the blocky white female.

The female had slowly, with slight humps and bumps, shoved the male from Je'leel's lap. Her lap was just not large enough for two cats to sprawl as they wished to sprawl.

Eulin popped through the door, still dripping water. She had been floating in the swimming pool and wondering whether she could convince the Vander to put one of these into their quarters at Magevern. And then began to listen and see what the small green had been listening to and seeing. The tiny dragon had been darting wildly about trying to be with them all, all of the time.

"It is called a Xylinth blade," she announced, leaning close to Je'leel.

They looked up at her. Two cats and Je'leel. The male shook his head. Eulin had dripped on him.

"What is?"

"An artifact in a drawing of a statue."

Je'leel nodded. She could tell from her sister's expression that there was more to tell.

Eulin told her everything that had happened, explaining that dragons didn't react to much that bothered anything other than dragons. And very little bothered dragons. So the small one had just watched and listened and waited for Eulin to ask.

"It frightened Mar," finished Eulin. "I am going home and search the archives." She was suddenly dry and dressed for traveling in very proper Vander attire.

"I will come," said Je'leel, "after talking with Mother." She marked her place in the book, scratched each cat behind the ears, and slipped from under them. The male had been attempting to reclaim her lap.

Walking into the large living room, she strode over to one of the many book shelves and gently rapped on an ornate ring with one fingertip. "Mother?"

A small figure materialized, yawned and stretched. "I was taking a nap." She had been sleeping since Tinker and the rest had left, two days ago. For an indjinn it was just a short nap.

"I am going to Magevern with Eulin. We want to look through her archives."

Dat nodded. "Big."

Eulin nodded. Dat stood next to her. Dat was taller. "I will take care of everything," said Dat. "Here." She hugged Eulin. "Say hello to them all for me."

"I will." Eulin stepped away, took Je'leel's hand. And they were gone.

Dat walked outside to look at the flowerbeds. Messenger always did such interesting things in the flower beds.

Winl Fzar. Not A Bad Day For Some.

Irinl stepped down into the room, glaring at the Guards standing by the door as she did so.

They winced.

Frahn followed her.

"Ma pot ram," snarled Irinal, glaring at the empty display case as if it was at fault for being empty.

One guard nodded at the other. It was an I told you so nod. But even so, he was shocked, a little, at her vile language.

The other guard, just raised from the ranks, blanched. He had never heard one of the nobles speak that way, especially a Princess.

The sharp sound of her boot heels warned them in time to look properly guard-like as she stomped back outside the room and down the hall and up the only stairs leading down to this deep room.

Frahn followed. He had decided that it was better to stay way back and be silent. She looked like mayhem waiting to fall upon someone.

Hahn Dohr Kahn.

The sun was low and to their left as they stood on the small balcony looking out over the great square toward the town. The Queen had one arm around his waist and was pointing with her free hand.

"Straight across and down leads to the Great Quay where all the vessels come to dock. It was agree that this was to be the Port Town for the Two Kingdoms. My Brother's realm does manufacture much and we carry. Thus each earns a fair share and none be in rivalry with the other." He nodded.

"When the sun is there, We will go down there and eat the first meal. Then stroll down there and . . . "

He nodded again. And every once in a while. And was glad his boots were comfortable and well broken in.

Then she pinched him.

"OUCH!'"

"It is improper for Our Lord to do that in public."

"In public?" He stared down at the ants walking across that vast opening directly in front of the palace.

"Our sea folk have far-seers. And are no doubt looking at us right this moment. With such a device it would be as if they stood right here."

"Really?"

"It is so." She laughed. "The sea folk are most rowdy and would believe thee are but one of them yet We feel that it is Royally improper. In public."

Lurin turned toward him. "However, a husband, high or low, may hug and kiss his wife in public." Her eyes twinkled as she slipped her arms around his waist.

Out in front of *The Clear Wet*, Hahn laughed

loudly and lowered the device from his eye and rolled his way back inside the gathering room of the inn. He thumped Parhn on the back.

"That rumor be true, you pay!" He ordered a large of the best. "Our Most Royal Queen be fair grappled by her King."

Parhn grabbed the far-seerer and ran outside to verify the fact. After all, it was a sizable bet.

So all joined him outside, taking turns, sharing the several devices among themselves. Then there was a collective sigh.

"Went inside," mumbled Qaphn, First of The Hart, the Queen's Own Vessel. "Thart be her though. Not mere servant tickling."

All deferred to his opinion. After all, he had been with The Queen all during the last sea exploration. He ought to recognize her.

"Think you The Pair will come here?" asked the inn keeper.

"The Prince and The Princess did," replied Hahn. All knew that next day was a Fest Day. And all knew that their Queen strolled and visited on Fest Days. And more than one lucky person had a boon granted. And a few had been lectured sternly if their home or their establishment was not well maintained.

No one wanted that. Not after the Queen, in a towering rage, had Prapna and all that he owned shipped back to The Old Kingdoms on the next fast ship. The Queen had talked to him once. The next time she had wacked him alongside the head with a serving bowl, charged outside, and had ordered the first soldier she had seen to do what she ordered.

The sea folk wondered where she had learned such language. She had sounded just like a mast-climber in a gale. Of course, after that, the sea folk knew that she was one of them. The fast ship, in one count, had sailed. Prapna had been paid full value for the building and everything left behind. Then she had given it to Tahn Trahn. The structure always looked newly built. Now.

The inn keeper had a barrel of the best brought up, telling one and all that it wouldn't be tapped unless Their Queen and Her King entered his establishment.

The sea folk grumbled and told each other that they would see to that. They told Qaphn that they expected him to see to that. At sea he might command, but on land, by the dragon, they were all equal. Then they drank and discussed what her King must be like.

Magevern. Deep Below.

Sa'ar met them as they shimmered in. "Short visit. Hello, Je'leel."

Je'leel hugged her. "Hello, Mother. We came to look through your archives." When Je'leel stepped back, Eulin asked, "Have you ever heard of a Xylinth blade?"

"No, what is it?"

Eulin told her all she knew. Especially about Mar.

Sa'ar frowned. "We have never heard of any group calling themselves The Gentle Eyes. Look for that as well And how to recognize them. You couldn't do anything?"

Eulin shook her head. "It was just like I wasn't." She grinned. "But it didn't stop the Shadow Dragon. However Mar did what she did, she didn't know that it was there."

Sa'ar's eyes went all soft focus. "I wonder whether she would be willing to visit here. And work with us. It would be interesting to see whether we could learn how she does that." She looked at Je'leel. "She went with them?"

"Father agreed to help her," said Eulin. "He could probably convince her to come here."

A smile tugged at one corner of Sa'ar's mouth. "He can be very persuasive. At times." She started to turn away. "I will speak with Cazor. We will see what she thinks of these Gentle Eyes." And laughed. "Don't let Eland order you around too much. She likes to keep things just so in the archives."

Winl Fzar. A Little Later.

Helf watched Irinl as she stomped into the room, Frahn trailing along behind. Helf hadn't seen that behavior from her since the Sword Master had made her practice all night long because she had failed to do what he had said to do.

"What did you learn?"

"Nothing," she growled.

"Father," said Frahn, "is going to come and look. Maybe then we will learn something."

"We," stated Irinl, "are going to visit the Grey Orz." She spun and glowered at a guard, who blanched. "Go find Sword, First Warrior, Ofend and tell him I want two sets from the First Band and himself to be ready to travel. NOW!"

The guard bolted for the door.

"It has been rather quiet since you left," laughed Help.

She bowed to him. "May I use them?"

"It will be good for them." He waggled one hand at her. "If you stay, your chambers are ready."

Irinl smiled and stepped close to Help and her sister Nandau, The First Princess, Help's Wife and Queen. "Have you ever seen anything that speaks of one of us wearing blue armor?"

She pulled a folded document from a pouch and opened it. "Like this?" It was a copy of the drawing of the statue on the wall.

Nandau gasped.

Help stared at the drawing of the statue. "That looks like the artifact."

Irinl told them about their discovery.

Hahn Dohr Kahn. Bright Morning.

Lurin sat up and looked down at him. "They are looking well."

He nodded, knowing who the they were that she referred to. "Everyone is fine."

"And who," she poked him with a fingertip, "is the new person?"

"Oh. Her."

"Indeed, Our King, her."

"She is Mar, The Gentle Eyes." He grabbed her hand. "And I do not know. We agreed to help her. Actually they agreed. I, as usual, am just being dragged along." He ran a hand over her ribs. "You have to be more careful. That is a very nasty scar. A new nasty scar."

She smiled. "We are careful. But We chose to work alongside Our People for We feel that this is the Right and Proper thing to do."

His finger was now drawing gentle circles elsewhere, having wandered away from her ribs. "Just be careful."

She leaned forward. "Am I still pleasing?"

He sighed.

She frowned. "Our King?"

"It took me years to convince them to stop asking that question."

"We would just know as We feel . . . "

"Stop!" He lurched upward, hooked an arm around her neck, and pulled her down. "OOOOOF!" He laughed. "You feel just fine. And not too heavy either. Before you ask."

Magevern. Deep Below.

Eulin looked up from her stack, a smudge of grey across the tip of her nose. And looked toward the open door of this store room. "She may keep things in order, but they certainly aren't kept clean. Find anything?" She looked over at Je'leel, half-hidden by another stack of material.

The stacks sat on the floor. So did Eulin and Je'leel.

"They are mentioned in this volume, The History of the Weth War. They were mighty warriors who wielded swords manufactured by Lyth. From the description I think they are the same ones. The account suggested that there were only a few of these swords ever made. Nothing is told of Lyth. Or what happened to those swords."

Eulin sneezed and glared at the stack of material she had been searching. "Were there Hephira involved?"

"Not mentioned"

Eulin stood. "Let's go get something to drink." She stared at all the stacks yet to be searched. "This is going to take forever."

Je'leel stood, holding a tattered volume. "Let's put this in our room."

Eulin nodded as they headed out through the wide door and through the main room of the archives. "Good idea."

Hahn Dohr Kahn.

The soft knocking on the outer door woke him.

"Enter," said Lurin, yanking on her boots. She was sitting on the edge of the bed, dressed, ready for the day.

The servant, holding a bundle of clothes in her arms, slipped silently into the bed chamber, glanced at him and bowed to her. Lurin pointed. "Just there." The clothes were set on the foot of the bed. "All wait in the dining room, Highness." Taking another look at him, she hurried from the room.

Lurin smiled at him. "Great Lord King, We would have thee dress in proffered garb." She indicated the clothes at the foot of the bed. "And leave monstrous weapon where it leans." His great two-handed sword leaned in the far corner. "It will not be needed for Our Royal Tour."

"Sure." He slipped from the far side of the bed and grabbed the clothes.

"Royal garb," she stated, standing. Her black trousers were draped over tan boots. Her shirt was rose with a stylized black dragon in flight embroidered on the left side, curling over the soft swelling.

He cleared his throat. "Nice dragon."

She grinned. "We did notice thy stare." And plucked at her shirt. "Our soldiers wear the same. But their dragons are outline, not solid. Only Our Royal Family wear the solid. Thus the folk will know." She nodded as he tucked in his shirt. "Nice dragon." And laughed.

Food does await, My Lord.

"Let's eat." He walked around the bed, took her hand, and headed for breakfast.

Eight happy faces beamed at him. The ninth, Mar, didn't look sure. The servants finished filling and handing around the plates as they sat at the large table. They cast subtle glances at him. The word had already spread through the servants ranks about their Queen and Her King.

"Most fair a'morn, My Lord." Chicken smiled at him.

"Eat hearty," said Lurin. "This day will be long. And Our People, on occassions such as this, tend to be." She paused. "Exuberant." And smiled. "A long and honored tradition."

As they ate, Lurin told them what they would be doing. It mostly consisted of wandering around and visiting. And they had no need for weapons. Everyone nodded. Chicken decided not to mention the knife tucked inside her boot.

Soon they were finished. And ready. As they stood, Tinker looked at Mar. "You don't have to come, you know. You could stay here."

"And get some more sleep," laughed Lurin. "We will probably not be back until first light next."

"I will come."

"Stick close," said Fair Mom.

The group headed out and down and out into the

main square. And the mob. People cheered, threw flowers, screamed, and called. Lurin hooked her arm around his.

He leaned close. "All day long?"

She nodded and tugged him forward. He found that if they walked slow enough that people made way.

"Which way?" Tinker nudged Lurin. She headed them toward the mouth of the main street.

Here they found that the press of bodies was less once they entered into the town proper. People crowded the balconies. They could see better from up there and could have a more private celebration. Those who had met The Prince during his Wedding Fest said that it was obvious that the Son was the King's. And everyone wondered how their Queen allowed Her King to wander elseplace when there was so much to do in Her Kingdom.

It was soon halfway to mid-day meal and the party had plowed deep into the town.

Sudden loud bellowing came from their right side. And a space opened up as three burly men pushed forward. They bowed and urged the King and the Queen to enter. Tinker looked up.

The sign read *The Queen's Cloak*. It was an inn.

Lurin tugged him that way. "Clothing Guilds prefer this one."

Inside there was an open space. The owner was holding everyone outside except Clothing Guild members. Everyone in the party was handed a mug of the local favorite beverage. Lurin smiled and took a swallow. "Very good."

Tinker tried his. It was good. A very fruity flavor.

"Brewed locally," explained Lurin.

She strode across the room, threw her arm around someone's large shoulders and held a low pitched conversation with him. Everyone in the room smiled.

The sun was directly overhead by the time they reached the intersection of the main road, the entrance to The Great Quay, and Waterway Road. The sea folk roiled around this spot.

Qaphn, The First of The Hart, The Queen's Own Vesssel, burst through the mob, smiling and bowing.

"HOP, QAPHN, HOP!" shouted the Queen in the joking manner and greeting of the sea folk. None but one of them would dare address them in this manner.

Qaphn smiled, threatening to bruise his cheeks as he urged them inside **The Clear Wet**. The inn-keeper served them from the special barrel. Then Lurin introduced her King to Qaphn and as many of the crew members that had accompanied them on her exploration as could crowd around them. And the mugs were refilled.

"If we don't eat soon, we are all going to be in big trouble," mumbled Tinker.

Qaphn who could see a shouted order through

the wildest storm leaned on the counter and bellowed at the innkeeper. Tables were hastily cleared and all the party seated and quickly served. As they ate, Tinker leaned close to Lurin. "You do this every Fest Day?"

She nodded and wiped something from his chin with a napkin. "It is Our custom." And grinned. "Fest Days are infrequent."

The outer door banged open as a large man lurched inside, one arm around a young woman with a wild gleam in her blue-green eyes.

Lurin smiled at the man as the pair headed toward their table. Two more chairs were dragged over. The pair sat. The woman had a tight grip on the man's belt.

"This, My King Lord, is The First Lord, the one who sees that everything runs well in this Our Kingdom."

The man carefully looked over all that he could see of Tinker. "Highness," he rasped. "My King." And gave a short nod.

Lurin laughed. "It appears you have fit all of this celebrations day into the mere beginning."

The First Lord nodded and threw his arm around his companion's shoulders. He had been leaning on the table top with both forearms. "This is Ferlan Pahn Drahn."

"Highness," said Ferlan carefully. "Great King."

"I seek a boon," said The First Lord, taking a pull from the mug someone had just pushed into his hand.

Lurin nodded. "During The Fest many ask. Some are given."

"I would have Ferlan to wife. But she will not." He held his mug up. "Because her father is naught but hired worker in wood."

Ferlan tugged at him, trying to get him to leave.

"It does not matter," growled The First Lord. "Not in this Your Kingdom."

Lurin nodded and beckoned over the inn-keeper and spoke in his ear.

"SILENCE," roared the inn-keeper. "I WILL HAVE QUIET IN MY ROOM!" He cleaned another table and offered his hand to Lurin as she rose, stepped on a chair and then onto the table.

The sea folk stepped back making a clear space all around the table, a silent pack of very large and very rugged men, watching her carefully.

Lurin pointed. "Ferlan, release that man!"

Ferlan jerked her hand away.

"Stand up here! DO IT!"

Sea folk stepped forward and hoisted the startled young woman up.

"Listen well," ordered Lurin in a stern no nonsense tone, "to what I do to this woman so all will know the truth of this event."

Ferlan's face slowly drained of color. She wobbled. Her eyes sought those of The First Lord, seeking help. He was staring at the floor.

"This is Ferlan Pahn Drahn. Do any here know

her father?"

A heavy set sea folk pushed from the far wall. "He is known." He stood, thick arms crossed over a massive chest.

"A good man?"

"Yar. Good as any, better than most."

"True?"

"Yar."

"If I grant a boon, is it truly given?"

"Yar."

Luring looked around the room. "Which rope climber among you here wants this woman?"

The First Lord's head snapped up. Deadly silence filled the room. Not a sea folk moved, all watched her. Ferlan gasped.

Qaphn shoved to the front. "We take no man's woman from him. Highness." He glared up at his Queen.

"Ferlan does not want him." She frowned around the room.

"Oh, NO!" yelped Ferlan. "That is not true." Her face flushed.

"As Queen of The Realm. I do so pronounce," stated Lurin, ignoring Ferlan. "That all will know your fate."

"Highness," whispered Ferlan. "Don't."

"In one hand of days," stated the Queen, spreading her fingers wide as she thrust her hand outward. "In the Grand Square, in the very center of the

Grand Square, with all in this room attending, I will see you wed, Ferlan Pahn Drahn."

Ferlan stared at her as Lurin's hand slowly raised, clenched into a fist, one finger pointing, drifting from here to there. "To that man!"

Ferlan gasped and toppled from the table into the arms of The First Lord. He stared at the tip of Lurin's finger.

Lurin glared around the room. "In My Kingdom, one of the two New Kingdoms, the citizens may marry who they choose. There are no barriers. UP! OR DOWN! You will remember this."

"YAR," roared the sea folk.

She jumped down. "I need a mug." She took one of the many thrust her way. Emptying it, she nodded at Tinker and headed for the outside, grabbing his arm in passing.

"Certainly hard on your citizens," he mumbled.

"They need to remember," she grumbled. And headed them through the throng and around a corner and into another inn.

It was *The Dragon Flag*. It was mostly full of men wearing royal garb. It was the inn of the soldiers. It was rather quiet in here. The troops celebrated quietly as they relaxed. They sat around tables and talked. But now were all on their feet, greeting her, eyeing him. And the others.

Her Commander bowed. "Majesty. Great King. Most welcome." He bowed. Soldiers offered mugs to all. And settled back around their tables. Talking quietly.

Lurin smiled at her Commander. "The First Lord in The Clear Wet will probably require assistance in finding his quarters."

Six soldiers hurried out and away.

"Good Fest," laughed the Commander.

"Good Fest," agreed Lurin, holding out her mug for a refill.

Tinker hastily followed suit. Whatever she did he felt he had better do as well. After all, he had no idea what royalty did, here, or anywhere else for that matter.

Soldiers nodded to one another. Her King appeared to be all right to them, but he was certainly not from Bahn Duhr Tohr.

A soldier, who had put away more mugs than he probably should have so quickly, lurched to his feet and surged over to his Queen. He stared down at Tinker. "Be he warrior? Or rug crawler?"

Soldiers suddenly sat straighter at every table. Rug crawler was a not very nice term, to put it mildly, for the courtiers who tended to flock around royal courts.

Lurin stared at the soldier. "A mighty warrior." She waved a hand at the Commander, waving him back.

"A test," demanded the soldier.

"Now what?" whispered Tinker, feeling the rest of himself getting ready to attack. The air soft crackled around the magic users. Mar stared from one to another.

Lurin laughed, stood, and stepped away from Tinker. "Do not injure my soldier too badly, My Lord King." She sipped from her mug and then reached for his. He handed it to her, moved to a clear space, and glared at her. She smiled. He set himself.

The soldier charged. Tinker side-stepped lightly, and kicked the feet out from under the soldier. And watched him bounce and tumble. Roaring loudly, the trooper scrambled to his feet and leaped back. Blocking the wild swing, Tinker punched him below the ribs on the side, grabbed the extended arm and flipped the man onto his back.

Dropping to one knee, the other resting on the soldier's chest, Tinker glowered at him, fist cocked back. "Enough. I think that is just about enough. No sense spoiling the Fest Day, is there? Soldier?"

"No, Highness," he gasped.

"You satisfied?"

"A warrior," said the soldier.

Tinker helped him to his feet, grabbed a mug from a table, and shoved it at him. "Here."

Lurin stepped up to them. "May thanks, Lord King. My soldier looks only slightly injured." She laughed. And spun around. "Be there any else who would judge Their King so?"

The Commander stepped forward and bowed. And smiled. "Never saw combat of such a fashion before. Perhaps, if I might impose, Our King, you would teach my First?"

Lurin swung an arm around Tinker's waist. "Next day. Late." She grinned at the soldiers. They grinned back and nudged each other. She held the mug high.

"A toast, Fierce ones."

Someone handed Tinker a mug. And all held their mugs high.

"To The Queen's Own." Lurin drained her mug. So did everyone else. Then she suddenly dropped to one knee and looked up at Tinker. The soldiers quickly did the same thing. "Hail, King of The Realm of the Dragon," she cried.

"HAIL!" shouted the soldiers.

The Commander waited until all were standing and all the mugs were refilled. "Highness, proud to serve Our Queen. And this, Our King. Warriors all!" Mugs were drained again.

"WARRIORS ALL!" bellowed the soldiers.

With a slight bow of her head to the Commander, Lurin took Tinker's arm and led him and the rest back into the thronged street.

"Well and truly Our King." She smiled at him. Everything was going well.

"Powerful stuff," said Tinker, squinting in the bright sunlight. "If we keep this up we are never going to make it. Eyes are getting fuzzy as it is."

Behind them Messenger started giggling.

"Whish, Our Kitten," slurred Chicken. "Thee be fou." She was wearing a very crooked grin.

Fair Morn nudged Mar. "Everyone better stop drinking toasts. Or we will have to find a wagon to haul everyone back in."

Mar blinked, and squinted at her. "These are a very happy folk."

"Certainly are."

Chantal leaned close to Smoke. "If that Lurin doesn't slow down with all that damn toasting all she is going to have in her bed is a snoring drunk." She looked at the rest of them. "It is just past noon and this whole mob is already getting pie-eyed."

Sha'gar had her arm thrown around the much shorter Szart's shoulders. Szart was humming loudly.

"Witch self," asked Sha'gar loudly. "Do you have an undo spell?"

Szart twitched and stopped humming. "Shurp!"

"Use it."

"Should have thought of that earlier," she grumbled.

"On us," finished Sha'gar. "Leave him be."

"By George!" gasped Chicken. "We do be sober as a judge."

Szart told them.

Mar also, said Fair Morn. *She is getting a goofy look in her eyes.*

Szart nodded. And cast.

Mar jerked and lurched into Fair Mom. "Who

did that?" Her eyes jerked from face to face. She was nervous having magic used on her.

Tinker slipped his arm around her waist. "Nice waist, also."

"Also, Great King Lord?"

"Yep. Nice dragon, nice waist." He gave her a little tickle on the ribs. "Ribs are all right too."

She tickled his ear.

He jerked his head. "Stop that."

"Most interesting an inventory."

"Didn't think that I had to list everything."

She laughed. And pointed. "Head into yon structure, the all blue one. It is The Farmers Guild."

"More toasts?"

"Of course."

"I will never make it."

"They make a mashed tree fruit drink. Very good for you. And it doesn't affect your body or your mind." Slipping an arm from around his shoulders, she tugged him into the building.

Chicken led the others to a cluster of small booths set around the nearby intersection. And bought them large cups of something that had chunks of fruit in it. And took a swallow. "Gazooks! Fierce concoction t'would fair remove wax from kitchen floor!" She unbuttoned the top buttons of her shirt. Leaning sideways she tossed an arm around Smoke. "Dark Self, need we trail after that Pair Royal?"

"Nope. They are safe. And will always be within

range."

"Then We do propose," stated, Chicken royally, waggling her cup for emphasis, "that We do stroll as We will. We would see Great Bridge. Up close."

Lelty. Not Entirely A Beautiful Spot.

The Grey Orz fussed and fumed, growling and snarling, and pointed at the wreckage.

"People did that. Looking for our treasure, the one you took." They all glared at Irinl. They had been demanding that she pay for the damages as it wouldn't have happened if the object had still been there. The debate, such as it was, had been going on for some time.

Tiring of it all, Irinl yanked a packet from her pocket, unfolded the drawing, and shoved it at them.

Hissing smoke and fumes, the demons began to back away in several directions.

"Who is she?" demanded Irinl over the din. And jangled a large sack of coins.

The speaker of the demon group stepped closer. "Thought that one died many times long before. What parzak did that?"

The rest of the Grey Orz snorted fire. Parzak was the vilest term in their language.

Irinl's eyes jumped to Frahn's and back to the speaker's. "Many times long before?"

"Pointy-eared zug, that one was before before before before before before my ancient egg parent!"

Irinl jabbed the sack into its mid-section. "Here."

She looked upward at it. The Grey Orz were several times taller. "Did she have a name?" She glared at the demon. Zug was an uneducated barely trained child.

"We were told that during the Great Tra'kan Battle, when the Krazak were eliminated, that one was called E'Nilt." It tapped the drawing with one red, hooked claw. "Is that a daughter many times after?" And for a brief moment it didn't glare at Irinl. "Doing things like that is what eliminated the Krazak."

Irinl blinked in surprise. "No. This is a drawing of a statue in a ruin."

Magevern. Deep Below.

"This is the third day."

Eulin stood and stretched and stretched and stretched, arching her back. "And there are still stacks and stacks."

Je'leel looked up. "Her armor was constructed from Blue Durl scales. From the caverns of Ler Thran." She watched Eulin as she twisted back and forth. "Ever hear of a durl? Or Ler Thran?"

Eulin grinned. "Let's go visit Mirf. Monetary Control has the most complete records of all. I'll bet that she will check the elseplace name for us."

Je'leel nodded. And rose to her feet. "We better bathe first. Everything here is dusty dusty."

They headed out of the Archives and down the hall. "If you'll scrub my back, I'll scrub your's."

Eulin threw her arm around Je'leel's shoulders.

Her hand reached down and began tugging the upper tie loose.

As they lounged in the hot steamy water, Eulin reached over and tickled her sister. Je'leel didn't react. She wasn't ticklish. "Time moves slower where Father is," said Eulin.

Je'leel nodded. "How do you know that?"

"The tiny blue-green is watching them. It is evening there. Of the Fest Day. Late evening. That day started late on our day before yesterday."

"It is what we have been told." Je'leel smiled at Eulin. "Remember, we gained several years on your wander and yet we were only gone a few days for our parents."

"Father and his Queen there are wobbling badly. The tiny blue-green says that the mothers went in another direction. They have that Mar person with them."

"Let's leave in the morning."

Eulin smiled. And jerked violently. Je'leel had tickled her.

Hahn Dohr Kahn. A Clear Pleasant Evening.

The two moons had sailed overhead and had long since set. The throngs had thinned down to an occasional small cluster of die-hard fest determined folk. They had noted that their King and Queen were still about, wandering rather badly from one side of the various streets to the other side, arms around each other's waists. And these late evening folk told each other than it was good to have royalty that joined the plain folk during a Fest Day. And that they knew how to be plain folk as well.

The pair lurched to a sudden halt.

"Water," said Tinker, staring outward at an endless sea.

"We are at the end of the Great Quay," stated Lurin.

"How'd we get here?" He released her and sat on the wooden decking, leaning back against a tall piling. The next one over had thick ropes tied around it. One of the sea vessels creaked as it shifted slightly in the gentle sea swells.

Lurin joined him, using his lap, and leaned against his chest. "Took a wrong turn." She set the large satchel down, slipping the strap from her shoulder. Then she opened it, fetched out a brown earthen jug and popped the top open. "Gift of the Artificer Guild."

She tipped it up, then handed it to him. "Purry good," she stated firmly. Her shirt had long ago come untucked from her trousers and was now mostly unbuttoned. She stared down past the end of her nose. The dragon on her shirt was making strange movements. "Looooooooord King?" She squinted.

"Ummmmm?"

"Be that you?"

"No one else here." He glared at her. "Better not be."

She held the jug to his lips and tilted it up. For just a moment. She didn't want to drown him. She sighed. "We can take a room at the inn just there." She pointed, her finger wandering vaguely in the correct direction. She tugged her shirt back together, lurching to her feet, dragging on his arm.

They started back toward town.

"Is that proper?" he asked as they wandered off the quay and into the street.

Lurin stuffed one corner of her shirt into her trousers. "We are The Queen. We are always proper." Her fingers clawed through her hair. Then she aimed him at the door.

They burst inside, a controlled stumble, laughing softly.

"I remember this place." Tinker squinted at the room. "I think."

"Majesty," gasped the inn-keeper.

"A room," she stated. "We do require a room."

Twirling away, he snatched a key from a pcg and beckoned at them. "The Captain's Pleasure. A room reserved for special guests."

The room was far back, in a corner isolated from the others. The inn-keeper quickly unlocked the door, swung it open, and handed the key to Lurin with a deep bow. "My pleasure." And hurried away. It was obvious that the King and the Queen had been doing Fest as heavily as any mast climber in the fleet. She almost wasn't in her shirt. He wasn't much better. It would be known far and wide by morning light. Those loose mouths in the main room would see to that.

She kicked the door shut and dragged him sideways, tumbling them both into the huge bed, the huge and soft bed.

At the next inn over, three doors down the central street, Fair Morn kicked the front door open and walked inside, carrying a noodle limp Mar in her arms.

The inn-keeper's mouth fell open as they all gathered around Fair Morn, lining up, more or less, along the counter.

Chicken had an arm thrown around Smoke's neck and was singing, softly for once, a rather bawdy song having to do with soldiers and willing maids. Her shirt was open to the waist.

"We need a room. Or rooms," said Fair Morn.

"Mooble," mumbled Mar.

Messenger was giggling happily as she watched pink things coming and going around herself and Szart. They were fun spells Szart had learned from R-Bar who learned them from her niece Shitar. Messenger had an arm around Szart's waist. Szart had a hand stuffed into one of Messenger's back pockets.

Sha'gar, her hand clamped on Sgenn's upper arm, was snarling at her. "Get rid of that thing." Something dark hung around Sgenn, yellow eyes searching hungrily.

"Imdak tik tik," mumbled Sgenn, leaning in Sha'gar's direction. Sha'gar shook her violently. The thing growled. But disappeared.

The inn-keeper peeked up over the edge of the counter at them. "Two rooms. I have two rooms."

"Fine," said Fair Morn. "We'll take both."

The inn-keeper hurried, almost running, down the hall. "This way, this way." And banged open the two doors. "Settle the next day," he near shouted, scurrying away, wondering what these females really were.

Dol Spar. A Small Office in Monetary Control.

They faded in, suddenly there. Frightening a clerk. She recovered fast. "Mirf is not here." She was one of Mirf's two clerks. And had become rather used to strange things happening. So had her sister, the other clerk. They were the only clerks to have lasted working for Mirf more than a few time periods.

"Where did she go?" Eulin sat on one edge of the desk.

"Out. I am Rema, one of Mirf's clerks." She had met some of the Vander before and recognized the costume. "May I help you?"

Eulin nodded. Mirf was selecting very good looking clerks. "We would like to know everything about an elseplace called Ler Thran."

Rema turned and ran from the room. Mirf's clerks always ran. Mirf didn't like to wait any longer than absolutely necessary.

Je'leel sat in one of the chairs lined up against a

wall. "Wonder where Mirf went?"

Another door opened and a clerk stepped into the room and looked surprised, for a moment. "Where's Mirf?" She had seen her sister racing down a hall toward the main files.

"Out," said Eulin.

"Oh." The clerk left, closing the door behind herself.

Eulin walked around and looked out the window. "Wonder how long we will have to wait?"

A door burst open and Rema shot into the room. She shoved a folder at Eulin as Eulin spun around. The clerk wasn't even breathing hard. She and her sister were in very good physical shape. Now. It was a side effect of working for Mirf.

Je'leel stood, walked over and peered over Eulin's shoulder as Eulin began to read the materials in the folder.

Rema waited to see whether they wished anything else.

There were only a few pages in the folder. One, a dirty, smudged sheet torn from someone's notebook. One was a note identifying the dirty sheet as a page taken from the journal belonging to Terl rin Hort. It was the only legible page that had survived. The journal fragments and the remains of Hort had been found on a ledge on Ler Thran. Everything had been badly weathered A red ring was found with the remains, inscribed Terl rin Hort so it was assumed that the remains belonged to this individual

The last page was a brief note which stated that the elseplace was never inhabited.

They looked at the crumpled sheet. Eulin didn't recognize the script. She nudged Je'leel. "Can you read it?"

Je'leel took the sheet and rotated it end for end "Not well. It says, I think, that the durl cannot be killed and that the author was trapped and waiting, expecting to die soon."

Eulin looked at Rema. "There is nothing describing Ler Thran?"

"It is the only folder," replied Rema.

"See what you have on the durl," said Eulin.

Rema ran from the room.

"I wonder what they are?"

They laid the folder on Mirf's desk and sat and waited.

Chapter Thirteen

Learning Something

London. Winnie's Home.

They had been there for four days.

Doc and Winnie had spent the time discussing various past projects and, every once in a while, the project that had brought the unusual artifact to the surface.

J. C. had gone to the British Museum and every other place that he could think of that might offer a clue as to that strange artifact.

Reep had come along, of course, watching her mate do what he did best, gathering information, absorbing everything he saw, read, heard, or experienced. But, there were no clues.

Four days later and still no-one had the slightest idea as to what that thing was. All they could agree on was that it was an anomaly with no apparent explanation.

J. C. and Reep, wandered into the great house and into the library, having just come from a prowl through a bookstore just down the street aways. Doc was standing, staring out the window, bouncing on his toes. Winnie sat in a chair, staring at a sheet of paper in his hand He blinked. And looked up at the pair just entering the room.

"Really quite astonishing," he said, shoving the paper at J.C.

J.C. walked across the room, took the paper, and read it. It was an analysis of the metal that the artifact was made from. The gist of the report was that this metal alloy was just not possible. Reep nudged J.C. very gently. "I know," he said.

Doc whipped around, eyes sparkling. Anything this strange was very, very interesting. "What, J.C.?"

J.C. shook his head. "Nothing. Just mumbling to Reep."

Doc stared at him.

J.C. looked at Winnie. "Telephone. I need to call home."

Winnie pointed. "Next door."

Doc watched them go, closing the room behind themselves. He frowned. Puzzled. This was most unlike J.C. Something different here, all right, he thought.

Grandeville, Tinker's Place.

She picked up the telephone.

"Hello?"

"It's J.C. Let me talk to Tinker."

"My Great Master is not here."

"Who's this?"

"Dat."

"Dat?"

"Yes."

"When will he be home?"

"I do not know."

"Why not?"

"He went to visit Lurin and Frahn and did not say for how long."

"Who?"

So Dat explained. It was all right to tell J.C.

"O.K. Thanks, Dat."

London. Winnie's Home.

J.C. set the phone on its cradle and threw an arm around his wife's shoulders. "Tinker is out there, visiting Lurin and Frahn."

"Hum hum," sighed the softest of shadows. "The Princess Lurin."

"Princess?"

"Yessssssssss. The Queen of Hahn Duhr Tohr and the daughter of Willawa."

"Ahhhhh, that one. Another looker, right? The one he had a son from?"

Reep nodded.

J.C. stepped away and threw the door open and leaped into the adjoining room. "Back in awhile." And jerked back, slamming the door shut. "Let's go to our rooms. You can take us there from there." He headed her out another door, toward the stairs.

"A very strange chap," mumbled Winnie, staring at the door.

Doc laughed. "J.C. is going to find out about that artifact. I'll bet on it. I recognized that look on his face."

"Doubt that, old chap." Winnie shook his head.

Doc flopped into a chair next to him. "If I was a betting man, you would lose your shirt." He smiled. "So tell me about last year's dig in Scotland."

Bahn Duhr Tohr. The Quarters of The Royal Advisors.

The beast had slipped silently into the room and dragged her down before she could react or call for help. She struggled weakly as it oozed over her. Her blouse was ripped open. It began to feed. She gasped.

"We would enter," whispered soft from above their heads.

"Ptar tik tik," she snarled. The beast disappeared as Hanred sat up and tugged her blouse closed. Ripple glowered.

"What?" He looked worried. They had not been doing anything unusual. For them, that is.

Ripple sat up, waved her blouse back into new, and said, gently, "Enter."

They appeared. Reep and J.C.

"What?" asked Ripple.

"Looking for Tinker," said J.C. Reep nodded.

"They are not here," replied Ripple. "They are with Queen Lurin in the New Kingdoms."

Reep looked at her sister.

Ripple explained, answering the unspoken question. Apparently Reep and her's did not know about that.

Reep nodded, held J.C.'s hand. They were gone.

"What are they looking for?"

Ripple shrugged. "Something is happening. Wonder why she brought him along? Strange strange." She sent a short call to Sook. Maybe she would have an idea. Ripple stepped around his outstretched legs and sat in the couch. Noting her expression, he fetched two mugs and a jug and joined her there.

Hahn Dohr Kahn. Early Morning.

They appeared in the great open space. And looked around. There were a few folk going here and there.

It was early morning. The sun was just beginning to pour slanting shafts of bright across the stone pavement.

J.C. beckoned at a man hurrying by. "Can you tell us how to find Queen Lurin?"

The man laughed, then stared at them. "Queen Lurin?"

"Yes."

He pointed at the gigantic structure looming up along the north edge of the vast square. "In there." And at a door. "Through there." He hurried away wondering how that pair could be so . . . uninformed.

"Big place," observed J.C. He started that way. Reep strolled by his side. It was the first time she had visited here.

Wake up! It was Smoke, gently speaking to him, in his mind.

"OOOOOMP?" One eye opened. It looked like very early morning to him. She mumbled something and waved one arm. His eye closed.

Wake up, MindMate! We have visitors.

Tell them to come back later. It is too early.

It is J. C. and Reep.

"What?" He jolted awake, fully awake, and snapped upright.

Her eyes flew open as the blankets flew here and there. Then she rolled onto her side and stared at him. "Lord King?" They were in her Royal Quarters having finally made it back there early in the morning.

"Visitors." He yanked the blankets back into some semblance of order and back up to her shoulders. "Unexpected visitors. From home."

She tossed the blankets aside, rolled from the bed, feet thumping on the floor. And snatched up her clothes. They were clean and fresh. Servants had slipped silently in and past the sleeping pair, replacing their yesterdays clothes with clean and new. Lurin was out the door and ordering breakfast before Tinker had his shirt buttoned. By the time he was finished, she had returned and began to hunt for her boots.

"You didn't have to get up."

"A Queen does not sleep when Her King is holding audience." Swinging her arms around him, she kissed him. "We fear we did Ourself over Fest. Our

King Lord did lead Us astray." She laughed.

"Humpf."

Lurin spun away and tugged on her boots.

A soft knock on the door announced that breakfast had arrived and was ready. The servants had been told to hurry.

They were well into their meal when a servant hurried into the room and announced, "Two strangers wish audience, Majesty?" He looked at the table. "They can wait."

"Send them in."

"Hi, guy," said J.C. as he and Reep entered. He smiled broadly at Tinker.

Tinker grinned a him. "Didn't expect to see you here." He cleared his throat. "This is Lurin, Queen of The Realm. Lurin, J.C. is one of my very best friends. From Grandeville." He waved at the chairs around the table. "You guys eat? Ahhh, and Reep, his wife."

"Hi there," J.C. said to Lurin as he and Reep sat. "It was mid-afternoon London time when we left. We need some help."

Then he explained what the problem was. And made a rough sketch of the artifact on a napkin.

Lurin sat straighter and looked at Tinker. "The Prince and The Princess must be brought here immediately." She called a servant in. "Send a message to Queen Sook to come here. Immediately. We have great need."

"Not required," sighed the sound of shadows.

Reep stared at the open space in the room.

Sook appear, glowering angrily. Then she saw Reep. "Aunt?" The servant hastily backed up against the wall.

A door banged open and they rushed in. Szart had felt the angry witch burst as had Sha'gar.

"Mother!" gasped Sha'gar.

"Father?" asked Sgenn.

"Sister?" Szart looked at Sook.

"Hi, daughters," laughed J.C., smiling at Sha'gar and Sgenn.

"All right," grumbled Tinker. "Everyone calm down." He meant the rest of himself. J.C. was always calm. Reep never seemed to react or worry about anything at all, as least as far as he was able to tell.

They did.

The servant hurried from the room.

Fair Morn sat next to J.C. and nudged him. "Pass the bread, please."

The rest had hurried in following the running magic users.

Tinker looked at Sook. "Can you bring Prince Frahn and Princess Irinl here? Now?"

Sook nodded.

And they were there. Dressed in full armour, swords in hands.

Irinl whirled around, snarling at Sook, "How dare you!"

"I told her to," stated Tinker.

Irinl whirled in his direction.

"Father?"

"Great King?" added Irinl.

"Thank you, Majesty." Tinker smiled at Sook. "If you wish to stay, you may."

Sook shook her head. And looked at Reep. "Aunt will tell, if necessary." She was gone.

"Sit!" said Lurin. Frahn and Irinl quickly did. Irinl still looked ready to hack someone into slivers.

"We have a problem," began Tinker. Then he and J.C. explained what the problem was.

"You should have brought it with you, here," snapped Irinl, jumping to her feet, striding back and forth. Then she whirled around and glared at J.C. and commanded, "You will go and fetch it back! Now!"

"Nope," said Tinker. "He will not."

"Lord King," she snarled.

"Simmer down, shorty." Tinker was getting irritated. He was really getting deeply bothered by what was suddenly becoming an ever expanding web of complication threatening to drag them all into something he didn't really want to do. All around the table they watched him very carefully, all the rest of himself.

"Calm down, calm down," hissed Chantal at him.

He sighed, clamped his mind shut, felt them relax, and explained, ever so carefully everything to J.C. and Reep

Irinl glared at Chantal. One didn't order a Great Lord around with that tone of voice.

Chantal glared back. And thought that some small Princess ought to get her butt kicked.

Fair Morn nudged her, and whispered, "Can't go around punching out our son's Wife."

"Needs to get her Princess butt kicked," whispered Chantal watching Irinl sit down.

"Someone want to tell me something?" J.C. looked from Irinl to Tinker. "How did that thing get buried under that site in England? Winnie said that the deposit it was found in was dated to around two thousand years ago, more or less." He winked at Irinl. "Nice ears."

Kazmar. Not A Nice Place To Visit.

The couple looked at Argar. He jerked. And wondered whether he would live long enough to state his business.

"So," said the man. "You think that we ought to help you?" He looked at his companion.

She smiled.

Argar felt his knees threatening to buckle. Maybe it had been a very bad idea, coming here. But he had been told that they wouldn't talk to a servant.

She peered at him. "Why should we do something for a merchant like you?"

Argar dropped to his knees. It was better than falling down. And began to stammer his reasons, promising them anything he had, or could acquire.

During his babbling tale, the woman reached over and took her companions hand in one of her's, her thumb gently stroking over the back of his hand. He stared into her eyes.

Argar gushed on.

London. Winnie's Home.

One moment the room was empty.

Then they were there. J.C. looked at the clock on the wall. They'd only been gone an hour or so. He hugged Reep. "Pretty good. Nobody should have noticed that little time lapse."

She nestled inside his arms. A slim woman that looked like she ought to be his daughter. It was because of his height. He was a good foot taller than she was. And her unlined face, all smooth moonlight pale skin, and great dark staring eyes.

He kissed her forehead. "Any ideas?"

She nodded.

He held her out at arm's length. "What?"

She told him.

Moments later, they burst into the library downstairs, startling Winnie. Doc was used to it.

Actually, J.C. burst into the room. Reep followed quietly behind him. "Let's go visit that site," said J.C.

Winnie snatched the pipe from his lap where it had landed and poked the stem back into his mouth. "Tomorrow, J.C. It is a goodly drive from here."

Doc watched J.C.'s face. And nodded to himself J.C. had learned something in some way only understood by J.C. And wanted more information. He knew that nothing would come out until J.C. was satisfied he knew what it was he wanted to say.

"Jolly good," replied J.C., being as British as he could. He grinned at Doc. "Think we will just pop off, stroll about, that sort of thing." He waved jauntily at Winnie and Doc and headed for the door, hooking one of his arms around Reep. "Ta, ta."

As the door closed, Winnie looked at Doc. "Rather strange chap."

Doc laughed.

Flinder's Green, England. A Bright, Mid-Morning.

Cup of coffee in hand, Doc had insisted they bring a thermos of coffee, one of tea for Winnie, Doc watched J.C. and Reep as they wandered out across the place where the archaeological site was. His arm was thrown over her shoulders, his head bent a little, talking to her. There was little to see. The excavations had been back-filled. The turf carefully reset.

Winnie sipped from his cup of tea and looked at Doc. "What is he doing?"

Doc shrugged. "He appears to be looking for something."

"For what?" Winnie puffed air through his thick handlebar moustache.

"Beat's me." Doc sat on the grass and leaned

back against the side of the left front tire of the car. And watched them walking slowly around.

J.C. glanced back and decided that they were far enough away that they could not be overheard. "You really think that you will be able to see anything? It was two thousand years ago."

"Yesssssss," hissed the gentlest of breezes.

J.C. consulted the map he had crumpled in one hand. He peered past her head to do so. "That rectangle just ahead. That's the pit where they found it. About three feet deep, more or less."

"Hum, hum, hum." She reached out and gently touched a strand only she could see. And put an anchor on it.

"What?" He watched her hands doing something. He knew she was one of the few witches that could see the faint magic strands left behind when a magic user appeared and disappeared. It happened whenever they moved from one spot to another.

"Not very old," whispered the soft air. She gently nudged his side with her elbow. "Not thousands of your elseplace years ago."

"This getting pretty weird."

"Very strong magic."

"Someone came here recently and stuck that thing into this site in such a way that it appeared to have been in situ when Winnie dug it up?"

She nodded.

J.C. sat on the grass and dragged her into his lap.

"Let's talk about that."

"By George," gasped Winnie, staring across the green at the pair sitting in the middle of where his excavation had been.

Doc nudged his leg with the thermos holding the tea. Winnie was leaning against the car. "Have some tea."

"What is he doing?"

"Hard to tell, Winnie." Doc squinted. "But from this distance I say that it appears that he is tickling her."

"Really now," huffed Winnie. "You mean to tell me that we have driven all the way out here just so your man could sit on the grass and tickle his wife, right in the middle of my excavation?"

Doc laughed. "He also seems to be having quite a conversation with her."

She stood next to the bed, dressed in a black robe, the witch proper dress for traveling when on witch business. She wobbled his shoulder, waking him. She had drifted shadow silent through the other bedrooms. All slept soundly.

His eyes flew open. "Time? We have only gone to bed, not all that long ago."

She nodded. Rolling from the bed, he quickly dressed, gave her a hug, and yawned. She handed him a large mug of steaming coffee taken from somewhere.

Three blocks away in a small, all-night restaurant, a waitress gasped, and blinked.

"Ummmm, good." He took her hand in his free one. "Let's go."

She nodded.

They stood in Flinder's Green right where she had seen the magic strand.

"Still there?" He took another sip.

She nodded.

He gently squeezed her hand. "All right, let's go see."

Grandeville. The Hardcastle Residence.

They faded into the bedroom, silent as silence. He stared into the dim. It was a large bedroom. With a large, bigger than king-sized bed. The whole thing was familiar.

"What are we doing here?" asked J.C. loudly. "This is Hard's bedroom."

Tajaar banged awake, rolled from the bed, long blade springing into her hand, as she came at them.

Reep banged halt over her and threw bright. Shem mumbled. He was a very heavy sleeper.

"It's not Hard," said J.C. "It's Shem!"

Tajaar stared at them. And relaxed. Reep released her. Tajaar put the blade somewhere and frowned at them. "True-mate friends?"

J.C. indicated Shem. "Better wake him up. I think that we have a lot of questions to ask." He sat on the end of the bed and nodded at Reep. "Couldn't you tell?"

She shook her head. Tajaar walked around the bed and began the process of waking her mate. J.C. held out his cup to Reep. "Want a sip?"

She took the mug from him and did, the slightest of movements at one corner of her mouth. It was a radiant smile for her.

J.C. laughed. And indicated Tajaar with a slight motion of his head. "Nice legs."

Tajaar was wearing only the top of a pair of men's pajamas, buttoned. It was on the large size, falling off one shoulder. It was Shem's.

The body in the bed was now being violently shaken. Tajaar grabbed his forearm and started to drag the body out of the bed. Finally his eyes opened.

"Morning? I didn't hear the alarm go off. Did I forget to set it? Again?" His eyes swiveled around, seeking the clock on the nightstand next to the bed. "It is one-o-clock! We just went to bed!" He lurched upright. And saw their visitors. "OH! Hi, J.C., Reep. What are you doing here? In here?" He reached over and pulled Tajaar close.

"We need to talk," said J.C. "And you need to get dressed."

Shem blinked. "Oh, sure. Meet you in the library."

J.C. and Reep headed out and down the hall.

Shem looked at Tajaar. "They say what's up?"

"No! Not-nice visit!"

He yawned. "It is rather strange, even for J.C.

Wonder why they didn't come over a little earlier?"

Ler Thran. Black. And Broken.

They faded in. Standing on the ledge and quickly checked their surroundings. The ledge was a narrow shelf of black rock, just part of all the other black rock.

This was the spot where the remains had been found. On one side the broken and split rock soared upward, on the other side, far, far below they could see the valley. Clouds mostly blocked the view of what might lie down there. A gaping hole was the only possible exit from the ledge other than jumping or somehow climbing down.

Up here, the wind blew soft whistling sounds as it hissed over the small openings in the shattered rock. That was the only sound.

Eulin nodded. "Wonder if the durl things live, or lived, in there? And how could anyone get up here? Monetary Control's records didn't say much, did they? Just the name and nothing more."

Je'leel peered inside. She didn't see anything. "We will be careful, sister."

Eulin laughed. And flicked the fingers on her left hand. Just so. The shadow dragon faded into the dark around her feet. Then she cast protection on Je'leel. And bounced light into the cavern. "Shall we take a look?"

Hahn Dohr Kahn. The Castle.

He looked around the table. She had finally

settled down. He reached out and refilled his cup. "J.C. and Reep will figure out what to do." He nodded at Irinl. "So, how about you tell us why this artifact is so important to you." Under the table, out of sight, Lurin patted the top of his thigh.

Irinl bowed her head. "Yes, Majesty." She realized she had forgotten her manners, her royal manners, again. Then she looked up and at Tinker. And told him all she knew. And all that she believed.

The Star-Cross Wand was the symbol of the Hephira kingdom. It was said that it dated from the very earliest beginnings. It was told, and was believed, that if the Royal House ever lost the artifact, forever, then that House would fall. And take the Kingdom down with it. She knew that this hadn't happened as the artifact had been missing for a long time. Still she believed that if they didn't recover it, this story might come true, and scatter the Hephira throughout the elseplaces, never to be reunited again. The recent past evil event was mumbled here and there that the loss of the artifact was the cause.

Long before records began, long before the earliest Hephira scribes began to record their history, a mighty warrior, wielding that artifact, had formed the Hephira kingdom after a great battle with something so evil that it had not been described. Neither the name nor the description of this first founder ancestor were known. The only link was through that artifact.

Only members of the First House kept it in The

Treasure Room. Yet everyone, regardless of place, rank, station, or locale, knew that it was the object that gave them their cultural meaning and law.

She took a sip from her cup, eyes frozen upon Tinker's. "It must be returned," she rasped.

Mar slumped in her chair, muscles in her face jumping, eyes switching from Irinl's face to Tinker's face, and back again. Back and back again. She clenched Fair Morn's arm in a rigid, white-knuckled grip. "Princess?" Her voice was the lowest of low whispers, urgent and strong.

Irinl's head snapped around. She stared at this woman who looked so ready to collapse, sweat rolling down her face. "Yes?"

Mar sagged deeper into her chair. Fair Morn looked at Smoke.

Struggling for control. lrinl's tale was quite a shock for her. Smoke gave a slight nod. *She will be all right. Soon.*

"We, us." Mar cleared her throat. "We, us, have one of those."

Irinl leaned in her direction. "Say that again."

Fair Mom refilled Mar's Cup and nudged her.

"We, us," said Mar, more clearly, taking a sip, beginning again. "We, us, have one of those. They are called Xylinth Blades." She leaned against Fair Morn and whispered softly, "I, me, killed for sure, Us."

Fair Morn slipped a protective arm around Mar's shoulders.

Irinl started to jump up. Frahn restrained her. "Don't," he hissed "You will frighten her into shock."

"I do not like this," grumbled Tinker. Lurin nodded. "A strange twist of events."

"Twists like that always get us into deep crap," He mumbled. "And beat up." He stood and left the room, to stand on the balcony and to stare out at the town.

Lurin hurried to his side.

He turned his head and looked into her eyes with wet glistening eyes. "And we have died." She wrapped her arms around him and held him.

"DAMN!" Chantal glared around the table. The rest of them had felt him react. Then she looked at Mar. "You better tell us about this Xylinth Blade of your's." And wondered whether she had brought enough ammunition along.

Ler Thran. Deep Inside.

"I wonder how deep this goes?"

They were deep inside the mountain, walking along the great tube that the cavern had become. It curved back and forth, totally hiding the entry mouth from their sight. The floor was clean, not dusty at all, which made both wonder about what it was that kept it so clean.

Other than their footsteps they hadn't heard any sound at all. This deep inside, they couldn't hear the soft outside wind.

Eulin's light spell illuminated the tube for a great distance in all directions. They walked along in a soft glow and had no problem seeing what little there had been to see, so far.

"Perhaps," said Je'leel. "The durl thing died long ago. That fragment we read in Monetary Control's folder certainly looked ancient."

"Hum," said Eulin.

"Huff," huffed Anamaxtor.

After they had walked for some time, Eulin had called him. The golden dragon, gifted to her as an eagle-sized dragonette by Sha'gar, was now larger than a large horse. He walked behind them. And had been silent talking with the shadow dragon. They had been discussing one of the favorite male dragon topics of conversation, after food. Female dragons. Not even Dragon Masters knew that dragons could silent talk. It wasn't really a secret. It was just that no one had ever asked them about it. Both dragons thought that the long red named Faken a'eb was rather active.

Grandeville. The Hardcastle Residence. Early Evening.

J.C. stared at Shem. Shem moved. Tajaar sat by Shem's side. Reep had slipped to the kitchen to make them coffee.

"You put it in there?" asked J. C.

Shem nodded.

"When?"

"Ummmmmmmm," said Shem. "Last week or

so."

J.C. sat straighter. "Winnie excavated it longer ago than that? And he dated it to around 2,000 years ago."

"Oh." Shem laughed. "Maybe it was longer ago than that." He stared at J.C. "No one was supposed to find it."

J.C. shrugged. "Winnie was testing a new metal detecting device for the military, by the site and that thing caused a real blip. So, he got permission and dug it up."

Shem slumped and looked unhappy. "Grandfather is going to be upset."

"Who?"

"Grandfather. Mother's father."

"Oh boy," said J.C. "You want to tell me what you guys are, or were, up to? Tinker's involved in this in some way and that guy was really looking unhappy about what ever is going on."

"Uncle?" gasped Shem. Tajaar tightened her grip on his arm.

"Hum hum," sighed the evening. Reep had arrived, bringing cups and the coffee pot. She cast protection over J.C., recognizing the magical agitation flowing from her nephew. She filled the cups and sat, shoving one into his hand.

"Thank you, Aunt," said Shem, being mage proper. He had felt her cast over J.C. And then he began to tell them what he had been doing.

Ler Thran. Deep Inside.

They strolled around a sharp curve, the tube bending almost 180-degrees, and almost bumped into it.

"Hum," said Eulin.

It was a body that had been dead a long, long time. It was obvious why it was dead. Something had chopped off the head. The head lay several feet away. The thing had a snake-like body about four feet in diameter. Unlike a snake, this creature had numbers of short legs, each ending in clawed feet. The legs ran the entire length of the body.

"A durl," stated Je'leel, examining the mumified carcass. A large patch of scale and skin were missing from one side of the body near where the head had once been attached. But the rest of the scales still adhered to the leathery skin. They were a deep, soft blue in the light, glittering purple highlights.

They walked around the body. It only had the one patch of scale missing. Eulin pointed at the bare place. "Those missing scales must be the ones like that statue."

Je'leel pulled, tugged and finally managed to twist one scale, hanging by a thin thread of skin, free of the body. She held it close to her eyes and examined it carefully. Then she stepped past Enlin and tapped Anamaxtor on the chest.

"Huff." He lowered his head to peer into her face.

She held the scale out and said, "Blow fire on

this."

He looked at Eulin. She nodded. He did, enveloping her forearm in a blast of angry red flame. It left a scotched mark on the far wall. Je'leel being indjinn wasn't bothered by the blast at all. Neither was the blue scale.

Eulin stepped close and looked over the scale. "Most dragons would have been injured!" She tapped the dragon on the tip of his snout and pointed at the dried husk. "'Do you know what that is, was?"

He shook his head.

Eulin called in an acid spiller and had it spit at the carcass. Exposed bones and part of the wall behind dissolved. The scales were untouched.

She took the scale from Je'leel and held it up in front of the dragon. "Give it a careful bite. I want know how hard it is."

The great monster carefully bit the scale. Nothing happened. The dragon spit it out. "Not edible."

Eulin sent her away. And stared at the head lying on the floor. "How could anyone chop off its head. She couldn't even dent that scale."

Je'leel looked in the direction that they had been walking. "I think that we should leave. We do not know how a durl attacks. But it seems that they are armoured against almost anything."

Eulin sent the dragons away. Then she took herself and her sister out.

The durl unfolded from a wall and wondered

who they might have been. It had been long long since anything alive had wandered this deep. She hadn't seen any of her weak cousins even beyond that. Sniffing the air, she realized that one of the hidden ones had been here as well.

Then she wondered why those two-legged soft meals hadn't been eaten by those two males. She headed deeper into the nest. The meals had only taken one scale. She decided that they couldn't have been related to that horror that had killed Uxorin and looted his body.

Ain. The Place of Training.

It was a rather ordinary looking village crawling up the side of a rather gentle hill. The streets wandered back an forth in graceful curves, following the contours of the slope changing elevation slowly. All the buildings were constructed of some soft, pale yellow, almost white stone.

It looked rather like a picture postcard Mediterranean village somewhere. Except that all the windows were triangular and the roofs covered with deep blue thatching.

They stood and looked at it. The town. It was where The Gentle Eyes kept the xylinth blade. The small group was armed with various forms of lethal, Tinker and the rest of himself. And Frahn and Irinl. And Mar. Except she wasn't. The Gentle Eyes did not carry weapons. It was foreign to their beliefs. But Mar was sticking close to Fair Morn.

Tinker looked his group over. Everyone was ready. "O.K., Mar, lead us to your House." He pointed at Irinl. "And you be quiet. We don't want any princess outbursts when we get there." He whirled away before she could respond.

Irinl fumed darkly at his back. Frahn carefully suppressed his smile.

The group followed Mar as she led them up and around until she stopped in front of a two-story building with a wide wooden front door painted a soft orange.

"Here," she whispered. "The Seat of The Gentle Eyes." And looked at Fair Morn. Fair Morn winked.

"All right," said Tinker. "Let's go visit."

Dol Spar. Late Afternoon. An office in Monetary Control.

Mirf stared at her clerk, "'Vat?"

"The Vander named Eulin and the John Tinker's daughter Je'leel were here and wished to see the files on," Rema consulted a slip of paper in her hand, "Ler Thran and durl." She wondered why she had to repeat herself.

Mirf sat behind her desk. "And?"

"And," stated Rema, again, "we had a thin file, a few sheets on Ler Thran, and nothing on durl."

"Get me that file," snapped Miff.

Rema whirled and ran from the room. Mirf looked at her two assistants. "So what were those two chickees up to?" It was rhetorical question. They knew it.

Mirf stared at the door. "Must be goofing off."

The door banged open as Rema charged inside. She shoved the folder at Mirf. "Ler Thran."

Mirf opened the folder and read the little information that it contained. "Humble bumble. Not much there is there, in there, there?" Her eyes jumped to Rema's face. "And we, in our vast files, have nothing, not a thing, bubkess, on this thing that frightened the author of this antique page?"

"Correct. Nothing. At all."

"Welllllll," hissed Miff, chewing on a thumbnail. "Somebody does."

Rema spun and ran, knowing what she ought to begin searching for.

"My, my." Mirf smiled happily. "Clerks like that I deserve." One hand slapped the correct spot on her desk top.

"Yes?" asked a very unctuous voice.

"Hoo boy," grumbled Mirf. "Fim Bee, what comes after Clerk, 1st Grade?"

"Clerk, dash, Prime," stated the oily voice.

"Vunderbar," chortled Mirf. "I like it!"

"Special Investigator?"

"My very own personal clerks, 1st Grade, both of them, are henceforth, Prime!" She glared at the desk top "Got that bubee? I have two, count 'em, two, Clerks, dash, Prime. Have a couple of new shirts, in their correct size, sent right away, tricked out with the new dodad insignia. NOW!"

"At once, Special Investigator."

"Good boy! Go shuffle paper." Her hand slammed the connection off. "They deserve it."

Rema banged back into the room and jabbed a slip of paper at Mirf. "Master Mio Ka'um Likzh, knowledge of rare creatures and their elseplaces."

Mirf read the slip and looked up. "Ready to travel? Where's Nema?"

Rema nodded. "Yes. Home. It is her day off."

"VAT!" gurgled Mirf. "I let her have a day off?" She shook her head. "Must be getting soft." And laughed a loud, rowdy laugh.

Someone knocked on the door. It was a very timid, faint knock.

Mirf looked at the door. "Such a knock that is."

The knock repeated.

"Come in, little mousey."

A young man carefully entered the room, eyes jumping from person to person. He clenched two bundles in his arms, to his chest.

"Yesssssssssssssssssssssss?"

He jerked. "SHIRTS!"

"You are one of Fim Bee's?"

He nodded.

She waggled one hand at him. Somehow it seemed disconnected from her arm. "Drop 'em on the desk and scurry away."

He did. Carefully, closing the door gently.

"Quan," barked Mirf, "look at the wall. Rema get out of that shirt."

Quan turned and stared at the wall. Fred's fingers did a quick dance on his shoulder, telling him that she was the only female that he ought to look at, unclothed.

"Off, off, off," snapped Mirf, shredding the paper wrapping from one of the bundles.

Rema hastily shucked off her shirt, wondering what her boss was up to this time.

"Oh my goodness. A real beauty bod." Mirf smiled at her clerk. "Neither of you wear anything but a shirt?"

"Too hot," explained Rema. All that running back and forth generated a lot of heat.

Mirf tossed her the new shirt. "Here, wear this one. Throw that other one away. It is out of date."

Rema stared at the patch over the left pocket. The gold thread glittered. Then she slipped on the shirt and tucked it into her trousers.

"So congradulations," gurgled Mirf. "You and Nema are Clerks, dash, Prime. With all the prestige and the money that goes along with that new title." She shrugged. "Not much prestige. Lots of money."

Bouncing to her feet, Mirf had been sitting on the edge of her desk, she beamed at her staff, and said to Rema, "When we return, you can take the other shirt to Nema."

Then she hustled them toward the door. "So let's give a go."

Magevern. Deep Below.

Eulin and Je'leel were sitting in one of the smaller gathering rooms, having a bite to eat, relaxing. The blue scale laid on the table between them. Every so often one or the other would pick it up and look at it.

Aada drifted in and joined them at their table. And poked at the scale with one finger. "What have you been doing, Young Heart?"

"Research."

Aada looked into her eyes. Eulin explained. And told her all that they had learned. So far. Aada picked it up and turned it over and over. "A durl scale?"

Eulin nodded. "We saw a dead one with a big patch of skin and scales missing. Something had chopped off it head. But we don't understand how anything could do that. Neither dragon fire nor dragon bite nor dragon acid could affect that scale."

Aada dropped the scale on the table. "You must be careful, Young Heart. You are our future."

"I know."

Aada reached over and took her hand. "Doesn't mean that you can't do things. Just remember your obligations."

"It is something that Father is involved in," added Je'leel.

Aada's eyebrows flew up. "Then you must be

extra careful," she demanded. "The Vander Lord gets pulled into events often caused by twisted evil." She stood. "Come, we had better speak with The Heart, your Mother. He may need our help."

Chapter Fourteen

Just A Little Surprise

Grandeville. The Hardcastle Residence.

"Your grandfather?"

Shem nodded.

J.C. slipped an arm around Reep and said, "Your grandfather wanted that artifact hidden because it is too powerful?"

"Yes."

"Not magic." sighed softest of voices. Reep looked at Shem. "It is not a magic thing. I could see feel nothing. But it is arcane crafted. Worked with some other principle."

"Grandfather didn't say how it came to be or why it was. He just told me where to find it. And then he told me to hide it somewhere where no thing would think to look."

Shem smiled at J.C. "I had been reading about interesting places to visit in England and saw that great open field. So I went there and buried it." He grabbed his wife's hand. "Tajaar and I. Grandfather told me how to do things like that during my training with him."

"Well guy, you certainly made a bad choice. Sir Winifred etc. dug it up and has it in his workroom even as we speak. Doc and I went over there to jolly old England to help him study it."

J.C. glanced at his watch. "And we have got to get back shortly before we are missed." He stood. "You guys better think of something clever very soon. I can't drag my feet much longer."

He looked at them and laughed. "And I certainly can't tell them what I know either." He tossed an arm around Reep as she floated by his side. "Let's go." And winked at Shem and Tajaar. "Better get moving."

Mak Sanspa. Not Much Of A Town.

"So it's a small place."

They stood at the edge of a cluster of neat buildings constructed from red, green, and white stone. The sun bounced reflected colors in all directions, a dazzle of neon color for daylight. From where they stood, they could the other side of town.

"Ten, twelve, more or less," observed Mirf. She consulted the slip of paper in her hand. And started walking into the cluster. "Can't be too hard to find."

And he wasn't.

They bumped into him as he came wandering along the street.

Literally.

They stood staring and he walked into them as he came around a corner. So he actually bumped into them. He was a rather nondescript man wearing clothes colored in soft blues and greens. He had strolled around a corner, deep in thought, and walked into Nema.

"Ashma gimli," gasped the man, looking startled and quite embarrassed.

"Oof," was Nema's comment.

So Mirf asked for directions to find the Master and they found out that they had found him. He guided them into his house, one house over. They had a short walk.

"Hum ha?" said Master Mio Ka'um Likzh. "Monetary Control?"

He looked at them, one by one. And carefully studied Fred. "Ah, boonda! A suk-dragon. A high level female." He shook his head. "NO! She is the high level female."

He stared at Mirf. "What is she doing so far from their encamphaunt? Working for Monetary Control?" He nodded. "You are in great danger, you know. Their warrior flock will pick you to pieces. She is the inexpressible value of her, ergma, group."

Mirf looked at Fred. "So, glitter eyes, you could have said something."

Quan leaned close to Mirf. "I will explain, ummm, later. She settled all that when we visited."

Mirf waggled one loose jointed hand at Master Mio. "Nuff about her. We need information on something called a durl."

"Ahhhhhhhhh, uncha!" said Master Mio. He stood and began to sort through various scrolls and folded documents stuffed into a large red box. There were a number of boxes sitting here and there of about the same size, all stuffed full. Each was a different color.

He finally pulled out what he was searching for, returned to his chair and beamed at the document he held in one hand. "They occupy Ler Thran."

Mirf nodded violently. And sucked in a deep breath. "Soooooooooo," she exhaled. "What are they?"

Mio shook out the document and turned it around. "Ahhhhhhh," he said. "Boo dooza!" And read it. And grunted to himself.

Mirf was beginning to seriously debate with herself whether grabbing him by the throat and banging his head on the wall might speed up the process when Master Mio looked up.

"Durl," he stated. "An ancient race of ardragons. Ardragons are vaguely related to the standard and well known, um, more or less, dragon, erglep, in certain aspects. The durl prefer caves. Caverns, underground holes to live and nest in. Like some sub-types of dragons they can eat rock. Durl are covered with blue scales. Fire resistant. It is stated even from dragon fire."

He stared at nothing and waggled a few fingers. "Imggle, I suppose molten rock would burn them though. Ah boonda, maybe not."

His eyes focused as he beamed at Mirf. "Durl are long, like snakes and worms. But they have many legs, umlee, unlike snakes and worms, which do not." He made fingers wiggles to indicate the many legs.

Mirf made hot-water hissing sounds.

Master Mio looked at her. "You do not look like a hob-goblin."

"Durl," said Mirf, squinting at him.

He stood, walked over and tilted back her head, peering at her eyes, his eyes also squinting, lines forming in his forehead. "How did you get hob-goblin eyes?"

"Long story," grumbled Mirf.

He nodded and went back to his chair. "My price for information is the story, long or short." And sat and watched her. He was very interested.

"So O.K.," sighed Mirf. "I'll tell you."

Ain. The Place of Training. The Seat of The Gentle Eyes.

They walked down a short hall and into large room occupying the central portion of the building. It was soft dim. Stark, almost empty. A single chair sat in the exact center of the room. A cone of light shown down from high overhead gently illuminating the chair. And its occupant.

She sat in aware stillness. She was an apprentice. All apprentices spent a day in the chair waiting to help visitors. Each apprentice took their turn, alternating days, one for each apprentice, until the apprentice became a complete person, one of The Gentle Eyes.

There were few visitors. So most just sat. And learned quiet contemplation. And had all the time they needed to work on the mental puzzles set to them by those who trained.

The apprentice stood. "How may I aid you?" And then she recognized Mar and dropped back into her seat in surprise.

Mar stepped forward. "Young Eye, I, we, us would speak with The One. Is she attending?"

"Most."

"Lead I, we, us."

The apprentice popped to her feet and did. Up a staircase, and then up another. To a room whose open wall looked down upon the central room and the solitary chair. The apprentice gently closed the door behind them after they were all inside the room. She hadn't said a word.

The tall woman turned from the railing and looked at them. And smiled. "Mar, you are free."

Mar began to quiver. "One, I, we, us will not die!"

Fair Morn stepped to her side and slid an arm around her. "Easy does it. Nothing will happen."

"Mar?"

"I, we, us told them of the xylith blade," whispered Mar.

The One rocked back on her heels. "What?" She stared at this group crowding around her Gentle Eyed Mar. She sensed magic users in this group but no-one was emitting. "Do you hold my Mar?"

"No," said Tinker. "She is trying to help us."

"Help? You?"

"Yes. Perhaps if we sat and told you what we

know you would agree to help us as well?"

The One sat and nodded at them.

"Irinl," said Tinker. "Tell her about that artifact and its place in the Hephira origin history."

Irinl pulled her chair close to The One and did.

Grandeville. The Hardcastle Residence.

Shem and Tajaar found Hard in the kitchen, working. They filled cups with coffee and sat at the table.

"Ummmmmm," said Shem. "Father?"

"Ummmmmm," replied Hard, turning and almost knocking the carton of eggs off the counter top. "Do I detect the sounds of some problem in that ummmmmm?" He filled his cup and sat and looked at his son and daughter-in-law. "Why are you up so early?"

Shem wiggled in his chair. "I think that I need help."

"Oh?"

"Yes."

Hard looked at his son. "Local, ah, trouble?"

"Father!" Shem frowned across the table. "Of course not!" He fingered his spoon and twisted it around inside the bowl of sugar, scattering white grains over the table top. "It's grandfather."

"Father?" gasped Hard. "You are in trouble with him?"

"No. Mother's father."

Hard sagged. "Oh." And shook his head. "I think that you had better talk with your mother then." He waved one hand. "I really don't understand most of what goes on out there." He looked up and smiled.

Ramp had slipped into the kitchen wondering why they were all in there, sitting and talking around the table. She laughed at their expressions. "Morning, Husband." And smiled at her son and daughter-in-law. And took another look at them. And sat. "What has my son been doing?"

So Shem began to explain.

Ain. The Place of Training. The Seat of The Gentle Eyes.

When Irinl finished the story of the artifact and the history of the Hephira, The One stood.

"I will take you down there. Then you will understand why you may not have that thing." She stepped around and past them. "Come!" And nodded. "You also, Mar the Gentle Eyes."

The One led them down the hall to a corner staircase. The wooden stairs took them down to the main floor.

The One unlocked a door, ushered them inside, closed it, and led them down. "Be careful, these have no rail or handhold." She crossed the basement they came to and unlocked a metal door whose hinges squealed rust as it was dragged wide.

Down they went.

And finally.

Nine doors later, nine level's later.

They arrived.

The One approached a door painted deep blue. It was, like many of the others, metal. Standing in front of the door, she turned to the group.

"Behind this door is the xylith blade." Her eyes darted from face to face. "I must have your word that no-one will try to remove it."

In the silence they could hear the door. It made a faint hum.

Finally, Tinker nodded. "No one will touch it unless you say so." He looked at Irinl. "Do you agree?"

For a moment it looked as if she was about to argue, then she nodded. "We agree."

Smoke, drop her where she stands if she tries to do anything.

Smoke nodded slightly and took a step back.

The One turned back to the door, pulled a broach from inside her blouse and lifted it and the fine chain it hung on from around her neck. She fitted the ornament into the appropriate hollow. Something clicked loudly.

She slipped the chain back over her head and dropped the broach back inside her blouse. And pushed the door. It swung silently inward.

The room they entered was round and high domed. The rock walls, ceiling and floor were polished mirror smooth. The light was soft and golden.

In the center of the floor lay a body, flat on its back, arms thrown wide, eyes open, staring. The xylinth blade stood vertical, a soft golden shaft driven through the center of his chest.

Irinl gasped. "It must have penetrated the floor as well."

The One nodded. "He is pinned to the stone. And is never to be released. From long before memory knows, The Gentle Eyes have kept this chamber."

She looked from face to face. "Never before has anyone not The One or a Gentle Eyes seen this." She indicated the chamber and its contents.

Frahn pointed at the body. "'Is that a statue?"

"Touch him," suggested The One.

Frahn cautiously stepped over, knelt, and did. With one careful fingertip. He looked at Irinl. "It is just like the one that we found."

The One gasped and stared at him. "What did you say? What did you find?"

Frahn stood. "A woman."

"A Hephira," added Irinl. She pointed. "Like him."

"Hanging on the wall in some ancient ruins," explained Frahn. "She had one of those sticking through her middle."

"And she wore blue scale armor," said Irinl.

The One thumped to her knees and swayed from side to side.

"Smoke?" snapped Tinker.

"Shock and surprise. She will be all right. Recovering fast."

The One sat back on her heels. And sighed. And nodded at the figure. "This is the evil that did that." She waggled one hand at them. "Sit. Now I will tell you a tale."

And the tale poured forth.

Long before before when many elseplaces were still isolated and the great interconnect had been hardly begun, the race of Ch'Karakzen boiled from their world, taking whatever they wished, enslaving whatever they wished, killing whatever they wished, doing unspeakable as they visited the unfortunate.

Battles and wars raged in more places than could be counted. But the Ch'Karakzen were too powerful and their evil kingdom spread.

On an elseplace now lost in the mists of time, there was a King, more clever than most, wise in metal working ways, arcane metal working ways, who crafted a small number of special weapons. They were the mightiest blades ever made. The Blades of King Lyth, call Xylith.

His son took one of them, and joined the Ch'Karakzen, wanting riches and land and power.

The brother's sister swore on her oath to kill him and to eliminate the evil pouring from the Ch'Karakzen. Taking the few blades left, she led a carefully selected group to do this deed.

And whole lands of armies followed these few. Slowly the Ch'Karakzen were pushed back. Back until the opposing forces faced each other on the great open plain known as Carcan on the elseplace of Zben a'copt.

During the Great Battle at Carcan, the Ch'Karakzen were eliminated to the last being. But not her brother. Somehow he escaped. And she pursued him, her blue scale armor protecting her from weapons and fire.

Many times later she found him and besieged him in the small town where he lived, planning how to begin again. Tricking her with oaths of brother and sister love, aided by others, he plunged his xylinth blade into her and fled even as the town fell into ruins around him and almost all of his followers died.

His father, The King, finally found him here, in this place. Then it was cleverly hidden.

She pointed at the body. "That is the result. The King did that. There lies the son." She looked at Frahn and Irinl. "And you have found the Princess."

She stood. "Now you know." And held up one cautioning hand. "Wild forces were used to make these weapons. And wild were the affects on the weapon users. After long usage."

One finger pointed. "He is not-dead, merely pinned in place for all time."

She sighed. "That is why, Princess Irinl, you may not take the xylith blade from here. He would be set loose upon the elseplaces again."

Frahn stared at the body. "Alive?"

The One nodded. "In a manner of speaking."

"The Princess also?" whispered Irinl, kneeling,

staring at the body.

"It is so."

Irinl walked on her knees over to her. "May we free her?" Tears ran down her cheeks.

The One smiled soft gentle. "I think that she would enjoy seeing what her people have become."

Tinker cleared his throat. "I think that we are done here." He smiled at The One. "Thank you. Ummmm, may Mar stay with us? For awhile? We, ahhhh, told her that we would do something about that guy that grabbed her."

The One nodded. "Mar may go where she wishes. We do not own The Gentle Eyes." She smiled. "We merely train them."

They trailed after her from the chamber and watched as she locked the strange door, sealing the opening once again.

As they began the long climb up to the main floor, The One asked, "Would you and your's take some refreshments, Chosen One." She laughed. "As soon as you introduced yourselves, I knew."

Halfway up, Tinker asked between heavy breathes, "What is the name of the Princess?"

"The Warrior Princess, Daish a'an'Nald ca E'Nilt, The Swordpoint of The Victorious."

Once back on the main floor, The One led them across the main floor, past the still figure sitting in the straight backed chair and into a comfortable furnished room. Three apprentices leaped to their feet.

"Sit," said The One. "We have honored guests. And Mar, The Gentle Eyes."

The apprentices stared at Mar. They had heard how she been taken. The One brought cups and served them. "It is my pleasure to do so," she said to Tinker when he started to protest.

London. The House of Sir Winifred Robson-Brown.

They strolled into the dining room, into the bright early sunlight streaming in through the windows. His arm was lightly draped over her shoulders. And sat. Servants quickly set breakfast in front of them. Winnie insisted that they eat in the dining room and stay out of the kitchen. It bothered the cook.

J.C. spread marmalade on his toast and looked across the table at his obviously aggitated host. Doc look a little excited as well. "What's up?" he mumbled around a bite of the toast.

"Bloody burglars," huffed Winnie.

"Comes from living in the big city, I guess." J.C. nudged Reep. She shoved the platter of sausages at him. "Grab your T.V.?"

"They took the artifact," snapped Winnie.

"Art thieves? Which artifact?" J.C. looked around. The house was full of them.

"The strange one," said Doc.

Under the table, Reep's fingers dug deep into his thigh.

"Well," laughed J.C. "They won't get much for

that thing." And thought that Shem had certainly moved fast. He looked at Doc. "Now what? The purpose of our visit has been snatched before we could figure it out." He looked at Winnie. "Called the cops?"

"Quite! They are inspecting the workroom and the exterior ground right now."

Doc looked at Winnie. "We could leave in a couple of days. Give J.C. a chance to show Reep around London some more."

"Of course," huffed Winnie.

"Really sorry," said Doc.

J.C. finished his breakfast and looked at Reep. She nodded. "Can we go take a peek," he asked.

"Stay out of their way," said Doc.

Right you are guv'ner." J.C. stood and tugged Reep toward the door. "Let's go watch. Never saw Bobbies in action before."

Winnie watched them go. "Not very excited, I'd say."

Doc laughed. "J.C. doesn't get excited about most everything. Although he is probably disappointed."

"Disappointed?"

"Uh huh. He hadn't figured it out. And now it is gone."

They peeked in through the open door. A burly policeman told them that they had to stay outside.

J.C. leaned close, bending slightly and whispered in Reep's ear, "Was it Shem?"

She nodded. She could feel a trace of his passage

in and out of the room. He, or Tajaar, had broken one of the windows from the outside and unlatched it.

A policeman peered into the room through the hole in the large window. "Rather small footprints. I'd say that it was a woman."

J.C. pulled Reep away. "Let me show you the big city now that we can loaf."

As they passed the open door to the library, J.C. waved at its occupants. "Ta ta. We're off to see this and that. Loverly day for a stroll."

Chapter Fifteen

One Problem Solved

Uata. The Land of Traders.

They stood there and stared at the front of the large and very gaudy building. Tinker et al, Mar, and Frahn and Irinl. Frahn and Irinl had come along as they felt they owed it to Mar.

The building they faced was four stories high with a wide porch running the full length of the front of the structure. Tall columns rose from the porch to the overhanging roof. They were painted in designs of violently clashing colors. Each column was different. There were twelve columns in all. Up above, standing all along the very edge of the roof were a row of stone statues. The front wall was painted in much the same style as the columns. More statuary stood on the porch.

"Damn ugly place." Chantal yanked out her revolver and checked it. And jabbed it back into her holster. "I'm ready."

Tinker nodded. "It is pretty bad all right." He looked at Mar. "The guy that took you lives in this place?"

"Yes," whispered Mar, stepping very close to Fair Morn, clenching her arm in a tight grip.

"I will need both arms free," said Fair Morn. "But you can stand real close, just back a little. You will be very safe there."

Mar reluctantly released her and stepped back just a little, one hand lightly holding Fair Morn's belt, right in the middle of her back.

"That'll work." Fair Morn nodded.

"Well," said Tinker, "shall we go in and talk with this person?"

"Indeed, Our Prince. Most forcefully." Chicken popped her blade up and down in its scabbard.

So, they did.

Up the stairs and across the porch.

Through the wide doorway, and into the large antechamber. This room was furnished in a manner that reflected the decor outside.

"Worse taste that we have ever seen," stated Chantal.

"Through that door," whispered Mar, pointing past Fair Morn.

A burly guard leaped in front of them, baring the way.

"Get out of the way!" snapped Tinker. "We have business with your boss!"

"Boss?" The guard frowned at him.

Smoke stepped sideways, grabbed the guard by the throat and slammed him against the wall. His head made a dull thump. She let him sag to the floor and started for the door. The watching merchants and the other guards made a wide space around this stranger group as they moved inside.

And they did move aside.

In a wave of bodies.

The man sitting in the ornate chair, on the high platform, glared at them. "I didn't ask for you!" Then he stood and stared at Mar. "How did you get her? I didn't hire you." He dropped back into his chair. "However, I will give you the reward."

He beckoned to one side. A servant ambled over and handed up a large coin sack.

"O.K.," said Tinker. "Let's have eyes everywhere. I don't think that this guy is going to listen to reason."

"He always gets his way," whispered Mar.

"Up here, Mar!" commanded Argar, bouncing the coin sack in one hand.

Tinker stepped forward. "We came to talk, not to trade."

Argar stared at him. "Trade or dic."

Tinker sighed. "Never fails."

The explosion inside the room hurt their ears. Argar jerked, slumped sideways, twitched and went limp.

"He wasn't going to be reasonable." Chantal straightened up from her stance, and looked at the rest of the people standing on the high platform. They weren't moving.

Levers clicked. Fair Morn fired. The chair, the

body, part of the platform, and a large section of the back wall silently disappeared. "That's that."

"Could have let me talk to him," grumbled Tinker.

"Father?" Frahn had never seen anything like this before. Irinl stood statue still, eyes as round as round could get. Mar wobbled and leaned against Fair Morn.

"Oh dear," said Messenger. "I think that she is going to urp."

Sha'gar stepped over to Mar and touched her cheek, gently with one fingertip.

Mar sucked in her breath and jerked. But the color returned to her face.

"Let's get out of here," said Tinker.

"Where sulda?" Sgenn looked around the room, watching the folk pressing themselves against the still standing walls, trying to have as much room between themselves and these strangers as they could get.

"Lurin's place." She nodded at Szart, who whirled them away. Sgenn didn't think that they would notice that she had left something behind. It would remove the entire structure and anyone in it that didn't run for their lives.

Hahn Dohr Kahn. Sunny Afternoon.

They swirled in, a cloud of black that twisted tightly. Into the main room of the Royal Quarters, Lurin's Royal quarters.

She jumped up, dropping her writing tool. She had been in the midst of preparing sets of instructions for the many activities that needed doing. A road extension. A new guild to charter. An order for five new ships.

"What is wrong with Our Princess?" Lurin stared at Irinl, checking for wounds.

Smoke looked at the Hephira. "Shock."

Lurin nodded. "Our son does look most strange as well. As does Mar."

"Same thing," said Smoke. She gently shoved Irinl into a chair.

"They killed him," explained Frahn to his mother, sitting next to his Princess, taking her hand, and frowning at nothing in particular.

Szart sat on the other side of Irinl and slapped her across the face, rocking her head to one side. And cast.

Irinl's eyes blinked. She sighed. And grabbed Frahn.

Lurin stalked over and stared into his face. "My King?"

"Ummmm," he said. "I think that it is because she comes from a sword wielding warrior culture. She understands swords and brawling that way." He sighed. "Ahhhhh, the guy that took Mar, ermmm, got killed."

He gently touched the side of Lurin's face. "Let's go out on the balcony and talk. I think that everyone will be all right in a little bit."

She nodded and walked with him. "My King, I also come from a sword wielding culture that understands swords and brawling."

Frahn looked at the rest of them as they settled around the table. "Mothers?"

Fair Morn kissed Mar on the cheek. "See, I told you that you would be safe."

Mar jerked. "What did you do?"

"Not much."

"I want to know," said Frahn, all Royal Prince. "What it is that my Mothers did back there! That was not much!"

"Cool it," snapped Chantal, still feeling the adrenalin rush.

"Our Prince, Sweet Princess," interjected Chicken. "You would not understand the technology and we do not believe that trying to explain is appropriate."

She drew herself up into her most Royal stance. "Suffice it to say that Chantal and Fair Morn did kill that villain most throughly and forever." She looked at Irinl. "And, we do most humbly apologize do we you startle with our actions."

Irinl nodded and began to look at them, to really look at them. Then she stood and slowly walked around the table, looking at each one of them, especially at the objects that they were carrying.

Smoke, Chantal, and Fair Morn each carried

strange things. She hadn't realized it before but now she knew that these things were weapons. She had assumed that they had been just peculiar decorations, strange jewelry of odd sizes and shapes, worn in peculiar ways. Regaining her chair, she looked at them. Again.

"Mothers of My Prince Husband, We begin to understand." She waved a hand to stop any comments from starting. "We had heard tales. Of The Chosen One. And his, ahh, associates. Fanciful, overblown stories. Wild beyond belief."

She smiled, a small tentative smile. "But now I think that not all were that wild as I had thought." Then she looked at them, face by face. "Will you help us visit the ruins? Come journey with us to the ruins?

He stood, his arm around her waist, on the balcony. "So, you see, we didn't really do that much."

They had been staring out over the great open space in front of the castle while he told her what had happened.

"Great King, your not much is more than most could imagine. Even this, Your Queen, stands in awe at what you so casually do. Be gentle with Our Son and His Princess. She has seen little and has barely traveled from her lands."

"Didn't mean to frighten anyone," he grumbled as he turned toward her. "What are we going to do with Mar? She is pretty, umm, confused."

"Perhaps we might just ask her what she wants

to do?"

He laughed. "You're right."

"She probably should go with you when you visit the ruins."

"Ummmmmm. Only if she wishes to."

Lurin smiled and twisted around until she totally faced him. "We wish a favor, We do." And saw a slight tightening in his face as he reacted to her tone of voice. "We wish to visit those ruins as well."

Before he could say anything, she stated, most firmly, "If need be, we will in full armor wear." And smiled. "From the reaction We saw in the other room, We feel quite safe, Fierce Warrior of Terrible Weapons, in accompanying you."

Something about her look and the tone of her voice told him that the only answer he could possible give was yes.

So, he said, "O.K. You come along. In full armor." And kissed her on the tip of the nose, and grumbled, "Taking no chances. Next day. All should be ready for travel by then."

She tugged him into the room they had left.

"O.K.," he said as all eyes turned in his direction. "Who is going to go visit the ruins tomorrow?"

"Father, it will take two full days just to prepare the expedition. And it is a many day walk from here."

"Umm," said Tinker.

"With hand-picked troops," added Irinl. "Great King."

"Ahhhhh," said Tinker.

"Lord King?" asked Lurin.

He looked at Frahn and Irinl. "Sha'gar and Szart can take us there in the morning." He looked over. "Right?"

Sha'gar nodded.

Then he looked at Irinl. "Do you think we will need, um, hand-picked troops as well?"

"Perhaps not."

He nodded. "O.K., we will just pop over there, let you yank that thing from her gut, and pop back." He dropped into a handy chair, mumbling, "Gonna be really glad when this is over and we can go home."

Lots of eyes watched him. Smoke slipped inside, checking Tinker. And said. "Let's rest for two days, MindMate. And make preparations." She glanced at Irinl. "One day, more or less, shouldn't make any difference. Not after all that time."

Irinl stood and bowed to Tinker. "As you wish, Lord." And bumped Frahn on the shoulder. He stood, and they headed for their rooms.

Lurin settled into the chair next to him as he turned and looked down the table. "Well, Mar, what do you want to do?"

She twitched. And stared at him.

Fair Morn nudged her. "Relax, he doesn't bite, you know." Then she laughed. "Ummm, strangers, that is."

Mar stared at Tinker for a long, long time. Then

exhaled a long prolonged sigh of breath. And sat just a little straighter. "We are trained to distrust magic and to prevent those who would use it from doing so." Her eyes danced from Sha'gar to Szart to Sgenn. "And yet, now, I know that this is always not true. Sooooo, I would see that Great Warrior Princess liberated by her kin. If I may, Chosen One?"

His eyes flowed from face to face. Then he nodded. "O.K., should be safe enough." And smiled at her and all the rest. "We will go in two days. Smoke wants us to rest."

Fair Morn nudged Mar. "That means you also. You really look beat."

Mar frowned at her. "No one hit upon me."

"Tired," said Fair Morn. "It is a term that means tired."

"Oh!" Mar nodded. "I am very tired. Since running to your home, I have been very, very tired."

Fair Morn stood and gently lifted Mar to her feet. "Nap time, Gentle Eyes." And pulled her toward their quarters.

Tinker stood. "Think that I will just go wander around town for awhile. After I get rid of this thing." And started for his quarters, swinging down the great black sword.

"Great King!" Lurin bent and tugged on her boots. "We will walk with thee." She followed him from the room.

Smoke stood and stretched. "He can't get out of

range." She looked at the servant still standing back against the wall, near the door. "We are hungry. May we get something to eat?"

The servant hastily bowed and rushed from the room as Fair Morn returned. "Me too."

Chantal laughed. "Maybe we ought to have some servants."

"No need," said Szart. "We can always wave in food, Sha'gar and I."

As they stepped from the servant's door and out into the great open space, Lurin took his hand. "Wither?"

He shrugged. "Just needed to walk."

She headed them across the vast square toward the main street. And the word raced ahead of them as friend told friend, worker told worker.

Several blocks later, he said, "Let's get something to eat." He knew that the rest of himself were having lunch.

It was only mid-day here. Smoke was correct. They needed two days. To prepare. To rest.

"There is a small shop, just there." Lurin tugged him in the right direction.

The pleasant odors made him aware of just how really hungry he was.

Bon appetite, said Chicken. Then they all closed off, providing him total privacy.

He smiled.

"It is plain merchant fare," explained Lurin, nodding at the owner who was anxiously waiting in the door of his establishment, kneading his hands. The owner waggled one hand at the interior. "Any table."

They took one in a corner.

"You order," said Tinker.

Lurin did. Warrior's portions. And a jug of the locally brewed beverage. She filled their cups. "This is made here, in this establishment."

He nodded, took a sip, then a long swallow. "I like it!" And smiled at her. "Shouldn't you be working, doing queen stuff?"

"A Queen may do as she pleases," stated Lurin. "Even entertaining her King."

"It was a joke."

She laughed. "As did We jest as well."

The food arrived, large bowls of it with large chunks of bread. "Fresh caught," said the owner, looking nervous.

"Fish?" asked Tinker.

The owner stared at him.

"Ahhhhh, from the water?"

"Rapin," he said. From the serving port his wife loudly cleared her throat, reminding him that these were not local merchants just visiting. He bowed and hurried away.

"Waterfolk catch them every day," explained Lurin.

He nodded as he sampled the dish. "Very good."

And grinned across the table. "The fish. The bread. The drink. The company."

Lurin smiled. "Sly talker."

He reached out and gently stoked the back of her hand. "You looked worried."

"I am."

"Why?"

"What if it does not work?"

He shrugged. "Then it was, is, just an interesting tale to be told."

"What if it does work?"

"Then we shall have to work very fast to keep her from dying. That is a terrible wound."

"How?"

"We shall have to talk to my Mothers about that."

"About what?"

"How to keep her from dying."

They had been discussing the same problem.

Irinl sat up. "Let's go. Now."

He shook his head. "They are resting. We will have plenty of time tomorrow for all manner of discussions about all manner of things relative to this expedition. I am sure that they will help in any way that we ask."

She ran her hand across his chest. "My Very Own Prince, the Hephira kingdom will owe them much."

He kissed her forehead. "My Very Own Princess,

they do not require anything."

Irinl smiled. "I don't suppose he would accept one of the Lessor Princesses?"

He choked on the beverage that he was sipping. "Don't even mention something like that to him. That is the kind of suggestion that will guarantee that my father will get angry and, perhaps, not want to help in this matter."

She frowned. "He seems to collect them."

"Not a good idea." It was a Princely statement.

She nodded. "Is he going to keep that Mar?"

"Probably not. Think of something else."

"Like?"

"A ring. Some object. Some special object."

She fiddled with his shirt. "Did you know that there is a very private garden up on the roof?"

"No."

"The Queen told me about it. And how to find it." She slipped from his lap and tugged at his arm. "It is a very private garden and it is a very warm evening. And your mother is in town. With your father."

They sat in the corner booth of another establishment, having dinner, sampling this and that, and the establishment beverage. The waterfolk that caught sea creatures and the sea folk who sailed the merchant and Royal Fleet and those who had sailed in The Queen's Own Ship studiously ignored them.

This was a lessor favored hangout for them, but

the word had spread. Many of the sea folk had recognized her on sight, having spent much time with her at sea. Many recognized him from The Fest Day. So, many had come to sit and drink and to slyly watch that pair.

"Pretty good stuff," he said, meaning the food and the drink.

"It is said by those who frequent this establishment that the drink here is the best in the kingdom." She waggled her hand in the air summoning refills. Then she changed her mind and ordered two jugs.

Once they arrived, she stood, holding one jug by the neck, she handed the other one to him. "You, My Lord King, have never seen Our Royal Vessel. It is tied up at the far end of The Great Quay." She tugged him to his feet and out the door.

They had a number of the drawings and sketches scattered over the table and had been discussing what to do once they got there. And had agree upon a course of action and what sorts of equipment would be required.

"Do you think that he will agree?" Fair Morn looked at the others.

"Damn well better agree," stated Chantal.

Smoke shrugged. "I think that he will."

"He will be safe," said Sgenn, looking at Sha'gar and Szart. Sgenn's eyes had a soft grey glitter to them.

"Careful, sister," hissed Sha'gar.

"Yesssssssss," added Szart.

Messenger gently turned the drawings around. "I think that the Princess is in the greatest danger spot."

"Indeed not," stated Chicken.

"Irinl," said Messenger. "She is going to pull that thing out."

Chantal nudged Szart. "Can you bring Dat here? That babe on the wall has a great blade jabbed through her gut. She won't survive long if she is actually alive once that thing is pulled free."

"Hum," said Szart. She motioned for Sha'gar to come to one of the other rooms.

Chantal looked at Smoke. "Think you will be able to hold her pain away?"

"No idea." She stood and stretched. "I am going outside and run laps around the square."

Fair Morn smiled and stood and headed out for the balcony. "Think that I will just flap around for awhile. It is late. It is dark." Later, when she returned, she decided not to mention what she had seen going on in the roof garden.

She leaned against the railing in the stern on the seaward side and said, "Give us a hug and a long kiss, My King Lord."

So, he set his jug on the small table fastened to the deck and did.

He shoved his dish away and grabbed his cup. It was two days later. And they had been taking it easy. And everyone was looking fit and well and ready to travel. Dat smiled at him. And he had stopped grumbling as soon as Chantal had explained why she had to be here. The ladders and all the other gear lay in the middle of the room, occupying much of the open space.

Frahn and Irinl were wearing their golden scale armor. Lurin glowed white in her plate armor.

Sipping from his cup, he finished his careful inspection of them, nodded to himself. Even Mar looked healthy. Lurin noticed his eyes flowing from person to person.

"We are ready, King Lord." She fingered the hilt of the great sword hanging from her belt.

"Right!" He emptied his cup. And stood. "Let's go."

They all gathered around the stack of gear.

And Szart and Sha'gar, working together, took them and their equipment out.

Chapter Sixteen

Another Problem Solved

Hahn Dohr Kahn. The Ruins. Bright and Sunny.

They swirled in.

Frightening three small animals that darted into the small heaps of tumbled rock.

Tinker smiled at Frahn. "Looks just like the drawings." And watched Smoke and Fair Morn organize their gear. He nodded to Frahn and Irinl. "We will follow you. You know the route inside. Just go slowly."

Frahn consulted a small drawing, looked up, located the path up and in, and started the careful climb into the ruins. The air was still and just beginning to indicate the heat that would come when the sun stood high overhead.

Eventually, they were in the cool of the room.

"Wow," said Tinker.

Mar gasped. "That is a xylinth blade." She started to walk forward and was yanked backward by Tinker.

"Nope! We do it just the way we planned it." He smiled into her startled expression. "Carefully."

Then he stepped to one side of the room, tugging

Mar along. Sha'gar waved in the first part of their gear.

She watched as Smoke and Fair Morn leaned their ladders against the wall. Fair Morn moved back as Smoke and Chantal climbed up until they stood high enough to grab the figure's arms. Smoke held a long knife ready to cut the rope of hair loose from the restraining knot if everything went the way that they thought it might.

Irinl and Frahn quickly assembled the small platform as soon as Szart waved those parts in from outside. Irinl would stand on it to pull the weapon free.

As they worked Fair Morn watched, then set, and reset her own weapon. She wanted a narrow enough beam that she could shoot and not hit either Smoke or Chantal. Then she carefully positioned herself. "Very high power," she said.

Lurin stepped sideways and stood near the entry door and positioned herself at the ready, one hand on the hilt of her great sword.

Dat walked up to the bottom of Chantal's ladder.

Finally they were ready. Everyone not required for some chore or other stepped to the side walls, their back against the chamber wall, ready for whatever might happen.

Szart yanked in a glittering bronze wand as Sha'gar pulled a flaming red one from somewhere. Something all dark shadow rose behind Sgenn.

"Don't interfer with them," Tinker whispered to Mar who was nervously looking at the activity, especially at the magic users. "We may need everything that we can get."

Frahn hurried away as Irinl climbed onto the platform and stepped close to the end of the strange weapon. She carefully positioned her feet, then even more carefully placed her hands on the shaft.

"Ready?" asked Tinker. And everyone answered they were. He took another slow careful look around the chamber, noting that everyone was exactly where they had planned to be, and nodded, mostly to himself. He sucked in a deep breath. And slowly let it out. "O.K. Do it!"

Irinl glanced over at Frahn and tightened her fingers. "I do not feel anything special at all." She glanced around and then up at Smoke and Chantal.

"We are ready," said Smoke.

Irinl yanked.

And staggered backward and off the end of the platform, still clenching the xylinth blade.

"Surprised," she gasped as she scrambled to her feet. "It came out so easily."

"Smoke?" asked Tinker.

Smoke tapped one arm of the being on the wall. "Still stone. Or something."

"Let's wait awhile." Frahn started over toward Irinl.

"Don't get in the way!" snarled Tinker. He waved. "Irinl, move over against the wall. Please?"

Frowning at him and his manner and manners,

she did, hurrying over to where Frahn stood. They both examined the blade.

"There was no resistance when I pulled it free. It was just like it wasn't stuck in anything at all." Irinl stared at the thing she held.

Tinker slowly walked over and climbed up onto the platform, making sure that there was plenty of room for Fair Morn if she had to fire. He bent and peered into the hole where the blade had been. Carefully he reached out with one fingertip and touched the stomach area and the small amount of exposed skin. Then just inside the hole. He spun around and leaped from the platform.

"MY LORD!" Chicken's sword slithered metallic his from its sheath.

He stared at his fingertip. And rubbed it against the palm of his other hand. "Better get ready, Smoke. She is either coming alive or we are gonna have a pilgrimage shrine here that will dwarf anything in Europe. This statue is bleeding."

Smoke tapped the arm. "No change up here."

Chantal reached over and touched the hair knot. "Smoke," she hissed. "Cut it!"

Smoke reached out and began to saw through the hair. "Pretty strange. Hang onto that arm."

"Damn right." Chantal grabbed the arm on her side.

Messenger scrambled up Smoke's ladder and tapped a peg with her black wand, ordering the peg to come out. In rapid order she had all four removed and scurried over to stand behind Fair Morn and to peer past her free side at Smoke and Chantal.

The pair pulled, lifted, and held the stiff limbed figure as she came free from the wall.

Smoke and Chantal eased themselves down their ladders, carrying their burden, And laid it on its back on the platform.

"Now what?" asked Tinker.

Smoke looked at him. "Something in there. I feel faint stirrings."

Chantal ran down the connecting corridor and then back, carrying the large medical kit. Popping it open she began yanking out bandages, tape, and anything else that she thought might be of some use.

Tinker waved Dat over. "What do you think?"

"Mostly stone." Dat nodded. "Someone didn't like her."

He looked at Frahn and Irinl. "Go check that other room. I am getting nervous." They hurried away.

"Cool it," snapped Chantal. "You are making us nervous as well."

He clamped his mind shut.

"Much better." Chantal, poked the bare forearm of the figure. "Soft."

Smoke stepped a few steps back, eyes predator focused on the Princess in the blue scale armor.

The statue screamed.

She screamed, arching her back, arms and legs

thrashing wildly.

Smoke pushed as hard as she could, forcing the terrible pain away. Blood ran from the gaping wound.

"DAT," yelled Chantal. "Get over here. I can't do anything. This is a real mess."

Dat walked over, bent and peered at the wound. "Yes, it is."

"Do something," urged Chantal.

"I am," replied the indjinn, stuffing one hand into the gaping wound. And then she set to work.

Chantal whirled away, gagging.

And in short while Dat straightened up and then began to work on the hands and the feet. And looked at Tinker and smiled. "Shall I make her more beautiful?"

"No. Leave her anatomy alone. Ahhhhhh, the rest of her anatomy, that is. Is she gonna live?"

Dat smiled. "She has all her parts. Again."

Smoke grunted. "She fights back." Sweat ran down her face.

"Release her!" snapped Tinker.

Smoke did.

The figure sucked in a deep breath and gasped, sat up, whipped a short blade from somewhere, and slashed at Smoke. Smoke's reflexes were faster.

Chantal grabbed the Princess by the hair and yanked her back, her head thumping loudly as it hit the platform. "STOP! THAT!" And punched her.

Something dark black held the dazed figure in its arms as Sgenn calmly walked over and stared up at her.

"I am Faan theurgist Sgenn, Princess. We just brought you back. It is not wise to attack my sister."

Tinker stepped close to them. "Get rid of that thing."

Sgenn sent it away. But not very far.

The Princess thumped, hard, sprawling on the platform as Frahn and Irinl raced back into the chamber.

"Nothing out there," reported Frahn. "Who screamed?"

Irinl gasped and stared as the statue sat up and began to carefully look at them. Then her eyes fastened on Irinl. "Who among the Hephira wears golden armor? And wields my weapon?" Irinl was still clenching the xylinth blade. "I know of no House thus attired."

Irinl bowed. "I am Nadarl ca Irinl, Princess."

The Princess tugged her legs around, sat cross-legged and bowed her head. "I am Daish a'an'Nald ca E'Nilt." Then she held up her hands and stared at them and ran her hand over her mid-section. "How is this possible?" She rubbed the side of her jaw. "That hurts."

Tinker slipped over to Irinl. "We, ahhhhh, helped The Princess free you."

E'Nilt stared at the sword sticking up past his left shoulder and the black clothes he wore and then back to Irinl. "These are the strangest servants that I have ever seen, Princess."

Irinl stood taller and straighter. "These are not

servants. He," she indicated Tinker, "is the father of My Prince, Prince Frahn." She waved her free hand. "And they are his, em eh, wives." And smiled. "They, em, helped me also. And fixed your wounds."

Mar stepped up alongside Messenger and Fair Morn. "I am not his anything," she said softly.

"Princess E'Nilt," said Tinker. "Let us return to our, umm, castle. There is much you need to know."

She nodded. "Perhaps we should. I would know how the war goes."

He glanced at Smoke. *Can you put her to sleep?*

E'Nilt sagged and toppled over. Smoke slipped over and picked her up, cradling the limp form in her arms. "Let's go."

They gathered up their gear and hurried through the corridor into the other room and up the stairs to the outside. Szart and Sha'gar took them away.

They swirled into the room, startling the servant who almost splashed soup over the Queen. It was the mid-day meal and he was setting the table in anticipation of the Queen and her guests returning. She had suggested that each meal was to be set regardless of anyone being in attendance. The servant ran from the room to order more food and to get some help.

"King Lord?" asked Lurin.

He nodded at Smoke and looked at Irinl. "Princess, maybe it would be better if she was with you for awhile. It would be easier when you explain, being her ancestor and all."

He pointed at a corner. "Ummmm, leave that thing over there. Just for now. Please?"

Irinl nodded and leaned the blade in the indicated corner and went with Smoke, who was carrying E'Nilt, to their quarters, Frahn went with them.

Lurin walked out of the room and hurried back shortly, minus her armor. "We need no weapons here."

They all hurried away and returned.

Tinker looked at them all and frowned at no-one. "That went so easy that I am worried."

Somewhere a door slammed against a wall. And Irinl bellowed, "HALT!"

E'Nilt hurtled into the room, wild-eyed, spotted the xylinth blade leaning in the corner, and lunged that way, past Fair Morn.

Almost.

Past Fair Morn.

"BLIZ FAR!" snarled E'Nilt, kicking and flailing wildly. Fair Morn had grabbed her by the collar and was now holding her in the air at arm's length.

"How dare you!" growled E'Nilt, twisting her head back and forth.

Fair Morn looked over at Tinker as Frahn and Irinl charged into the room and skidded to a halt.

"Don't drop her," ordered Tinker. He walked over and stood in front of the cursing, struggling Princess. But not too close. She glowered at him and kicked.

"What do you think you are doing?" she demanded.

"My question exactly," he replied. And looked at Irinl. "What happened?"

Irinl stalked over and glared up at the dangling E'Nilt. "I started to explain, everything, and she called me a foul name and a supporter of evil, and ran away, saying that she would slay us all."

Sgenn walked over and stood by Tinker's other side. And looked at E'Nilt, a small half smile forming. "That is not-nice." She nodded. Something vague folded around the xylinth blade and took it, somewhere. Sgenn nodded. "You could follow it."

E'Nilt kicked wildly at them. "RELEASE ME!"

"Nope." said Tinker. "Not until you promise to sit and listen to everything that we have to say."

"I make no promises to demon fiends." She folded her arms over her chest as well as she could and glowered at him. "I am unafraid of death."

Chantal pushed past them and slapped E'Nilt's face. "You are dumber than the dumbest, ahh, peasant. We unhooked you from that wall. We healed your wounds." She slapped her again. "You Hephira Royal Princesses are a Royal pain in the butt." Chantal's head snapped in Irinl's direction. "And don't you say anything, dinky!"

Stepping to one side, she glared at Tinker. "Cowboy, these pointy-eared little babes all need to have their butts spanked."

Lurin walked over and said softly, "King Lord, may We speak with Princess E'Nilt?"

He nodded. "Why not?" Fair Morn grumbled at them. "This is really dull, just holding her in the air."

Lurin stepped close to E'Nilt and looked into her eyes, their heads were on the same level. Fair Morn had lifted her captive a little.

"I am" stated Lurin in her most formal tone of voice, "Lurin, Queen of this Kingdom, Hahn Dohr Kahn, Realm of The Dragon. This is My, ah, castle. These are My Friends. And this, My Husband, The King. You, Princess Daish a'an'Nald ca E'Nilt, are abusing Our Royal hospitality. Did Your Royal Parents still live, We would send most strongly worded scroll to them. We know of you and your exploits. It is time for you to learn of us and our's."

Lurin smiled past the startled face at Fair Morn and commanded, "Drop that insolent child, she is interfering with our meal." She stepped back.

Servants had arrived and were busily setting the table, adding another place setting.

E'Nilt hit the floor, sprawling.

"Will you join us," asked Lurin sweetly, watching E'Nilt stand. "And you will take off that armor. Nothing on this table will attack you." She smiled. "Just put it all there." One finger pointing rigid sword at the appropriate corner.

E'Nilt spun, stomped away, yanked off her armor and tossed it into a heap. And spun, glaring at them all, and stalked over to the table, thudding heavily into a chair.

"Oh, my!" gasped Messenger. "She is really, ummm, pretty."

E'Nilt only wore the thin under armor garment.

"Very nice," observed Dat. "Even if I didn't do anything."

Then, as they ate a very leisurely meal, Lurin had each of them tell E'Nilt of their exploits.

And over dessert, Lurin looked at her. "So, Princess of Legend, do you now understand?"

"Yes. I do." E'Nilt was staring at the food in her bowl, shoving it around with her utensil. "I do." She looked up, great azure eyes wide, staring at them. "Humblest of apologies to all."

She looked from face to face. "What am I to do?" She waggled one hand loosely. "Nothing is . . . I . . . am what? A living legend myth . . . " She blinked. "I should have stayed on that wall."

Irinl's fist thumped on the table top. "Nar frn!" Her face flushed. "No, Princess."

"Ummmm?" said Tinker.

"Tis conundrum," agreed Chicken.

"Ummmm?"

"A problem can always be solved," stated Lurin.

"Ummmm?"

"Spit it out, Cowboy." Chantal refilled her cup.

"Father?" asked Frahn.

Tinker looked at Irinl. "Do all the Hephira live in

your kingdom?"

She shook her head. "After the great scatter not all have returned. It has not been that long since you cleansed our lands of that evil."

E'Nilt's head snapped around to stare at Tinker.

"So," he said. "E'Nilt could be from some far flung, far away place, newly arrived, couldn't she?"

Irinl nodded and looked at E'Nilt. "It could explain her armor and, aaaaaa, behavior. My sister, The First Princess, would probably agree to claim her as a Princess cousin of great stature and standing." She smiled. "If the Princess E'Nilt would agree to that."

E'Nilt looked at Tinker. "Tell me of this thing that you did for Our Kingdom."

"Say on," murmured Lurin, nodding at Chicken.

"Well," began Tinker. "It wasn't much."

He told E'Nilt what happened.

When he finished, she stared at him, just stared.

"What?" he asked.

"I am a Princess with no kingdom and no resources, Mighty Warrior Lord. How am I to debt relieve? For my life? For my, sssssss, cousin's Kingdom?"

She stood and walked around the table to stand near him. And smiled warmly.

He blanched. And rasped before she could say a word, "No!" His eyes jumped to Chicken's. "Tell her, Princess."

"What?" asked E'Nilt, frowning at his strange

behavior.

Chicken quickly suppressed her smile. "Our Lord wishes Us to say, with great cordiality, that if The Noble, and beautiful, Princess E'Nilt, Mighty Warrior, has some desire to debt relieve, it may not be done by Arranged Marriage as He is, at this very moment, most occupied pon other most pressing matters whose delicate nature may not be disturbed."

"Oh." E'Nilt stepped closer to him. "Most perceptive, Lord. But we shall speak with Our, sssss, Cousin Irinl on this matter." She spun away and flowed smoothly back to her chair.

He sighed. And mumbled, "Never stops."

Lurin squeezed his thigh and nodded at a hovering servant who hurried to refill all their glasses.

E'Nilt leaned sideways and began to talk to Irinl in very low tones. Their eyes kept jumping to Tinker's face.

"I think that it is time for us to go home," he mumbled.

"Not quite yet, King Lord."

"Ummmm?"

Lurin leaned close and started to speak to him. They faded in.

A man. And a woman.

They smiled at each other and looked around the room.

"Ahhhhhhh, Mar," said the man.

"We have looked long and far," said the woman.

E'Nilt surged to her feet, eyes blasting hate, face contorted with rage. "YOU!"

They stared at her.

"It can not be!" the man said.

"Long before before, we fastened you to that wall," said the woman.

"Merde!" Tinker looked around the room. No-one was carrying weapons. And there wasn't anything handy that would serve as one.

Mar sat straight, eyes seeming to grow more and more round as she stared at this stranger pair.

Sha'gar and Szart snarled. Mar had blanketed them all, including the couple starting to look confused by this new feeling.

Sgenn nodded. And sat still as still.

Something dark reached up from the deep below.

E'Nilt felt it bump gently into the side of her leg. She jerked and looked down. And grabbed it. The xylinth blade.

She leaped at them.

The blade sang blood angry as it was swung in a great arc.

"NO!" shouted the man.

The woman didn't have time to say anything.

They toppled over, gore splashing over E'Nilt, those nearby, the table, and the floor. The top halves fell one way, the rest the other way, arms and legs thrashed, twitched, and stopped.

Stomping through the mess, E'Nilt slashed off their heads. "All that time," she snarled, "all that pain."

She kicked the heads across the room. And whirled around, the fire fading from her face. She bowed to Sgenn. "You may take the blade away. Now." She held it out.

Sgenn shook her head.

Mar toppled from her chair.

"Shock," said Smoke as Fair Morn knelt by Mar's side and rearranged her arms and legs.

"Those." E'Nilt waggled the blade at the remains. "Things were the brother and sister Ramday, vile twisted life energy takers. They betrayed me after the great war."

She wiped her face with her free hand, smearing her face even more. "My Brother and I were at our outpost, Parantor, resting." She frowned darkly. "His magic held me to the wall." Tears began to wander down her face. "And she took my blade from . . . my hand. . . and . . ."

"ENOUGH!" snapped Tinker, interrupting her. "Princess," he said softly, gently, "go take a bath." He pointed in the correct direction. It was toward Lurin's quarters. "Goes for anyone else that got messy."

Lurin snapped orders to a servant and smiled at them. "Let us retire to another room while this one is cleaned." She tugged Tinker into her quarters and out onto the balcony.

We will see to Fair Mar, said Chicken.

"That was certainly a surprise." He flopped heavily into the couch-like piece of furniture.

Lurin sat, handed him one of the mugs, and filled them from a jug. She had carried everything from the other room.

"Most true." She leaned against his side. "Princess E'Nilt is a most fierce warrior."

"I'll say." He tilted up his mug.

She nudged him and refilled his mug. "Great King, We wish Thee to do a Royal thing."

"Sure. What?"

"Go scrub most be-grimed Princess Fierce."

He slumped. "Send a servant."

"It will not do."

"Why not?"

"Our Princess Irinl did tell us that among the great Warriors of her kingdom, that it is an honor, warrior to warrior, to do this. And none worry, in this instance, whether the body be male or female warrior."

Lurin sat up. "And it is the worst breach of manners to do anything else. Or to tell others of what one sees. Very private, very special, warrior to warrior."

He sighed. "Why me?" And looked over. "Send Irinl. It is her cultural thing." He laughed. "Or Frahn."

"E'Nilt sees this Great King as her equal. Not any other."

Do your job, grumble butt. Chantal laughed. *If she*

gets out of line, you can drown her, or we can punch her lights out later.

Nosy butt. He lurched to his feet. "Care to come along?"

Lurin laughed. And watched him walk away.

"Hello in there," he said into the billowing steam.

"Who speaks?" she demanded.

"I do. Tinker."

"What?" she snapped.

"Scrub your back? Wash your hair? Warrior to warrior, Princess?"

Water sloshed. "You may. Enter!"

He stepped into the steam filled room and walked cautiously in the direction where he knew that the deep tub was set flush to the floor. And stopped. "Like hot water, huh?"

She looked over her shoulder at him, face just above the thick layer of soap foam. "Yes. More is coming. Get in before the servants arrive.

Grumbling softly to himself, he sat on a bench, yanked off his boots, and then set his clothes in a neat pile. And slipped into the tub.

"Ugly scar," said E'Nilt, glancing around and up at his side.

"Stuff happens." And pushed her forward, a little. "Where's the washing things?"

"Here." She tossed the cloth over her shoulder. It hit him in the face.

"Lean forward," he mumbled, starting to scrub

her back. Her skin became a soft golden glean again.

"Certainly managed to get covered in it, all right."

She arched her back. "A gentle touch for such a large warrior. Scrub harder. I am not fragile." So he did. "Uuuurrrgh," she sighed.

"Close your eyes." He squeezed water over her head. And did it again. He began to scrub her hair, and, finally, he patted her shoulder. "All right. Rinse off."

E'Nilt slipped down and under the water. And surged up, wiping her hair from her face. She was facing him. "Bend forward. I will wash your hair."

"It is clean."

"Bend over!" she ordered. So, he did. And she washed his hair. Whether it needed it or not.

"Rinse!"

He did and sat up, wiping his hair from his face. She watched his face.

"What?"

"Warrior to warrior," she said.

"What?"

"Am I pleasing to the eye, to look upon?"

He sighed. And cleared his throat. "Sure."

"What?"

"Yes. You are very, ummm, pretty."

"Many folk think we Hephira are an ugly folk with funny ears."

He shook his head. "Wrong."

"Warrior to warrior?"

"Yes. Warrior to warrior."

E'Nilt sat straighter and stared at him. "Then, warrior to warrior, how is it that my offer was refused?" She smiled. "And do not tell me that court tale your slim warrior related."

He sighed, heavily. "It is hard to explain."

She spun around and slipped back, leaning against him. "We shall be Princess patient." And laughed. "You may even dare to put those large arms around me while you explain what is sooooo hard to explain. Warrior to warrior."

With great reluctance he slipped his arms around her. "O.K., sneaky. Let me explain, warrior to warrior." And he began.

"That princess is going to get her pointy ears boxed," growled Chantal, spinning the cylinder of her revolver around. "If I don't shoot her in the butt first."

"She is not going to do anything," said Fair Morn. She smiled at Mar. "Feel better?" She sat on the bed next to Mar and tugged the blanket into order, just a bit.

"Indeed," agreed Chicken. "Most Royally proper."

Mar heaved herself into a sitting position and pointed a quivering finger at Sgenn. "What are you?"

"Eh?" Sgenn looked at Smoke.

Smoke shrugged. "Very upset, confused."

"What?" asked Fair Morn. "It is only Sgenn."

"I dampened them all, all the magic and all the

magic users in that room." She stared at Sgenn. "It did not work on her."

"Hum," said Sha'gar, tilting her head to one side as she looked at her sister.

"Hum hum," added Szart, casting a glance at her clan cousin.

"I am not a magic user. It is not magic," stated Sgenn. She smiled, a soft half-smile. "Those are commands." She walked over and sat on the bed and gently took one of Mar's hands in one of her's.

Mar twitched.

"A theurgist has only to command, by voice or thought, and the servants always hear and obey. It is not a spell." She nodded at Szart. "Or an incantation." She nodded at Sha'gar. "Just a command. My training took me down deep. And down deep recognizes my voice, however spoken, out loud or in my mind. And does what I ask."

She gently kissed the back of Mar's hand. "So I have no magic to dampen." And smiled that soft half-smile again. "Only a thought."

Mar slowly shook her head. "I can not stay around you folk. There is too much violence." She looked at Fair Morn and began to sob. "But I do really like you all."

Fair Morn smiled. "We know. Maybe you could stay here with Queen Lurin. She seems to lead a fairly quiet life. If building a new kingdom can be described as fairly quiet." She hugged Mar as Sgenn moved out of the way. "You probably won't have anything to do, I suspect."

He laughed.

"What is funny?" she demanded.

"Ummmmm, just some other business." He sighed. "So, are you satisfied? Know why your offer had to be refused?"

"I do." She laughed. "You are very comforting, however."

"Seems so."

"I do not think living in Irinl's kingdom would be a good thing to do."

"Why not?"

"I am Princess E'Nilt. I have been pinned to a wall while all I knew dissolved into dust and legend. How could I live among folk who will only see that? How could I live in a kingdom whose history I do not know? How could I live in a kingdom whose customs and manners I do not know?"

"Well?"

"What?"

"You could become part of Lurin's court. The people here have gotten used to seeing Irinl. They would just think that you are from her kingdom and would never know the difference."

She twisted and half-turned in his arms. "Very clever." And smiled. "Does the Queen have another son?"

"Nope."

"Release me. I would speak with the Queen." She stood and clambered out of the tub. "Get towels. My hairs requires drying."

Tinker stood, found towels, dried off and dressed. Then he walked into the other room where E'Nilt waited, tossed a towel over her head, and began to dry her hair. "Might as well be at home," he grumbled.

They all gathered in the newly cleaned dining room. And settled around the table.

"Mar," said Tinker before E'Nilt could begin, receiving a Princess scowl for doing so.

Mar stood, bowed her head, and explained what she wanted to do.

"You may," said Lurin, beckoning over a servant and speaking to her. "Go with her, Mar. She will show you your rooms. And tell her anything that you might wish to have. It will be Our pleasure to have you at Our court." The Queen watched them walk from the room.

E'Nilt sprang to her feet. "Great Queen, we seek a great favor!"

"Speak."

"I, the Princess Daish a'an'Nald ca E'Nilt, would become part of your Most Royal Court. If The Queen would have me." She watched Lurin from an expressionless face, still as the statue that she once was.

Lurin suppressed her smile. "It will be a rather dull place for such a fierce warrior."

"I would help The Queen build Her Kingdom."

Now Lurin smiled. "Welcome, Princess of The Realm of The Dragon." She beckoned over another servant. "Fetch Our Princess the appropriate garb."

E'Nilt turned to Irinl. "My armor and the blade are your's. Put them in the kingdoms treasure vault." She stood, bowed to Irinl, and then to Frahn. They stood and bowed in return.

E'Nilt spun back to Lurin. "I would rebuild those ruins and live there."

"Most lonely a place," observed Lurin.

E'Nilt smiled, a rather sly smile. "There are deposits of rare red-green fanar gems in a carefully buried mine whose mouth could be reopened. I would oversee that endeaver and the small town that will soon appear as those ruins are rebuilt." She bowed to Lurin. "If My Queen so desires."

"We do. And will have a road begun this very day. From Wurm north."

A servant ran in, arms full of clothes.

"Your new clothes, Princess." Lurin looked at the servant as E'Nilt took the garments. "Take Princess E'Nilt to The First Lord. She has much business to talk with him about." She looked back to E'Nilt. "The First Lord will start all in motion. Work with him, plan with him. He is very good at it. We will speak later."

E'Nilt hurried away, toward an adjoining room to change into her new court wear. "Come with me," she said to the servant.

Tinker slumped in his chair. "I think that we are

ready to go home."

"First light, next day," said Lurin. She stood. "Let me show you my private garden." And tugged him to his feet and toward the staircase that led up to the roof.

Irinl walked to the corner with Frahn and handed him the blue scale armor. She held the blade. And looked at Sha'gar. "Send us to my kingdom, please?"

Sha'gar nodded and grabbed Szart's hand.

They were gone.

Frahn and Irinl.

"Whoosh," stated Chicken, refilling a large mug that sat on the table in front of her.

"Right," agreed Chantal, shoving over her mug.

"Gosh," said Messenger, looking at Smoke, as she felt Tinker's mind clamp shut.

"That Queen is a strong pouncer." Smoke winked at Chicken. "Must be a Royalty attribute."

They went off to wander about the town.

Grandeville. Tinker's Place.

They swirled in, settling onto the rear deck.

"Boy, am I ever glad to be home." Tinker turned and smiled happily at everyone.

Violet haze formed at one end of the deck. Eulin and Je'leel stepped out.

"Mother told us." said Je'leel, walking over to them, Eulin by her side. "That you were coming home."

Dat hugged Je'leel.

Eulin kissed Tinker. "Mother sends First Greetings."

"Everyone healthy?" he asked.

"Very. They worried about you."

"Well. Everything went pretty easily, considering."

"Right," laughed Chantal, throwing an arm around Eulin. "He fended off two babes. Let's go make coffee and cocoa. You can tell us what you and Je'leel were doing." They headed toward the kitchen.

"As soon as I get rid of this thing, I think that I will take a walk. Look around." Tinker gestured at the great sword that rode on his back.

"I will go with you." Smoke slowly winked at him.

And they did.

And everyone scattered.

To do this and that.

Individuals Of Note

Grandeville.

Tinker's Place
John Tinker -- the individual used as an intermediary by Big Red in his ongoing activities to maintain the balance of the universes. During his initial time on Mirk Wild Weald, Tinker was told by The Thought that he is The Chosen One of legend. Now merged telepathically into an entity with the rest following the cultural values of Smoke's people.

Smoke of the Velvetmist - a gigantic, telepathic carnivore, now transformed into a human shape by Big Red. She was selected from her home, a hidden and never visited elseplace, to be one of the original companions to aid and journey with John Tinker. Now MindMate to Tinker, Chicken and the rest.

Princess Chicken - an Easter Season fluffy chicken toy from an Easter basket, transformed by Big Red and placed as a traveling companion and aid for John Tinker.

Messenger - Once "The Messenger" of her people but joined with Tinker and the rest when she began to fold inside herself believing Tinker and crew were monsters and demons from her folk's mythology come alive.

Fair Morn - a one-time mythological jest created by the magical force, Big Red. Messenger severed her magical bonds changing Fair Morn from a jest into a real person.

R-Bar - a witch of The Faan clan, joined into the polyorganism of Tinker and the rest by Smoke. (Deceased).

> **Sedeem** - her daughter, a magician.
>> **Farth** - Sedeem's mate-for-life, a Silver Ranger.

Ferrelden - of the Risshar, a Night Runner from Zhorndar'h. (Deceased).

Flar - one time owner of a Magical Items Shop. (Deceased.)

Chantal Baire - a Veterinarian with a clinic near Grandeville.

Ranfer - witch of the Tanpak clan. Preferred to be called Ran. (Deceased).

Sha'gar - Faan magician, daughter of Reep and J.C.

Sgenn - Faan theurgist, daughter of Reep and J.C.

Dat - an indjinn, gifted to Tinker when the group bought a ring, The Eye of Dat.

> **Je'leel** - her daughter by Tinker.

Szart - Faan witch - chosen by R-Bar to be Tinker's mate-for-life.

Chantal's Friends

Frederica Hensler - "Freddie" - lives in Portland.

> **Ralph Andervante** - her husband

Sandrew Sherl Sandermeyer now **Anderson** - "Sandy" - Tinker's Attorney.

> **Red** - her husband, a member of the Grandeville

Police Department.

Janine Teacate - "Streak" - Sandy's secretary.

Chen's Chinese - The Building.

Adam Lieu Chen - Master Chen owns and operates *Chen's Chinese*, a restaurant located in Greater Downtown Grandeville. He also trains Tinker in the martial arts.

Dragon Ranch - not far from Tinker's Place.

Prince Goose - a windup plastic toy transformed by Big Red into a traveling companion for John Tinker. He is a brother of Chicken.

Chen Gum Lung - The Golden Dragon of the House of Chen. A sometimes amulet gifted to Tinker by Master Chen.

Doc's Home

Kappa "Doc" Heckmann - anthropologist and adventurer. A friend and neighbor of John Tinker's.

J. C. Smith - one of Tinker's close friends. He works for Doc in many capacities.

> **Reep** - of the Faan witch clan, married to J. C.
>> **Szaifeh** - her daughter, a witch.
>> **Sha'gar** - her daughter, a magician.
>> **Sgenn** - her daughter, a theurgist.

Membrane - one of Doc's "associates." He run Doc's stores, *Cactus Spine*, specializing in cacti and succulents.

Badnews Treefalls - another of Doc's "associates." He

is Doc's constant companion.

The Hardcastle Residence.
Alandale Fredrico Hardcastle IV, known as "Hard" by all his friends.

> **Ramp** - of the Faan witch clan, a magician, his wife.
>> **Sa'ar** - her twin daughter, a magician.
>> **Shem** - her twin son, a magician, also known by his parents and grandparents as **Alandale Fredrico Hardcastle V.**
>>> **Tajaar** - his wife.

Grandeville Police Department (GPD)
Red and **Green** - two very large men who once played football together on the local college team. They function, usually, as the late night patrol. They are good friends of Tinker, J. C., and Hard.

The Elseplaces

Paradise.
Big Red - a pure force of magic personified. He is primarily concerned with maintaining the balance and order of the universe of universes. And, more often than not, has some influence over the events that plague Tinker.

> **Dancing-All-The-Day** - Big Red's wife.

Silly-All-The-Day - their son.
Treena - the wife of Silly.

Various - depending upon mood.
Dram - an individual often called The Evil One. He began life on Murk Wild Weald as a magician-in-training. But after long and secretive study in The Library of Arcana he slowly was transformed by his knowledge and his ambitions into one of the few pure forces in the universe of universes. Dram has a tendency to work at living up to his title.

Stumpf.
The-Mountain-That-Walks - an individual most often addressed as Mountain by his traveling companions. He is one of the original companions selected to aid John Tinker.

A Place Unnamed.
Macabre - who specializes in killing things. He is usually accompanied by his pets: The Vipers, and the Sparkling Tigers.
Gyre - his female companion, created by his vessel, Gyreship.

The Six Lands.
Sorrowful Mistidings - a professional Teller of Tales, selected from The Six Lands, as one of the original companions to aid John Tinker. He lived with his wife

and sons. Now deceased.

Tears Trimblechin - his grandson, a growing Teller of Tales, trained by his grandfather.

Clear Bandler - The Land of Magicians
The $1.98 Magician - trained by Big Red and told to aid Tinker in whatever manner he could.
Plum Duff - a magician and consort to $1.98.

The Old Lands - Bahn Duhr Tohr.
Willawa, The White Warrior, Queen of all the lands, New and Old.

Toucan, The King - he is the brother of Prince Goose and Princess Chicken and once was Tinker's advisor.

Hanred, Ripple's mate-for-life - he is a Master Illusionist who once traveled widely through the universe of universes and is also known by many of the folk as "Old Hanred."

Ripple, Advisor to the Royals - she is the Clan Head of the Faan witch clan.

The New Lands - Aahn Duhr Tohr

> **Frinda** - son of Willawa and Toucan, now King of Bahn Aahn Tohr.
>> **Sook** - a Faan witch, now his Queen.
> **Lurin** - daughter of Willawa and Toucan, now Queen of Hahn Dohr Kahn, The Realm of The Dragon.
>> **Frahn** - her son by Tinker.
>>> **Nadarl ca Irinl** - his wife.

Daish a'an'Nald ca E'Nilt, The Swordpoint of the Victorious.

Dol Spar - Headquarters of The Monetary Control and Mirf's home.
Mirf - The Special Chief First Inspector, often sent on special assignments by The General, the overall director of The Monetary Control and her boss.

Fred - a suk-dragon, her Assistant.

Quan - Fred's mate - Mirf's Assistant.

Magevern - home of the Vander mage Guild.
Sa'ar - the Heart of the Vander, who made Tinker The Lord of The Vander.

Clans, Guilds, and Other Organizations.
(known individuals listed)

Anaza sorcerer Phylota - located in Far Corner.
> Netanada -- Elixa (Clan Head), Sorceress.
> Abadoda -- Three Rank Sorceress.
> Hatopa -- Three Rank Sorcerer.
> Important Artifacts.
> > The Ancient Book of Songs.

The Divineal of Thantala - located in Murklan Obscuratan. A Place Never Visited.
> Lady Grimtouch - The Glimmer (Clan Head) of The Divineal of Thantala.
> Lady Fairdeath - traveling with Sluba mage Ransapal.
> Lady Dawnmort
> Lady Softtouch
> Lady Nightreaper
> Lady Final Kiss
> Lady Lastgift
> Clan robe color - forest green almost black; carry a short gold staff.
> Important Artifacts
> > The Book of Death.

Potri witch Clan

Turintor

Clan robe colors - grape and green design.

Faan witch Clan - scattered widely throughout the universe of universes.

Ripple - Clan Head - The fifth Born.

Hanred, the Illusionist, her Mate-For-Life.

Shitar - their daughter, a witch.

Mantara - Grenzanr warlock - her mate-for-life.

Santar - their daughter, a witch.

Sook - their daughter, a witch.

Sepanix - their daughter, a witch.

Szart - their daughter, a witch - mated to Tinker.

Ranna - The First Born

Anjan - her mate, Death Warrior

Adarlak - her mate, Hacto mage.

Riz - The Second Born.

Rekel - The Third Born.

Ap Kar - a Hinta warlock, her mate-for-life.

Rbat - The Fourth Born. At one time thought by many to have gone far.

Reptar - The Sixth Born.

Rumtah - The Seventh Born. Known as The Lucky One.

Reep - The Eighth Born. Known as The Silent One.

Married to J. C.

Szaifeh - their daughter, a witch.

Sha'gar - their daughter, a magician.

Sgenn - their daughter, a theurgist.

Rotak - The Ninth Born.

Raft - The Tenth Born. Known as The Fast.

Mrrinar - a Catfolk Healer, her mate.

R-Bar - The Eleventh Born. (Deceased).

Tinker - her Mate-For-Life

Sedeem, their daughter, a magician.

Ramp - The Twelfth Born. A Magician.

Married to Hard.

Sa'ar, their daughter, a magician.

Shem, their son, a magician.

Important artifacts.

An immense collection of volumes dealing with the arcane collected by Hanred during his many travels through the universe of universes.

Talair witch Clan - located on Tanadra.

Motaiss - a warlock

Mendurra - a witch.

Clothes colors - black with just a hint of faint grey in an ornate design that runs down the outside of each sleeve.

Sluba mage Guild, one member located in Three Trees Town.

>Ransapal- studied the Dark Under and ancient witch history. Traveling with Lady Fairdeath.

Vander mage Guild - located in Magevern.

>Sa'ar - the Heart of the Vander.
>
>>Eulin Dragon Force - her daughter by Tinker, a mage and Dragon Master.
>
>Tobtz - the Soul of the Vander.
>
>Cazor - mage warrior.
>
>Moonda
>
>Aada
>
>Bant
>
>Andovar - the Farseer.
>
>Imdar - the Healer.
>
>>Rorx - Vander warlock - her son by Tinker.
>>
>>Szaifeh - a witch, his Mate-For-Life.
>
>Imten - the Artificer.
>
>Tinlee - the Adept.
>
>Xanx - Apprentice Healer.
>
>Marl - the Seeker.
>
>Galron - The Bent.
>
>Zulan - The Brave.
>
>Clothes color - they are always dressed in garb of the faintest purple. It is from the color of their

garments that folk often call them "The Purple Magicians."

The Wood With - located in Newlar, relocated from Blurratha. Hidden. In Plain Sight.

Fairlan - Cluster Head

Ringlan - Cluster Head

Clearlar - Cluster Head

Faerlar - Cluster Head

Flerlan - The Observer

The Wood With are always accompanied by their beast. When the Wood With are present one might notice the smell of blooming flowers on the air.

The Garden Gnomes - located in Growing Green.

Phineas Grass

Hiram Toadstoll

Franny Waxflower

Franelken Vetch

Tiny Rosebud - the emissary

Rose Perrywinkle

Monetary Control - located on Dol Spar.

The General - Head of Monetary Control.

Mirf - Head of the Special Investigations Office.

Fred - a suk-dragon - First Assistant.

Quan - Fred's mate - First Assistant.

Rema - First Clerk.

Nema - First Clerk.

The Nagar
Kartz - Head
      Raj - a Medical Doctor - her mate.
Reslar - youngest sister.

The Silver Rangers - located on Fandor's Dan.
Farth - Tindar (General) of the Silver Rangers.
Sedeem - Faan magiwitch - his wife.

Bits and Pieces of Cultural Data
(From the files of Monetary Control)

The Garden Gnomes.

The Garden Gnomes are a small folk, perhaps the smallest of all the folk. As their name implies they are fascinated by gardening and frequently visit those gardens that they recognize as being above the average in terms of arrangement and care, whether ornamental or functional.

At some point, in their past, one of them had been seen while visiting a particularly well designed ornamental garden. This kind of happening was not something that they liked to happen nor did they like to talk about it. This garden, as things seem to happen to this folk or that folk over their histories, belonged to a sculptress of some skill and very fast eyes. She made a statue of what her eyes saw as just a fleeting glance and set this statue in and among a artfully organized patch of flowers.

And as things so often happen, a visitor saw this statue and asked the owner to make one for him. And so it went. And so it went. Much to the consternation of the Garden Gnomes.

And eventually an entire industry sprang up around these statues and their production. People even wrote fanciful books about the culture of these things. They were all wrong, of course. None of the authors had ever talked with one of these small folk or had ever visited a Garden Gnome village.

The end result of all this was that the Garden

Gnomes retreated deeper and deeper into areas where they would not, or could not, be observed.

Young Garden Gnomes, every once in awhile, on a dark, a particularly dark night, would steal one of these statues and hide them away.

Of course, this had no effect on the overall population of these fake garden gnomes. That industry was to well intrenched.

The Divineal of Thantala.

In time before time almost before memory it is told that the Divineal were there, passing through the universe of universes upon business that none dared ask about and few would dare challenge. The few that did, died. This rare occurrence, challenging one of them, and the result of that challenge, was told one to the other, and thus was the tale spread, and The Divineal were left to pursue their own interests. Most of these interests appeared to have something to do with Death. Death as a being, not merely as the end of something.

All the folk of the elseplaces recognized them as none else would dare to wear a deeply hooded robe of dark forest green that was almost black. And none else would presume to carry a short gold staff.

It is said among the many cultures in the universe of universes that few have ever seen the face of the individual hidden in the blackness of the deep hoods. It is also said that to see that face is to die. But, if one had ever done so and survived, none had ever so stated.

It is known and understood by most folk that one does not approach one of The Divineal and start a conversation. One does not watch one of The Divineal closely. One tries as much as possible to ignore their existence. One hopes to stay alive. It was this understanding that brought into being the label used far and wide for them, "The Sisters of Death." But it never, ever, was used when of them could hear it.

None knew where their elseplace, their home place, was located. None knew which of the many elseplaces, numbers beyond counting, would be the one wherein they resided. And even if one could find out, in some mysterious way, none would dare chose to go to such an elseplace.

The Divineal were polite and very soft spoken, if and when they might chose to speak to someone. And all, but the foolish and soon to be dead, would do all that they were capable of doing, if asked to do something. That is what the folk in the universe of universes believed. And none knew of anyone that had been asked and who had refused and survived.

None knew how many Divineal there were. None knew why or what they were about and most folk felt that the best place to be when one of them was around was to be somewhere else.

The Divineal were like a pebble dropped into a still pond whose action caused ripples to flow out in all directions. And like that pebble, they were totally unconcerned about those ripples.

The Witch Clans.

The Potri witch clan came into existence, as did all the witch clans, during what all the clans call "The Great Migration." From where this migration came is a great matter of debate and argumentation, but not why.

The ancestral clan, or clans, also a matter of intense debate and argumentation, had, through arcane knowledge, come to understand that a disaster beyond the control of any user of magic was about to happen to their homeland.

So they fled out into the universe of universes and over time the witch clan, or clans, splintered and grew into the myriad of clans that are now present.

The long ago seen disaster happened in a single violent explosion that removed their homeland as their sun erupted and ate everything within reach.

Some thing, some event, during that long ago migration and scatter brought into the witch culture a sense of authority coupled with a powerful magic that each clan cultivated. Each clan developed their own clan interests and evolved their own unique concept of magic. The end result of this was a somewhat provincial sense of proper witch attire and proper witch behavior. The pairing of these beliefs with their sense of authority meant that the folk living in the many elseplaces in the universe of universes knew that any witch tended to be rather short-tempered and had a predilection toward violent behavior when the behavior of other folk, witch, magician, or non-magical user, was felt by the witches to be engaged in improper behavior, undesirable behavior, or were just plain irritating.

Most witch clans dressed in wardrobes of midnight black, the exact style of their clothing varying widely. Some of the clans, in the long before before, had, for reasons they chose not to reveal, settled on wardrobes of other colors.

The Faan witch clan is unique. Among all of the witch clans scattered across the universe of universes, they are the only one that does not maintain a clan house. And, unlike all the other clans, the members are all and only generationally linked. The magic of the Faan flows down the female line from mother to daughter.

The Faan clan, unlike the other clans, are trained almost exclusively by their female relatives, mainly by their mother and their aunts. But if a sister has learned some new and unique twist, it may be shared, sister to sister. It is due to this multi-generational sharing and training that has made the Faan noted throughout the witch clans as being the most powerful clan and to be avoided if at all possible. And some few understand that at some point in the long ago long ago, in their mating with their chosen mates-for-life, from other witch lines, that something unusual happened that twisted and transformed their genetic material.

The result of this event was that, at times, their offspring are born with new and unique abilities. This tends to explain why the Faan do not maintain a clan house. Members of their clan, most often, prefer to wander mostly by themselves and to study and collect magic and magic spells. And other things.

The Mage Guilds

The mage Guilds apparently came into existence in the long ago long ago in a manner none understand or thought to record as this event was in a time when such occurrences were not seen as being important enough to warrant special note.

Magicians are, in one sense, at the opposite end of the magical spectrum from the witches. That is why the magicians and the witches tend to avoid each other whenever possible, especially physical contact. The magic of each tends to be unstable in contact, often resulting in fatal results. However, there is the fact that, at times, in a manner none truly understand, that magicians and witches may have close association, even mates of the others, without dire affects.

The Vander mage Guild, as written in the Histories of the Arcane, was once a sub-Order of the Fanderlaine mage Guild. Little is known of the Fanderlaine and what they thought to specialize their skills upon. The Vander sub-Order eventually split away from the Fanderlaine and pushed deep into the arcane knowledge that was of particular interest to their members. The Vander became the most radical of the experimenters of the mage Guilds and explored many areas of interest to them. This was considered most strange in the mage communities as the Guilds tend to be extremely conservative in their outlook and mage knowledge. Unlike most Guilds, the Vander are almost exclusively female, each member carefully selected for skills and aptitude.

The Anaza Sorcerers.

The Sorcerers were, and are, a small clan and have forever lived in small isolated elseplaces rarely relocating. Small isolated elseplaces were more common in the universe of universes than most of the folk realized. And that suited the Sorcerer clan quite well.

Why they preferred to live this way is lost in the dim reaches of an ancient history begun in a time almost before time itself. Various of the First Sorcerers at numerous points in time in their long, long history had searched their book of lore and learning, The Book Of Songs, for clues as to why this was the way it was. But each had failed. None of them realized, or knew from the oral traditions of the clan, that the Book Of Songs had come into existence long past the time when the reason why could be remembered.

So, as these things happen, the Sorcerer clan has remained reclusive and unknown to the larger universe of universes, not really hidden so much as just being very remote and private.

There was one piece of information known to the clan, a piece of information never allowed to be transmitted to anyone not a member of the clan. And similar to the reason for their preferring small, isolated elseplaces, the acquisition of this piece of information, the how and the when and the why of it did happen, was lost in the time long before before.

Someone, way back then, had learned to recognize the presence of a folk never seen and poorly understood. This recognition was not visual but rather a matter of odor, the odor of blooming flowers. With such an olfactory clue, this small clan of magic users, the Sorcerer clan, knew when the Wood With were around. They had never seen one but the delicate and pleasant odor told them when these folk were about.

The Wood With knew of this strange thing. So they tended to keep a watch on this small group more from a matter of curiosity than of any fear of what that clan might do.

The Sorcerer clan, of course, knew when these other strange folk came and went so they, the Sorcerers, tended to keep Sorcerer business very carefully hidden from these others. And in some strange and subtle way, the clan felt that the Wood With were not to be trusted. It was a cultural tradition, never to be questioned. The reason for this was also lost in the dim historical past. And, of course, they would never attempt to affect the behavior of the Wood With. Tradition also stated that this was not to be done.

The True History of the Magic Users as Discovered by the Divineal.

Many of the witch groups, whether the Witch Clan, the Sorcerer Phylota, the Nagar sort, or the Divineal, have a tale from a time long before long before, and long before written records, of fleeing their homeland before it was destroyed by an event that no magic could prevent. This tale was passed member to member as an oral tradition and eventually was written down. It appears that this event happened.

But, as the magic users scattered into the universe of universes, their knowledge and identities became unique, group to group, and most felt that they were different than all the others.

However, all the groups so far mentioned are witch, even though some felt that others were not and needed to be hunted down and destroyed.

What none of them knew, or understood, is that the magicians were also from this same single event. Witch and magician fled from the same homeland, although, in some manner not understood, the magicians lost the remembrance of that past happening.

The witch and magician groups on that homeland

attempted to cast a great spell of prevention. It failed and they fled. None knew that the failure of that spell caused a great change in their magic, with witch and magician forces becoming polar opposites of each other, hence the great danger, now, of mixing, one with the other, magic or personnel, most of the time.

The Wood With.

The Wood With are a small folk. If anyone saw one of this secretive group from a distance, an event so unlikely as to be in the realm of never, it might be thought that what was seen was a very young human child of ten or twelve years of age. Of course, few human children are accompanied by a beast as tall as they are.

The Wood With, from a time before forever, have remained unobserved and unknown, which is exactly what they wish. As a group they are, for the most part, uninterested in the affairs of other sapient beings in all the universe of universes. But, every so often, there occurs a one that attracts their attention. This event is a rare, but not unusual, happening.

The Wood With prefer to live in and among the big trees, taking comfort one from the other. They and the environment blur together where ever they might be. This skill, this cultural attribute, is the main reason, but not the only reason, why they remain unseen and unnoticed.

Their beasts are as unique a species as the Wood With. From an early age one finds the other and from that instant the pair are inseparable. The beasts blend into their surroundings with the same ease as their constant companions.

It is a peculiarity of the Wood With that their presence leaves a faint odor of blooming flowers in the air. In all the time of their existence only one small group have ever realized this fact. But that group's mythology and cultural values are such that the fact that they know this is all that they know. Every thing else they believe, everything else are tales from antiquity with all the error that derives from that.

The Kingdom and Kingdoms of Bahn Duhr Tohr.

The Kingdom of Bahn Duhr Tohr had been, until its most recent merging into a whole, a series of large and small kingdoms, each with a unique name and a unique color scheme. These color schemes were relegated to their Royalty and to their armies. It was very useful to combatants to be able to recognize friend from foe in the chaos of massed combat.

Many of the kingdoms, but not all, could trace their existence back into the dimly remembered past. Some even argued that they existed long before written records came into use. The kingdoms large and small, frequently merged, or broke apart, as the normal political intrigues and royal wheeling and dealing created large kingdoms out of smaller ones, or as so often happened, smaller kingdoms out of larger.

But, in spite of the usual turmoil over boundaries and royal household alignments, all the kingdoms were dependent upon each other as no single one had all the resources necessary for true self-sufficiency.

The bonds between the rulers and the ruled are tight and mutually advantageous. Rulers who did not keep the needs of their folk foremost did not last long. Of course, the occasional battle with a neighbor was accepted as just part of life. Battles were, for the most part, short. This was due to the usual approach to warfare that assumed that most of the fighting would happen between the royalty of the houses in contention. The knights and lessor troops often suffered nothing worse than broken bones. Most of the time this occurred during the first melee and charge.

Grandeville.

Grandeville is a small, rather isolated, rural community of 8,000 population (more or less) tucked away in the mountainous corner of northeastern Oregon. It survives in a provincial unawareness of many things, being overly conscious of the ancestors who settled the place long after the westward migration brought California, Washington, Oregon, and Idaho into statehood.

The town sprawls down from "The Bench," a shallow bench along the edge of the next door mountain slope, to The Blue River, named after the color it has after the first snow melt surges from the canyon and out across the valley proper, always threatening to jump its banks and flood the surrounding farm land.

There are two newspapers published in town, a weekly and a daily (except for Sunday). The Daily, The Grandeville News, tends to ignore anything happening outside the edge of town. The weekly, The Mountain View, tends to ignore anything happening in Grandeville and prints whatever the publisher happens to feel like publishing.

There are a number of local establishments of note:

- The Two Bags Full - a grocery store.
- The Railroad Bar and Grill - also known as The Rail.
- Big Darlene's Bar - the home of the Annual Chili Cookoff and Arm Wrestling Championship Event, All Comers Invited.
- Johnson's Everything Shop.
- Chen's Chinese Restaurant.
- Leonard's Outdoor Supply Shop.
- The Always Open Gas Pump.
- The Romp and Stomp Motel
- Randy's Truck Corral.

About the Author

George R. Mead began to study anthropology in 1962 after being discharged (honorably) from the U. S. Army, Combat Engineers. He eventually received a B.A., M. A., and Ph. D. in his chosen field. And many years later an M. S. W. in Clinical Social Work. He was worked in aerospace, taught at the college and university levels, worked in a community action agency, ran a restaurant, been unemployed, and worked for the U. S. Forest Service. He is now retired from the work-a-day world but does a certain amount of consulting, writing, and research. He lives seven miles outside of the small town of La Grande, Oregon, with his wife, one cat, and a German Shepard dog named Katy who firmly believes that staring into his face at nine-o-clock in the evening is a statement that popcorn should be made. A new dog joined the house as an eight-week old puppy found by Katy under some brush in the middle of the American Southwest desert. Rez is now four years old and weighs 107 pounds (some puppy).

www.ingramcontent.com/pod-product-compliance
Lightning Source LLC
Chambersburg PA
CBHW072256020726
47501CB00002B/293